Almost a Goddess

"Ms. Degodessa?"

Kyra leaned back in her chair and looked up. Way up. "Yes."

Jake Lennox strolled in and stood across from the desk. Dressed in khaki slacks, a navy sport coat, and well-tailored white shirt, he looked more like a wealthy customer than a man on staff. And when he smiled that *come here, baby* smile, her insides started to itch.

He held out his hand. "We haven't formally met. I'm Jake Lennox, Mr. Themopolis's nephew."

She accepted the handshake, ignoring the jolt that shot straight to her core. Though no other mortal man she'd met had zapped her with his physical presence in the same way as Jake Lennox, it was nothing she couldn't take in stride.

"Do you have a minute? I need to ask you a few questions."

"I'm ... ah ... busy," she answered. "It's only my second day on the job."

Mesmerized by his eyes, she stared, noting they weren't brown, as she'd first thought, but a very dark and intense blue.

"Kyra?"

"Hmm? What?"

"I was hoping we could talk."

"Talk?" The blue practically purple, close to the color of the mountains on Mount Olympus ...

Avon Contemporary Romances by
Judi McCoy

ALMOST A GODDESS
WANTED: ONE SEXY NIGHT
WANTED: ONE SPECIAL KISS
WANTED: ONE PERFECT MAN

JUDI McCOY

Almost a
GODDESS

AVON BOOKS
An Imprint of HarperCollinsPublishers

This is a work of fiction. Names, characters, places, and incidents are products of the author's imagination or are used fictitiously and are not to be construed as real. Any resemblance to actual events, locales, organizations, or persons, living or dead, is entirely coincidental.

AVON BOOKS
An Imprint of HarperCollins*Publishers*
10 East 53rd Street
New York, New York 10022-5299

Copyright © 2006 by Judi McCoy
ISBN-13: 978-0-06-077425-7
ISBN-10: 0-06-077425-8
www.avonromance.com

First Avon Books paperback printing: June 2006

Avon Trademark Reg. U.S. Pat. Off. and in Other Countries, Marca Registrada, Hecho en U.S.A.
HarperCollins® is a registered trademark of HarperCollins Publishers Inc.

Printed in the U.S.A.

10 9 8 7 6 5 4 3 2 1

This book is dedicated to the goddess in every woman, no matter where she resides. Though if Mount Olympus really does exist, I imagine it wouldn't be such a bad place to live.

I owe a special thanks to Erika Tsang for keeping me on the straight and narrow with this book.

And, as always, to Helen Breitweiser and her stellar story expertise. Yes, Helen, romance authors swallow tons of chocolate when they plot. It's the only way to get the job done right and still remain sane.

Chapter 1

Mount Olympus, present day

"Am I late?" gasped Chloe as she burst into the great hall.

Kyra offered a hesitant smile and shook her head. After tucking a wayward curl of red behind her ear, she resumed her pacing. This was her second performance review in as many centuries and she was a mass of jangled nerves, as were, she imagined, Chloe, Zoë, and the rest of the muses. The thought of Zeus judging their successes and failures always left them flustered.

She'd be the first to admit she'd become a bit lazy over the past millennium, but it wasn't her fault mortals had grown suspicious of good fortune. Nobody on earth believed in luck or serendipity anymore. No matter how wonderful the incidents that occurred in their lives, they focused on their woes, most of which were mere trifles compared to the plagues and pestilences that had once befallen mankind.

"Have you heard from Zoë?" Chloe hopped into step beside Kyra. "Why do you think Zeus wants to see the three of us at the same time?"

"You know how single-minded Zoë gets when she's worried. She probably couldn't resist rearranging the flowers in the dining hall. As to why he summoned us here together—"

The demi-goddesses stilled at the sound of frantically tapping sandals. Sable tresses askew, Zoë skittered to a halt next to them.

"Had to stop and straighten the sash on one of the graces' gowns," she wheezed. "Aphrodite gets so bent out of shape when her handmaidens are in disarray." She cocked her head in the direction of Zeus's office. "Has he called for us?"

"He's with Polyhymnia. Poor thing looked frightened to death when she arrived for her appointment," said Kyra.

Chloe folded her arms. "Well, why wouldn't she? Fat lot of use there is for sacred poetry—sacred anything—these days. It's a wonder he doesn't put us in a soup pot along with the chickens who refuse to lay."

2

"I hear he's reassigned most of our sister muses, so maybe he plans to do the same with us," suggested Zoë. "You know, have us inspire something that fits better in today's world. I wouldn't mind being the muse of high adventure. Maybe rock climbing or spelunking or—"

"You're terrified of heights," Chloe reminded her, fluffing her golden curls. "Personally, I've been thinking I might have more success at inspiring good judgment. Someone with a brain needs to influence the movers and shakers of the mortal world."

"If Zeus complains about the way we've carried out our tasks, we can simply tell him we'll try harder," said Kyra. "It will give us another hundred years to come up with a decent defense."

"I blame these ridiculous 'performance reviews' on the twentieth century. First there was the telephone, followed by the radio, then that miserable box with sound and moving pictures—"

"It's called a television, Zoë, and it's a form of entertainment. You need to loosen up a little," lectured Chloe.

Zoë rolled her eyes. "Maybe so, but have you seen his latest gadget? He signed onto the Internet so he can be in touch with the *real* world. Even conjured a dozen computers." She bent and whispered, "We're all expected to use one."

"Use a computer?" echoed Kyra.

Chloe gave an exaggerated shudder. "What does he intend to do with a computer?"

3

Judi McCoy

"Probably send out a virus that will cripple mankind's ability to communicate," answered Zoë. "Calliope said Zeus came down hard on every muse he's reviewed so far. Claimed mortals needed a calamity of global proportions as a reason to write the poetry she's known to inspire. He's ready to instigate a cyberspace war just to get the ball rolling." She hissed a frustrated sigh. "The last thing Earth needs is more war."

Thunder rumbled. A bolt of lightning split the cerulean sky. The massive doors opened and Polyhymnia raced out in tears. "I've been reassigned," she sobbed. "No more sacred poetry. I'm supposed to be the muse of *blogs*." Continuing to sob, she wobbled from the landing. "How can I inspire something when I don't even know what it is?"

Kyra sighed at the news. At least Zeus was willing to explore the possibility of different tasks. In truth, their father was nothing but a bag of bluster and howling wind. After complaining he had lost the respect a deity of his magnitude deserved, he'd become testy and sour trying to adjust to the latest breed of humans. Since the arrival of the twenty-first century, he treated Mount Olympus as if it were a corporation and he its CEO.

She didn't mind the new order. But she did mind being lumped with two other muses, as if she weren't good enough to merit an appointment of her own. She loved her sisters, but Chloe had always been a self-centered diva, spreading happiness willy-nilly

4

to whatever mortal struck her fancy. And Zoë was more a fusspot than a muse. Though Zeus would never admit it, deciding that mortals had to be inspired to properly plan a meal or brighten their personal space was a dumb move.

Righting the skirt of her flowing white chiton, Kyra peered around the doorway. What was once a beautifully appointed dais with magnificent marble thrones now resembled an office straight from the pages of one of Earth's many design magazines. Zeus sat in a cushy chair that seemed to be massaging him mechanically, drumming the fingers of one hand while he guided a mouse with the other. The fax machine was spewing pages, while CNN blared from an overhead television.

Squinting at the screen, Kyra gasped. The diabolical deity was playing solitaire! She ducked when he raised his head of flowing white hair.

"Don't stand there gawking, daughter. Enter. And bring those two good-for-nothings with you."

As one, the trio threw back their shoulders, pasted smiles on their faces, and walked into the royal suite. Zeus spun his chair around and shuffled papers on the blotter, then gazed at them with a raised brow.

"I assume you know why you're here?"

"Yes, sire," they chorused.

Chloe snapped to attention. "And we're thrilled to report our accomplishments over the past one hundred years. I've inspired seven humans to find true happiness—"

"The divorce rate among mortals is staggering," he responded, causing Chloe to hang her head. "As is their suicide rate and the number of pills they ingest for depression."

"Thanks to Martha, at least their home décor is exciting," Zoë chimed.

"Martha?" Zeus sounded as if he'd never heard of the home décor maven. "What about bustles, plastic shoes ... toe rings! Each was a terrible idea. You haven't inspired a thing of value since washable wall paint."

"But everyone loves Martha," Zoë continued. "And they especially like my most important contribution: 'It's a good thing' has become a worldwide catchphrase."

Thunder rumbled, its sound as ominous as Zeus's growl. "Oh, that Martha," he groused. "Perhaps you should have given her stock tips instead of decorating advice."

"The lottery is a huge success," Kyra interrupted, hoping to lighten the moment.

Zeus wrinkled his already craggy forehead. "Poverty around the world is on the upswing. Many people can't make ends meet, and have declared bankruptcy in lieu of paying their bills. Most are positive the world is against them." He frowned. "The three of you are not going to talk your way out of your failures this time. I'm still top god around here."

Kyra opened and closed her mouth, but was at a loss for words. Any moment now, she expected their father to throw up his hands and banish them from the room. Instead, he shook his leonine head.

"You three are the least successful of my daughters. None of you has inspired much of anything, therefore mortals have never taken you seriously. I created a dozen muses, but the history books only speak of nine. Not only have you lost your edge—you never had one to begin with." He tapped a bony finger on the desk blotter. "Perhaps a bit of time as handmaiden to Hera . . ." He appeared to consider the thought. "No, no, not after the last altercation."

"But sire—" Kyra began. Would they never live down the incident with Hera and the pig . . . and the pigeons . . . and the ambrosia?

Zeus raised a hand. "Hear me out and be grateful for my benevolence. You have two choices. First, you may stay on Mount Olympus and accept a loss of status. Instead of gossiping or flirting the day away, you can muck out the stables, toil in the kitchen, or work in the dairy. There are any number of chores that will allow you to earn your keep."

The sisters moved closer together, as if united in fending off the disgusting tasks.

"The second offer is more challenging, therefore of greater risk, and eventually of more value, as well. Each of you may go to Earth and take a final stab at fulfilling your destiny, which means doing the things for which you were created—to inspire mankind. If you succeed, you may return here and live forever in splendor—no more performance reviews—just frolic and fun. But if you fail . . ." He leaned forward. "You will remain on Earth and live as a mortal until your dying day."

Kyra tugged her sisters into a huddle. "What he's offering is impossible."

"Handmaiden to Hera the Harridan is *impossible*," moaned Zoë. "The other choice threatens our very existence."

"I have no intention of pulling udders or shoveling horse droppings until the end of forever," said Chloe. "We are demi-goddesses, created to inspire. What else can we do?"

Closing her eyes, Kyra weighed the options. If they did nothing, an eternity of boredom and toil awaited them. If they accepted the challenge and failed, their fate was the life and death of a mortal. But, if they should succeed, they would reap rewards of splendor and enjoyment forever. She whipped her head around and asked, "Is that all?"

"Well, there is one more thing." Zeus stroked his snowy beard, a hint of evil glinting in his ebony eyes. "Falling in love with a mortal is not allowed. Dally if you must, but keep your mind strictly on your work, so I'm certain you're taking this challenge seriously. Dire consequences await you if you return here more impassioned by a mortal than your job."

"Fall in love? Not bloody likely," said Zoë, more to herself than her sisters.

"It'll never happen," muttered Chloe.

Kyra shrugged in agreement, silently vowing to keep her mind on the required task.

The sisters locked gazes. After joining hands, they stepped closer to the desk. "We accept the challenge," they said as one.

"And are grateful for it?"

They nodded.

Zeus smiled, though it appeared more of a grimace. "Good, good. Now here are the conditions."

Kyra bit her tongue to keep from screaming. With Zeus, there were always *conditions*.

"You shall live independently of each other, hundreds of miles apart, for a single earthly year. During that time, Kyra must inspire mortals to achieve and believe in good fortune; Chloe, you must help however many mortals you meet to have a future full of happiness." He raised a brow in Zoë's direction. "You, daughter, must find a way to enhance their lives through appearance or design, but no more idiotic ideas or tainted mavens." He raised a finger skyward. "And above all, remember the love thing." He leaned back in his seat. "If you fail in these tasks by midnight of the final day, beware my wrath. Are there any questions?"

"How many mortals must we inspire?" Zoë asked.

Zeus raised a bushy eyebrow. "I'll decide how many when I'm good and ready, and not before. Do I make myself clear?"

"Yes, sire," she answered in a dour tone.

"And you'll need to learn the use of one of those." He jerked a thumb over his shoulder, indicating the computer. "So we can stay in touch."

Chloe stuck out her lower lip. "Why can't we use Hermes?"

"That boy hasn't taken wing since the day I installed the telephones. He's in charge of networking the system. I'll allow you a day to become proficient, so we may communicate via the Internet."

Chloe stomped her foot. "That's not fair. The others don't have to—"

Zeus shot to his feet and lifted his arms. Thunder shook the clouds around them. "Silence!"

Without warning, Kyra rose like thistledown, floating, swaying, cresting on waves of cool dry air. She looked left and right and saw her sisters do the same. Thanks to Chloe's disrespectful actions, they'd lost the time to prepare.

Darkness overtook her as she felt herself spiraling downward, a lone leaf tossing in the wind, unable to control her destination.

Chapter 2

Monte Carlo

A wave of satisfaction rippled through Jake Lennox's stomach as he turned over his cards in a gesture honed through years of self-control. Though he considered himself a minnow, maybe a marlin on his best day, in the world of high rollers, he'd out-lasted four of the five whales who had started this big-money poker game several hours ago, and won enough to pull ahead a hundred thousand for the night.

"A full house, aces and jacks."

Socrates Themopolis shook his bald head, his smile that of a benevolent godfather. "You never cease to

11

amaze me, son. Just when I'm positive you're bluffing, you manage to show a winning hand."

Grinning inside, Jake stacked the mound of thousand-dollar chips. "What can I say, Mr. T? You're a worthy opponent. It's always a pleasure sitting at your table." *And taking your money.*

The man some thought should top Bill Gates as the world's wealthiest, tapped steepled fingers to his lower lip. "We go back a long time. What were you—eighteen—when your father had an aneurysm in my casino? Still say it was a damned shame it happened on your birthday."

Jake remembered the gracious treatment he and his mother had received from the hotel magnate on one of the worst days of their lives. He'd always thought it fitting that Themopolis had paid for his father's funeral. Hell, his dad had lost so much money at his casino Mr. T should have named a slot machine in his honor.

"It was thirteen years ago. I've come a long way."

"You certainly have, and I've developed a lot of respect for you since then. The way you've taken care of your mother, learned to play a thinking game, never got in over your head . . ."

"The respect is mutual, Mr. T. It's the reason I stay out of your casinos when I'm in the States. It wouldn't be polite to take advantage of a mentor."

His gaze fixed on Jake, Mr. T leaned back and spoke to the dealer. "I think we're through for tonight, Jimmy. You can close the game room."

When the dealer left, Jake started to rise, but Themopolis gestured that he remain seated. "You're a hard man to track down. To be honest, one of the reasons I'm here is because I heard you were in town. I want to ask you something."

Curious, Jake settled back in his chair. Men like Mr. T usually acted first and asked questions later.

The billionaire opened an exquisitely carved humidor resting at his side. Taking out a Havana, he lit up and worked the cigar until gray-blue smoke floated in the air. "You travel in the right circles. Have you caught wind of a problem I'm having at my Las Vegas hotel?"

Jake had heard rumors of some minor cash flow troubles at the Acropolis I, but hadn't given it much thought. The gambling grapevine was full of gossip, most of it exaggerated or untrue. "There's buzz on the street, nothing I took for gospel."

Mr. T narrowed his gaze. "Someone's skimming money, but I'm not sure from where. The casino is always packed, so is the hotel, yet revenue is down by a million a month. My accountants are stymied, as is the GM."

"Have you called the gaming board?"

"I will, once we've caught the culprit. Whoever is running the scam is clever; the lost revenue could be from anywhere."

"What about hotel security?"

"Mel Turcotte was forced to retire after his stroke. His second in command, Rupert Ardmore, is competent and expects to be named Mel's successor. He claims he's investigating, but I'm not confident he's doing a good job." Mr. T set the cigar in a cut-crystal ashtray. "Things have escalated over the past month. At the moment, the only person I trust is my surveillance chief, Herb Molinari. He's been with me since I started in Las Vegas."

Jake didn't believe in Lady Luck. Proficient gamblers won using their brains, instincts, and wiles. So why was it he had a gut feeling the elusive female had just taken a seat on his shoulder? Lately, he'd been pondering a new career, something that would allow him to come clean with his mother. But all he knew how to do was play the odds in cities far from upstate New York. If Socrates Themopolis were indebted to him, there'd be no limit to what he could achieve.

"And you're telling me this because . . ."

"Last time we talked, you intimated you were getting tired of the gambling life. Is that still true, or have you changed your mind about leaving the business?"

"Let's just say if the right opportunity came along, I'd give it serious consideration."

"Good to hear, because I've decided to slip someone into the Acropolis I can trust, someone who knows his way around, but isn't familiar to my employees or the regular players. The old-timers might remember you because of your father, but Vegas is overflowing with new blood. With the cover I propose, people will figure they've seen you around, but I doubt they'll remember where."

"I'm flattered, but I have to ask, what's in it for me?"

"How about the chance to use the business degree you earned in college and manage a casino, instead of trying to beat one? And a percentage of the nightly take."

Jake thumbed his stack of chips. Earning a steady paycheck while being part of a business he enjoyed and understood, inside and out, suddenly became a heady lure. "You just said you have a competent manager."

"Competent, but not stellar. I want stellar, Jake." Themopolis took a long drag on the cigar and blew a smoke ring. "I want you."

Kyra faced Rupert Ardmore across his impressive desk. She'd seen the hotel manager around, even delivered coffee to this office when he'd met with her ex-boss, Ms. Simmons. In the eleven months since her arrival in Las Vegas she'd done her best to take mortals at face value, but there was something off-kilter about this man, something she couldn't put her finger on, and it made her uncomfortable.

"You understand Ms. Simmons left us in the lurch. With little more than a week before the grand finale of the Voice of Vegas competition, there's no time to hire a replacement. Since you were Ms. Simmons's assistant, I assume you know as much as she did about the project and the other giveaways we offer our patrons."

"Yes, of course." When she'd first begun her life on earth, the only employment Kyra had been able to obtain was the arduous job of a cocktail waitress in the huge casino. A few months later, she'd brought Ms. Simmons a drink and offered her a shoulder to cry on when she'd found the woman flapping around the lobby over some promotion gone wrong. Ms. Simmons had been so grateful, she'd given Kyra a position everyone considered a move in the right direction: personal assistant to the special event coordinator.

Since accepting the assignment, she'd done nothing more challenging than fetch files, take messages and, when she'd finally learned how, answer e-mails. Ms. Simmons had treated her as more of a glorified go-fer, but the job was still better than standing on her feet and serving drinks for hours on end. It also allowed Kyra, as the Muse of Good Fortune, to indulge freely in her favorite pastime—walking the casino floor, chatting with guests, and offering luck.

"Las Vegas is celebrating its one hundredth birthday, hence the new, updated ad campaign. I expect the singing competition to run without a hitch and make a name for the hotel. If you handle things with competence, I'm prepared to offer you the title and salary of special events coordinator permanently. If the night is a disaster, you'll be fired on the spot." Ardmore sat back in his leather desk chair and gave a smarmy smile. "Do you have any questions?"

Then and there Kyra decided she had no use for the man. Zeus had been threatening, but he held her fate in his hands. Ardmore was a puffed-up rooster with a lame my-way-or-the-highway attitude she despised. Working here had given her the ability to inspire good fortune in mortals. If not for that opportunity, she'd walk out now.

"And I'd still be in charge of the Wheel Deal and other promotions?" she asked, making certain her time remaining would continue in the same pleasant manner. The singing competition was scheduled for the night Zeus was scheduled to summon her back to Mount Olympus. Surely, with so many mortals winning money and prizes, she'd inspired enough to believe in good fortune. Only after she returned home would she know if her father saw it the same way.

"Absolutely."

Kyra held back a grin. By the time the Voice of Vegas was over, she'd be back to her world in a flash of glory. "Then I'll take the position."

"Very well." Ardmore scribbled on a notepad. His phone rang, and he frowned. "That's all, Ms. Degodessa."

Though the hotel manager hadn't said so, Kyra assumed Ms. Simmons's office now belonged to her. Which meant she no longer had an excuse for why she occasionally missed answering Zeus's weekly e-mails. It was a minus for the new job, but she'd worry about it later. First, she had to tell Lou the good news.

She took the stairs to the casino floor and headed to the service bar, hoping to find her best friend with a few free minutes to chat.

"Hey, Kyra. What's shakin'?" asked Eddie, a vertically challenged bartender with spiky black hair.

"Nothing much. Is Lou around?"

"She's serving drinks. And from her cranky attitude, I think she's having trouble at home again."

Louise Chandler, the sole support of her eighteen-month-old daughter and frail mother, lived in an outlying town in a shabby but neat two-bedroom duplex.

"Who was it this time? Her daughter or her mom?"

Eddie shrugged. "Hard telling."

"It's tough trying to lend Lou a hand when she won't accept what's offered," Kyra said more to herself than the bartender. "Are you still slipping extra chips on her tray?"

"I do my best, but she's sharp as a tack." Eddie's eyes narrowed. "Ixnay on the situation, doll."

"Here's a new order list, Eddie." Lou sighed as she placed her tray on the bar, then turned tired eyes on Kyra. "Last night was rough."

"Katie get another earache?"

"Yeah, and she woke my mother, which set them both to complaining. Kids and their health—it's

18

tough enough keeping them in clothes and toys, add doctor bills and it's a guaranteed trip to the poor house."

Kyra had never spent much time with children, as each of the gods and goddesses had been born fully formed by Zeus. But she'd heard enough of Katie's antics and ailments from Lou to know kids were a handful, especially toddlers.

"Then this is for you," said Kyra tucking a twenty-five-dollar chip into Lou's fanny pack, all she knew the waitress would accept. "I found it over by the slot machines."

"You are the luckiest woman I know. But you can't keep giving me chips you find on the floor. If the hotel hears about it, you'll get fired," Lou chided.

Before Kyra could respond, Eddie brought over a drink-laden tray. "All set." He gave Kyra a hopeful grin. "Sure you don't want to have dinner with me after work?"

"No thanks, maybe tomorrow."

He rested his knobby elbows on the bar. "Why do I get the feeling 'tomorrow' is never gonna come around?"

"You're too sensitive," Kyra said. "I told you I don't mix business with pleasure. And speaking of business—"

"I heard Ms. Simmons quit this morning. Something about not being appreciated." Lou caught Kyra's smile and jumped up and down. "Oh my

19

gosh, you got her job, didn't you? You're the new special events coordinator!"

Enveloped in the woman's childlike glee, Kyra was suddenly proud of the position, even if Ardmore's offer had come in a backhanded manner. "I'm on trial. It won't be mine permanently unless the Voice of Vegas goes off without a hitch."

"Congratulations. I know you'll do a top-notch job," said Eddie. He scanned the area with a practiced eye, then raised a brow. "Here's another bit of news. Have either of you met Mr. T's nephew?"

"Mr. T has a nephew?" asked Lou.

"So goes the rumor. He's the straight arrow standing by the cashier windows—reminds me of a cop. Name's Jake Lennox."

Kyra's scalp prickled, but she managed to stay calm as she glanced casually to her right. The man in question was dressed in a white shirt, red striped tie, and perfectly tailored gray suit. Tall, with thick dark hair, black eyebrows, and a scowl, he appeared the direct opposite of the hotel's convivial owner.

She recalled seeing Mr. Lennox as he strode through the casino this past week and remembered that, more often than not, he wore a smug expression, as if confident and secure in his abilities. He'd intrigued her when she'd first seen him from afar, and caused her to wonder at the reason behind his superior grin. When she'd found herself thinking about him as she lay in bed at night, she realized she'd broken her one and only personal rule—never dwell on any mortal man—and pushed him from her mind.

Viewing Jake Lennox tonight placed him right back on center stage. "How long will he be here?"

As if to prolong the anticipation, Eddie busied himself wiping down the counter. In the time Kyra had worked at the casino, she'd found the brash bartender to be a fount of information, much of it correct.

"No telling," Eddie finally said. "Word is, Mr. T wants him to learn the business, so Lennox will be conducting one-on-one interviews with a few of the employees. He has full access to any area of the hotel. I didn't know the old man even had a nephew, so I'm checking my sources. The whole setup sounds fishy to me."

Lou hoisted her tray. "He's good looking, in a brooding sort of way."

Kyra had determined months ago that she couldn't spare a serious thought for anyone of the opposite sex, brooding or otherwise, while residing on earth. She wasn't about to get involved with a mortal and risk falling in love when she had the chance to return to Mount Olympus and live forever in splendor. As hard as she'd worked, she wasn't sure which of the mortals in whom she'd inspired good fortune would count with Zeus.

"Which employees?" Kyra asked, concerned about being alone with a man who might be trouble in a very personal way.

Judi McCoy

"Management, a few peons here on the floor, even the guys in valet parking if he wants."

Just what she didn't need to hear. "Interesting." Kyra turned in the direction of the women's lounge. "Well, I'm heading for home. Tomorrow's my first full day in charge, and I can't afford to be late." She waved a good-bye. "See you in the morning."

As she passed the bank of cashier windows her skin tingled. When tiny bumps rose to attention on her arms, she knew immediately she was being assessed by Jake Lennox, and not as a co-worker, but as a woman.

You wish, was her first thought.

She'd had plenty of chances to date, and almost as many offers to skip the courting ritual and get right to the nitty-gritty of down-and-dirty sex. Throughout the ages, the citizens of Mount Olympus had dallied at will, with each other as well as with mortals, enjoying the freedom of a no-strings arrangement. Unfortunately, as centuries passed, people lost belief in the gods. These days, when a deity came to earth, it was usually to make mischief instead of love.

Chloe had slid into the habit of consorting with men soon after arriving here, insistent that she would never be involved in a complication of the heart. Kyra had stayed celibate. She had no need to resurrect a flaw haunting her since birth. Though her sisters thought it was in her mind, Kyra knew it to be true. Whenever she gave her body, she couldn't help but give her heart. When the time came to end the affair, it always took her forever to move on.

She'd already decided that the next time she got involved, it would be for eternity. And it would be with a man of Olympus, where she could spend *forever* in the company of gods. Not a mortal with dark eyes and wavy hair . . . and a brash killer smile.

Though she hadn't talked to Chloe or Zoë in a week, she was certain they would tell her that, imagination or not, she had to guard her heart. With only a short time left of their exile, each sister was determined to return home in triumph.

As a daughter of the mighty Zeus, she would not—could not—fail.

Chapter 3

Jake left the two men he'd been chatting with and ambled to the bank of surveillance monitors used to keep tabs on the entrances, exits, and interior of the hotel. Peering over Herb Molinari's shoulder, he frowned. "What the heck is she doing?"

"Don't have a clue, but it's a daily ritual . . . and it gets better. Just give her a second."

Jake glued his gaze to the monitor and again took note of Kyra Degodessa's eye-catching figure and sexily tousled hair. He'd seen her the first day he'd arrived at the Acropolis, sitting behind a tiny desk next to the concierge, and had immediately wanted to slide his hands over her silky-looking skin, taste her ripe lips, run his fingers through those russet curls and spread them out on a pillow . . . preferably a pillow in his bed. And his reaction to her remained the same.

Kyra stood as rigid as the marble statue of Zeus she was observing in the entryway. When viewed from the rear, she had long shapely legs, a well-rounded bottom, and a nicely indented waist. Jake recalled an ID photo that showed her heart-shaped face, smoky gray eyes, and high cheekbones. Not to mention a mouth made for sin. All in all, a woman who looked like she could bring a sane man to his knees.

She appeared bright, personable, and according to those he'd talked to, able to handle herself in any situation. Though he'd heard she was recently promoted, he didn't understand why she'd been wasting her time running interference as the personal go-fer of the hotel's special events coordinator.

From the information he'd compiled in his online investigation, he'd learned Ms. Degodessa had started out as a lowly cocktail waitress, and those women still trusted and admired her. While the dealers and pit crew adored her from afar, the busboys, bartenders, and roustabouts jockeyed for a date. Even the customers she'd served seemed thrilled when she paid them attention.

After two days of digging, he'd had zero success ferreting out information on her past. She had no credit history, no police record, and no prior job experience. The "who to notify in the case of an emergency" line in her employment application was blank, and she lived alone with no visible love interest, either male or female. If he didn't know better, he'd think she had magically appeared on earth just eleven months earlier, because there was little data on her before that point.

He'd made a few subtle inquiries and found that, besides the promotions manager and Ms. Simmons, Kyra was the only hotel employee who had intimate access to the implement used in the daily Wheel Deal. Now that she was in charge, he planned to look into the event to make certain the Acropolis wasn't experiencing a loss in that particular area, as well.

Right now, due to her ritual on the gaming floor, Kyra Degodessa was his sole suspect in the casino's lost revenue problem.

"I keep asking myself what she's thinkin' when she stares at the great and mighty Zeus," said Herb, interrupting Jake's train of thought.

Jake studied the twelve-foot-high god. Every inch of both the Acropolis I and II was decorated in a Grecian motif. The largest ballroom here had been christened the Mount Olympus room, the restaurants were done in carved stone and imported marble, and the lobby was filled with elaborate columns and giant statues of males and females dressed either in flowing gowns or fully nude.

The statue Kyra inspected was the latter.

"At first, I thought she was some kind of pervert," Herb continued. "The way she always checks out that statue's private parts gives me the creeps."

"You can only see her from the rear. How do you know what she's looking at?"

The guard shrugged. "What do most babes stare at when they see a naked guy?"

Straightening, Jake stuffed his hands in his pockets. He pitied Herb, who had just signed the final papers on his divorce decree, and was down on women in general. Jake was divorced too, but with him the opposite was true. He was happy they were free of one another, and Corinne had found someone else.

He was about to tell Herb to keep his speculation on Ms. Degodessa to a minimum, when his quarry moved. Hands on hips, she bent forward as if calibrating the statue's formidable genitalia, raised the middle finger of her left hand, and shot the stone god the bird. Then she tossed her head of curls, and flounced off toward the casino floor. A surprise, because Jake had expected her to use the morning to formally ensconce herself in her new office.

"Does it every time she comes through the door," commented Herb. "You want me to follow her with the zoom lens?"

"I can handle it from here." Jake walked from the surveillance center in the basement to the elevator, and punched the button for the main floor. On the

27

ride, he perused the flocked wallpaper and gold-veined mirrors decorating the car walls. Depending on what part of the hotel you were in, the Acropolis resembled either the inside of a Greek diner or a bordello. Socrates Thermopolis had interesting taste—whorehouse tacky with an ethnic twist.

He entered the lobby completely at home in the bright lights and almost deafening racket of a fully functioning gaming establishment. The buzzers, whistles, bells, and tuneful ditties of the slots and other electrified games of chance that filled the center of the floor were as familiar as the air he breathed.

This was the heart of the casino. Roulette wheels end-capped the room, flanked on both sides by craps tables, of which only one was in use at the moment. Blackjack stations finished the outer ring, cradling pit bosses who watched over their babies. Right now, the low-ball tables were moderately busy, while the bored dealers at the big money stations stood and shuffled the cards, fanning them in hopes of snaring a sucker. To the rear were glassed-in chambers housing poker and other card games. Even with air purifiers running day and night, the atmosphere was smoky, congested, and thick.

He didn't like to dwell on it, but the playing area reminded him of a past he longed to forget. His father had died at a craps table in this very casino. Thanks to Socrates, Jake had gone to college and gotten a business degree, but jobs had been scarce when he'd graduated. With a widowed mother to care for, he'd drifted back to something he knew well—the life of a professional gambler.

Now Socrates was again giving him the opportunity to rise above his dad's failures and make something of himself. Something that wouldn't garner snide comments or looks of disapproval. Something fulfilling.

Something that would earn him respect.

He propped himself against a wall at the first service bar. A few of the change handlers nodded politely, but for the most part the staff paid him no mind. Herb had introduced him around and given orders Jake be treated as they would Mr. T. Jake had concentrated on building a friendly relationship with the employees. He'd been making his way through the list, until someone mentioned Kyra and her habit of walking the casino when she wasn't working for Ms. Simmons.

Over the years, he'd seen plenty of weird good luck rituals used by various gamblers, but when he'd learned of the strange hand jive Kyra shared with some of the customers, he'd decided to give her a closer look.

He perked up when he spotted Ms. Degodessa across the floor. She'd shed her coat and wore fitted black slacks, a black turtleneck sweater, and a gold-colored blazer. Her red hair was pinned on top of her head in a mass of ringlets and, now that he could see her, he noted she wore only a minimal amount of makeup to enhance her natural beauty.

Jake strode across the room in a zigzag pattern and paused behind a kiosk housing a variety of million-dollar slot machines when Kyra stopped beside an older woman sitting at a flashy one-armed bandit. With her unkempt appearance, baggy pants and cigarette dangling from bloodless lips, the customer resembled a typical loser.

"Now, Marie. I thought you promised to quit." Kyra plucked the offensive item from Marie's mouth and stuck it in a standing chrome bucket. "I told you I wouldn't be able to wish you well if I caught you smoking again."

The woman gave a snaggletooth grin. "Ya shoulda checked, missy, because it wasn't lit. Guess you owe me another hit."

Kyra removed the cigarette from its sandy grave, inspected the tip, and returned it to the can. "Sorry, I jumped the gun." She tapped the older woman's shoulder with two fingers. "I wish you the best of luck, Marie. I'll see you later."

When she sashayed away, Jake was tempted to go after her, but suspected he'd find out more if he observed the customer. Marie slid three one-dollar tokens into the "Mining for Gold" machine and, grinning broadly, pulled the lever. Without sparing a glance at the row of bars that would mark her a winner, she placed her bucket near the trough and waited.

A half-second later, lights flashed and bells rang a crazy jingle of success. Dollar tokens clanged, and

Marie scooped them into her plastic container. Giggling like a six-year-old who'd just unearthed a treasure, she clutched the bucket to her chest and headed for the cashier.

A bolt of unease tripped down Jake's spine. Raising a hand, he flagged a floor manager. The jackpot hadn't been more than a couple of hundred, not large enough to post on the casino wall, but several unscheduled wins a night like this one would add to Mr. T's loss line.

Phil Riley trotted over, his expression curious. "Something wrong, Mr. Lennox?"

"I want this box sent to the equipment room for a complete overhaul. Take it apart, and let me know if you find anything out of the ordinary, even something as simple as a loose screw."

"Sure thing," said the manager. He shut down the slot machine, then used a hand-held radio to contact maintenance.

Jake searched the area and spotted a pile of burnished copper curls in the distance. Adjusting his tie, he strode in Kyra's direction.

Why was Jake Lennox following her?

Kyra had spotted him right after she'd reached Marie's side. She was surprised to see him in the gambling room at this early hour, but he'd definitely been on her tail.

From the way he'd homed in on her last night, she suspected he'd taken an interest in her, as had most of the single men who worked here. But if that were the case, why didn't he simply introduce himself and ask her on a date? Unless he was one of those perverts who lurked around women just to enjoy their panicked reactions.

She recalled his dark sexy eyes and brooding smile and shook her head. Jake Lennox had to realize the effect his *come here, baby* smile had on women, so why was he lurking after her like a would-be mugger? Checking her out as a hotel worker was totally ridiculous. She'd been a lowly step-and-fetch-it assistant until a day ago, and she certainly hadn't done anything to merit his suspicion . . . except talk to Marie.

She swallowed. Had someone told him of her "good luck" reputation or the effect it had on a few chosen customers? No, that couldn't be it. It made more sense to believe he was just one of those men who were so full of themselves they preened like peacocks until a woman noticed. Typical of the male mortals she seemed to attract.

Relegating the incident to the farthest recesses of her brain, she stopped at her old desk to pick up a file, then climbed the stairs to the mezzanine level. When she worked for Ms. Simmons, the woman must have had her extension on speed dial, because there were some days when Kyra's lobby phone never stopped ringing. Now that she was in charge, she thought it might be fun to give a stellar performance, then leave Rupert Ardmore in the lurch as had her superior. Besides, she needed all the help she could get where Zeus was concerned. If she did a commendable enough job, he might add points to her review.

She closed the door, sat at the polished cherry-wood desk, and took in the space around her. Large, with a window overlooking the parking lot, the office had a surveillance camera angled from an upper corner in order to pan the area. Even though the décor consisted mainly of red flocked wallpaper, crimson draperies, and a large leather couch, the room seemed sterile. She scanned the desk and drawers, taking note of their pristine, dust-free condition. It was clear housekeeping had already scooped up anything personal the last owner might have left behind.

Spinning in the chair, she swung around to the credenza and blinked at the glaringly vacant space. She'd hoped to begin her morning using the computer to send her weekly report to Zeus, as she sometimes did when Ms. Simmons wasn't around. What had happened to the annoying machine?

Turning to the phone, she punched in a hotel extension and left a message on Rob Garrett's voice-mail. "Hey, Rob, it's Kyra. Did you hear, I've got Ms. Simmons's old job? I'll tell you about it when I see you. In the meantime, her computer's disappeared and I need it. See what you can do, okay?"

Rob Garrett was one of the few mortals she'd met who was a truly nice guy. He lived in the apartment below her at the condo complex, and over time they'd become friends. By day, he toiled as a computer professional at the Acropolis; in the evening, he practiced the song he'd be performing in the competition for the Voice of Vegas, and in between he saw to the care of his aging grandmother. One night, after his clear baritone had drifted up from his apartment, Kyra suggested he try out for the contest. Rob had won the hotel's competition, and made it through the elimination rounds to the finals.

Thinking of the big event reminded Kyra of her charge—the supervision of the Voice of Vegas. First prize was a year's recording contract and the high-profile job of singing a song composed specially for Nevada's Division of Travel and Tourism. The chosen singer would handle the TV and radio voiceovers for the city's promotions as well as record the song to be released nationwide.

Each hotel on the strip had been encouraged to hold in-house auditions to find an unknown in their employ to represent the casino. After that, the participating venues held a string of eliminations, until the contestants were whittled to six, one each from the Acropolis, Tropicana, Luxor, Bellagio, Mirage, and Circus Circus.

The casinos had drawn lots for the rounds, and the Acropolis had scored the coup of hosting the grand finale. With Ms. Simmons gone, Kyra was in charge.

She knew the guest judges' names by heart. Dr. Slick, a noted rap artist, Missy Malone, a famous pop singer, and Simon Cloud, a British recording executive, were scheduled to arrive a day before the competition. It was up to her to cater to their every wish, and interface with the television crew and the emcee of the event, a local lounge entertainer by the name of Buddy Blue.

Sorting through the file she'd compiled on the event, she reread the details Ms. Simmons had given her. She was so involved, she didn't realize someone had knocked at the door until she raised her head and met Jake Lennox's steely gaze.

"Ms. Degodessa?"

Kyra leaned back in her chair and looked up. Way up. "Yes."

Jake Lennox strolled in and stood across from the desk. Dressed in khaki slacks, a navy sport coat, and a well-tailored white shirt, he looked more like a wealthy customer than a man on staff. Not pleased that she had to crane her neck to make eye contact, she rose to her feet. Thanks to her five-foot-nine-inch frame, his six-foot-something height wasn't as noticeable as when she'd been sitting. But when he smiled that *come here, baby* smile, her insides started to itch.

He held out his hand. "We haven't formally met. I'm Jake Lennox, Mr. Themopolis's nephew."

She accepted the handshake then quickly sat down, ignoring the jolt that shot straight to her core. Though no other mortal man she'd met had zapped her with his physical presence in the same way as

Jake Lennox, it was nothing she couldn't take in stride.

"Do you have a minute? I need to ask you a few questions."

"I'm . . . ah . . . busy," she answered. In truth, being this close to the man made her itchy all over—including some extremely personal places she didn't want to think about. "It's only my second day at this job."

"I heard."

News really did travel fast in a hotel. "So if you'll excuse me . . ."

"How about lunch?"

"Sorry." She tapped a finger on the file. "I plan to eat at my desk."

"Ms. Degodessa, I'm in the process of interviewing various employees of the Acropolis to get an idea of staff morale and satisfaction. Someone mentioned you might be a good person to speak with."

Mesmerized by his eyes, she stared, noting they weren't brown, as she'd first thought, but a very dark and intense blue.

"Kyra?"

"Hmm? What?"

"I was hoping we could talk."

"Talk?" The blue was practically purple, close to the color of the mountains on Mount Olympus . . .

"I just need to ask you a few questions."

Coming to her senses, she folded her arms. "I think it best you make an appointment," she said, annoyed she'd been close to stammering. And why was she finding it so difficult to breathe? "I'm swamped until after the Voice of Vegas."

"It won't take long." He stepped closer. "Later this afternoon? In my office?"

In *his* office? "Fine." Anything to get rid of him. "What time?"

"How about six o'clock?"

"I work the Wheel Deal in the lobby at four and it usually lasts until six-fifteen."

"Six-thirty then?"

"I'll try."

He extended his hand again, and Kyra thought seriously about rejecting the offer. Then she realized how ridiculous she must look with her hands tucked securely under her elbows. Clasping his fingers, she gave another cursory shake. "I'll see you later."

"I'm in the basement."

"The basement?"

"Make a left when you leave the elevator. I'm across from the surveillance room." He quirked up a corner of his mouth. "I'll be waiting."

The door closed and she heaved a breath. How dumb could she be, agreeing to meet with him privately, where she'd again be under the scrutiny of those laser-sharp eyes. Considering her libido's reaction to him, Jake Lennox should be put on the back burner and forgotten.

Figuring any number of things could happen by the appointed time, she concentrated on the Wheel

Judi McCoy

Deal. The hotel promotions manager had started the contest to bolster attendance between 8 A.M. and 4 P.M. Each day, slots players had the opportunity to win fifty thousand dollars. Numbered tokens were placed at random in the machines and dropped into the troughs when a player won. Players were instructed to turn in their tokens between four and five. It was her job to line up the players and give each one a single spin of the Deal Wheel.

Small monetary prizes and gifts peppered the ninety-nine numbers, while slot one hundred indicated the grand prize of fifty thousand in cash, to be paid on the spot to the winner. If the first person in line won the money, the rest of the contestants continued to spin for lesser prizes.

Kyra spent time choosing the week's offerings. Ms. Simmons had no imagination when it came to the giveaways, but Kyra liked to mix things up a little, sometimes adding gifts she knew would mean a lot to certain patrons. Of course, that was after she had a chance to speak personally to those who turned in a token. If she had her way, everyone would win the fifty thousand, but that would arouse suspicion, so she made sure the grand prize was awarded at least three times per week. The other two days, she spread small bits of good fortune in place of the big win.

After completing the task, she ate a light lunch while she phoned the assistants of each of the Voice of Vegas judges, introducing herself as their new contact. On her final call, she left a message on the machine of Buddy Blue, the king of lounge lizards. She'd met him several times, and shuddered whenever she recalled the way he'd licked his reptilian lips as he'd stared at her chest.

At 4 P.M. Kyra went to the lobby and sat at her old desk. A line had already formed with hopeful players, which in itself made her smile. Many people left before trying the wheel, which meant the ones who stayed already believed in the *possibility* of good fortune. But every so often she found a customer who needed her inspiration.

She spoke with a husband and wife from Duluth, a boisterous man who wore a half-dozen gold chains around his neck, a grandmother who came to Vegas once a month because she thought it kept her young, and many more who hoped they were lucky. Though she enjoyed meeting the customers, there were usually a few with whom she felt a kinship, that indefinable link of the heart. But not today.

Just when she decided to let fate make the choice, a young woman ran to the table, panting like a marathon runner.

"I'm not too late, am I? There's still time to exchange my chip for a spin?"

Plainly dressed and wearing Coke-bottle lenses, the girl appeared so full of hope it made Kyra's eyes hurt just to look at her eager face. "Nope, we have one more minute."

"That's good, great." She held up the chip, engraved with the number thirteen. "When this coin dropped into the nickel slots trough, I had a gut feeling tonight was my chance to hit the jackpot."

"Really?" asked Kyra. "Do you believe in luck?"

"To tell the truth, no. I've never been to Las Vegas before. I don't even play the lottery. I should be home waiting tables to pay off my college loans, but a friend talked me into coming, so I said to myself, 'Why not?' and here I am."

Kyra led her to the correct spot in line, pleased she'd found her cause for the day. "I wish you the best of luck," she said, tapping the woman's shoulder with the first and second finger of her right hand.

One by one the customers took their turn. A crowd gathered to cheer them on, commiserating with groans when the jackpot slot was missed. Then came the female college student, who gave the wheel a downward push and stared at the spinning circle of color. Several rotations later, bells, buzzers, and whistles clanged. Lights pulsed in time to a garish blast of music. The crowd cheered, and well-wishers patted the girl on the back.

She grinned through tears at Kyra. "Th-thank you. Thanks so much." She dried her face with a tissue. "I can't believe how—how—"

"Lucky you are?" asked Kyra.

"No, I mean, yes, I am lucky. I'm going to use the money to pay my loans. Then I'm going to lighten my work load so I can concentrate on my studies. The money will be put to good use, that's for sure."

Kyra led the girl to the front desk and left her filling out paperwork with the clerk. Returning to the wheel, she handed out certificates, one spin at a time, to be exchanged for other prizes. When finished, it was past six-thirty and she was exhausted. She'd done her good deed for the day. It was time to go home.

Then she remembered her appointment with Jake Lennox. Since she'd said she would *try* to make the meeting, she figured she hadn't made a commitment. She'd apologize tomorrow, give him a few minutes, and forget about him.

Out in the blustery January desert wind, Kyra passed guest parking and hurried to the employee lot, shivering as she walked. Halfway to her car, the hairs at her nape stood on end. Cocking her head, she forged ahead as she reached into her bag and found her pepper spray. After a few weeks on earth, she'd learned the noxious mist was the best protection a lone female could carry.

Gravel crunched behind her. Damn, why hadn't she taken Howie up on his offer to put her car in the parking garage at no charge? She hadn't wanted to owe the valet the type of favor he suggested, but anything was better than being mugged or raped. Or worse.

Almost to her BMW, she hit the button on the automatic lock. The moment she whipped open the door, strong fingers clasped her shoulder. Spinning

41

on her heels, she held up the aerosol can. "I'm warning you, I know how to use this."

The figure ducked and weaved. "Hey, hey. Careful with that stuff. It's me. Jake Lennox."

Her stomach fluttered, and she slouched against the car. "What do you want?"

"We had an appointment, remember?"

"Oh. Sorry. I was so busy it slipped my mind," she lied, dropping the pepper spray into her bag.

"I guessed as much, but I wanted to catch you. I saw you leave on the surveillance monitor and decided to check the lobby. You blew past me like one of those speed walkers in the Olympics."

His mention of the ancient Greek games made her pine for home. "I'm really tired," she explained. "Besides, it's too cold to talk out here. I'll phone you tomorrow, first thing, and we can set up another appointment."

He stepped closer, as if protecting her from the bracing wind. "Maybe we could go somewhere to discuss things tonight instead," he suggested, giving her one of those killer smiles.

His blue-eyed gaze seared a line of heat straight to her insides. In return, she gave him her best I-don't-think-so glare. "If it's a date you're after, I don't get personal with co-workers." She slid behind the wheel, started the engine, and powered down the window. "If you'll excuse me, I have to leave."

42

Jake placed his hands on the car roof and leaned in. "I don't mess around with co-workers either. I just want to talk."

"That's what they all say," she said under her breath. Since arriving on Earth she'd been hit on by almost every man who had crossed her path, and the idea that she'd been wrong about this one stuck in her craw.

He hunched down and stuck his head inside. "Ring me tomorrow, as soon as you get to your office."

His mint-scented breath caressed her cheek, and Kyra sighed inwardly. It had been a long while since she'd allowed herself to get this close to a man, and Jake Lennox was prime. Too bad he knew it.

"I'll do my best." With nothing more to say, she threw the car into reverse and stepped on the gas.

Chapter 4

Jake followed the Beemer's tail lights until they disappeared from view. Jeez, that was close. With her killer body, sultry smile, and smoky lashes, Kyra Degodessa oozed sex appeal from her toes to the top of her wind-blown hair. Even after her gaze had turned from frosty to frigid, he'd almost lost it for a couple of seconds and actually thought about kissing her through the open window of her car.

Her car! Absentmindedly, he ran a thumb over the spot on his jaw that had brushed one of her curls. She'd had this position for less than forty-eight hours. How the hell could a second-class assistant afford to drive an expensive, late-model import? And where did she get the cash to pay for what he suspected were designer clothes and shoes? Did she have a wealthy benefactor or had she bought the luxuries with the money she'd skimmed from the hotel?

Mentally adding the possibility to his list, he returned to the Acropolis, still trying to figure out why Kyra was so cool to him. Okay, so he'd pushed until she agreed to meet today, then backed out of the commitment until tomorrow, but hey, he was only doing his job. As an employee of the hotel, she should have been more cooperative, even if she suspected he had dating on the brain.

And that was the problem. As curious as he was about Kyra Degodessa, he couldn't deny he wanted to get her alone, and she'd somehow figured that out. Which meant he had to stay grounded. If the Acropolis was losing money because of her, it was his responsibility to gather the data and turn her in. He just had to ask questions in a way that would keep his mind out of the bedroom.

Jake pushed through the casino doors and strolled to a bank of elevators. On the way he spotted Rupert Ardmore, his competitor for the permanent position of hotel manager. Ever since he'd arrived on site, the short, slight man had made it a point to let Jake know he was out of his league. He had yet to figure exactly what the interim man-in-charge was doing to find Mr. T's missing cash, but it didn't matter. Once he bagged the culprit, Ardmore would be standing in the cold with egg on his face, and he would have the job.

Judi McCoy

The manager veered in his path, as if daring Jake to run him down. "A moment, Lennox, if you please."

Well, hell.

Jake stepped to the side and continued on his way. "This is a bad time. I have a lot on my mind."

He planned to escape his nemesis, as he had on more than one occasion. From the day they'd met, the creep had bombarded him with e-mails suggesting things Jake could do around the casino to make himself useful, as if relegating him to errand boy. It had been a balancing act, ignoring the creep while he stayed friendly.

Ardmore followed on his heels, then darted in front of him. Obviously frustrated, he raised a hand. "It's important."

Jake doubted it, but figured he'd never get any peace if he didn't cooperate. Then he remembered Kyra's evasive tactics. Was this how she felt when he'd pestered her for a meeting? If so, no wonder she acted annoyed.

"How about five minutes in your office?" he offered. That way, he could walk out the door whenever he wanted—like right after Ardmore sat down.

"I don't think—"

Jake glanced at his watch, an intimidation trick he'd picked up from Mr. T. "That's all I can give you tonight."

His opponent pursed his thin lips. "Fine, follow me."

They took the stairs to the mezzanine level where the important offices were located. Ardmore led him into a large, well-appointed space. "Why do I get the feeling you've been avoiding me?" the man asked once he settled behind his desk.

Jake shrugged. "I think you're oversimplifying it. I've been trying to immerse myself in the day-to-day operation of the casino, so I don't have much time for chit-chat."

"It's a sound idea, but you need direction. Being Mr. T's nephew doesn't mean the running of a hotel is in your blood. I have an MBA from Wharton and two years of working with Mel Turcotte, one of the best in the business. I'd be happy to give you a few pointers. Couple more years and maybe you'll be ready for a promotion."

"It's a generous offer," Jake responded, neglecting to mention his own business degree. Instead, he activated his *charm* gene. "I'll have to think on it."

Ardmore narrowed his eyes, and nodded at a poster displayed on the wall advertising the Voice of Vegas competition. "Tell me, do you enjoy that type of entertainment?"

Suspicious of the guy's wheedling tone, Jake said, "It's okay, but not really my cup of tea."

After opening a drawer and pulling out a manila folder, Ardmore linked his hands on the blotter. "Well then, maybe it's time you learned to drink a different brand."

Huh? "And what makes you say that?"

"Since you're here to learn the ropes, I thought you might want to do something constructive. I'm handing you the reins of coordinating certain aspects of the Voice of Vegas alongside Ms. Degodessa, our new special events coordinator. Your job will be security, crowd control, the voting process, things of that nature. It'll be an important night for the Acropolis, so both of you are needed." He pushed the file across the desk. "The details are in here."

Well, shit! Handling crowd control for such a huge circus would be nothing but a waste of time, mostly because it would take him away from his investigation into the casino thefts, which would stymie his quest to be the new GM. Did Ardmore suspect that was the reason he was here, and had thought up this stupid idea just to sidetrack the competition?

Jake collected the folder and pasted an eager grin on his face. "Thanks for the honor."

The man's expression turned to one of confusion. "Honor?"

"It's the opportunity of a lifetime. Gives me a chance to meet celebrities, get the hotel in good with the media. I might even swing a spot on television. And if I ace the job, it's sure to impress my uncle."

He stood, clutching the file to his chest. From the look on Ardmore's mug, he could tell the guy had segued from pompous to poleaxed in under five seconds. As soon as he got to his suite, he was going to call Themopolis and plead for release because he'd bet his last thousand-dollar chip the magnate wouldn't approve. He had no time to supervise a contest when he had to concentrate on the missing funds.

"I'm going to my room and ordering a bottle of champagne to celebrate," Jake lied. "See you around."

Ardmore stood. "If you don't mind, I'd like an update on your progress every other day or so."

"Sure, no problem."

In the hall, Jake huffed out a breath. It was natural for the smarmy bastard to resent his presence; a new alpha male on the turf would alarm any red-blooded man worth his salt. He had planned to win the manager's position honestly, not through subterfuge. As of tonight, the gloves were off—and there'd be snow in the desert before he'd give the ass a single progress report.

He marched to his suite and flung the folder on his bed, then stripped out of his tie and suit jacket. Taking a seat at the desk, he dialed Mr. T's private number. The droning ring gave him a chance to think and, in a flash of brilliance, he realized he'd been handed a prize, not a punishment. If he accepted the task of coordinating the contest, he'd be able to prove to Mr. T he could succeed at any aspect of running the hotel, including the supervision of major events. More importantly, he'd be working closely with Kyra Degodessa. It was the perfect excuse for tomorrow's *talk*. He just had to keep his mind on business, and he was set.

Voicemail answered and Jake knew he had to say something. "It's Jake Lennox. Ardmore just assigned me to co-direct the Voice of Vegas. It could put a crimp in my investigation, but I'm going to work through it. Please give me a call so we can discuss the details."

He set the phone in its cradle and ran his fingers through his hair. Then he checked out the room service menu. Nothing on the list caught his attention, so he turned to the desserts. His mouth watered at the picture of a triple scoop of vanilla ice cream covered in plump, juicy strawberries. The decadent concoction caused his thoughts to glide to a sassy redhead with a centerfold body.

By the end of day tomorrow, he'd have Kyra Degodessa all to himself, his to question and observe whenever he wanted. Until he got the answers he needed, what could it hurt to fantasize a little? Or a lot?

He picked up the phone and ordered the sundae . . . with extra whipped cream.

Kyra pulled into a parking space in front of her condo complex, still thinking about Jake Lennox. She recalled the confident set of his broad shoulders, his superior grin, and the bone-melting way he'd sized her up from head to toe. His every action signified a man who was self-assured and proud of it.

Almost a Goddess

He'd made it clear he didn't want to date her, yet he continued to tease her senses. Rarely was she wrong about a man, be he god or mortal, so Jake had her flummoxed. What was so important about a simple interview that had him at her heels even when she was on the casino floor?

She stepped into the condo lobby and, clear as water from a mountain spring, caught the flow of another idea. Instead of looking for a way to avoid the man, perhaps she should encourage him. Her sisters kept advising her to have at least one interaction with a male while she was on Earth. She could never fall in love with a guy like Jake, so maybe, just maybe, she could go to bed with him and still be safe.

Having a fling might take his mind off of what she did with the customers, and he could be exactly what she needed to erase the loneliness she'd experienced of late—without the complications. It had been so long since she'd allowed a man to touch her in anything more than a friendly manner. After months of celibacy and inspiring good fortune, a mindless *affaire* could be just the thing. No strings, no hurt feelings, just plain old, no-holds-barred sex.

After entering the building, Kyra unlocked her door, took off her coat, and hung it in the closet. Though the condo was nothing like her rooms on Mount Olympus, she enjoyed the apartment's clean lines and trendy furniture.

Upon arriving here, she'd awakened from a deep sleep and found herself lying on a queen-sized bed. Perusing the condo, she noted it contained everything she'd need to live comfortably, right down to a closet full of designer clothes. She'd come across a lease for one year's occupancy marked "paid in full" sitting on the kitchen table, along with a handbag. Inside was a credit card and a collection of documents needed to exist on earth without suspicion. There was even a sporty automobile waiting in front of her building.

She glanced in a corner of the living room and grimaced at the pile of computers and other smaller devices that magically appeared there on a monthly basis. Zeus had been determined to have her use each cursed form of modern communication, and she'd ignored his every attempt. It was only after she'd been promoted to special events, and Ms. Simmons had insisted she learn the basics of e-mail, that Kyra agreed to familiarize herself with a modicum of modern technology. Her father seemed to know the very moment it happened, because the first personal communication she'd received had been from *topgod@mounto.org*.

Zeus, the wily old fox, had seen to everything. She had no one to blame but herself if she failed in this final chance to inspire.

In the kitchen, she turned on the heat under the kettle, intent on brewing tea. She was hungry, but it was too late to eat . . . well, maybe a cookie or two, but no more. She heard a knock as she poured boiling water over the tea bag in her cup and carried the steaming brew to the foyer. After peeking into the peephole, she opened the door.

Rob Garrett, his expression sheepish, smiled broadly. "Hey, Kyra, I heard you walking around and thought you might appreciate a little company."

"I just heated water for tea. Would you like a cup?"

"If it's not too much trouble." He followed her into the kitchen and sat at the table. "Got any cookies?"

"You read my mind," Kyra teased, taking a package of Orange Milanos from the cupboard. There were a few *good* things about living on Earth, and this particular delicacy was one of them. After fixing his drink, she placed it and the cookies on the table and took a seat across from him.

Rob was young and strapping—at least six-four—with curly blond hair and lovely brown eyes. Kyra was proud of the fact that she'd talked Rob into entering the Voice of Vegas with other contestants from the Acropolis. The judges had liked him so much he'd won without her wish of good fortune.

"Sorry I couldn't get back to you this afternoon. Ardmore had me in his office, setting up a new top-of-the-line computer system. He's such a stickler about the details, it took me hours to finish the job."

"You're forgiven," said Kyra, taking a sip of tea. "I didn't have one second to worry about it after I started work."

"Your message was a high point. Congratulations on the promotion." He popped an entire Milano into his mouth and chewed. "Does that mean you're also in charge of the singing competition?"

Kyra conjured a look of innocence, then let her smile grow. "Oh, I don't know. Probably . . . since Ardmore said it was up to me to make the show a success."

"Wow." He swallowed the cookie in a gulp. "Fantastic. It'll be great. You'll do great."

Kyra reached out and covered his meaty hand with her smaller one, hoping to give him courage. In past discussions, Rob had confided his worry over his lack of experience and his occasional bouts of stage fright. Though he'd made it through to the final round, he continued to have doubts before he went on stage. She feared he would be his own worst enemy and blow his big chance at stardom.

He sighed. "I could really use a win. Putting my grandmother in a nursing home ate up all of my savings."

Rob was his grandmother's sole support and a very caring grandson. "Just think. You'll triple-quadruple your money once you win."

His expression grew serious. "I got the name of a singing coach and thought maybe I should take a couple of lessons, but the man is expensive. I tried asking Ardmore if the hotel would foot the bill, but every time I brought it up he changed the subject."

54

"Then you have to make him listen," said Kyra. "Your success will bring positive publicity to the Acropolis, and that means more business."

Rob set down his mug of tea. "Since you're in charge, maybe you could ask him for me."

Kyra didn't want to speak to Rupert Ardmore about anything, but she'd learned to take a challenge in stride. Rob was a nice guy who deserved a win, and he'd been there when she needed a few lessons when she'd lied and told Ms. Simmons she could open, save, send, and answer e-mails. If singing instructions would give him confidence to make the grade, then she'd do her best to see he got them.

"I will. First thing tomorrow."

Rob grinned from ear to ear. "Thanks, Kyra. Maybe someday I'll be able to repay you for the help. It if wasn't for you, I wouldn't have entered the contest in the first place."

"Just get a computer up and running in my office by the end of the day tomorrow." She was already late with her weekly update to Zeus. "Anything else I can do to help?"

"Um . . . maybe you could talk to Grandma for me? Tell her how you think I have what it takes to win."

Blindsided by his request, she blinked. "I'm not sure that's a good idea. I mean, she doesn't know me, so why would she care about my opinion?"

Rob's complexion turned red as a stop light.

Judi McCoy

"Um . . . uh . . . because I told her . . . you were . . . special."

Special? The word did not bode well. In the time she'd known Rob, he'd never offered to introduce her to his grandmother.

"Did you lie to your grandmother about me?"

Cringing, he took a long drink, then swiped his hand across his mouth. "Sort of."

Kyra tried to stay calm. There was no need to panic. "What does that mean?"

"I told her we were going together."

"Going together? As in dating?"

"Sort of."

"I am *so* beginning to hate those words. Please be more specific."

He slumped in his seat. "Promise you won't get mad?"

"I can't promise anything. But if you're truthful, I'll think about it." She picked out a cookie, realized she'd lost her appetite, and returned it to the bag. "Now what did you say about me to her?"

"I told her you were . . . the one."

"The one!" If news of such close involvement with a mortal got back to Mount Olympus, someone—like Zeus—might assume she'd fallen in love, which meant she'd been too busy to do her job. The father god might negate the good she'd done simply because she'd canoodled with one special human. Inhaling, she slid her palms to her cheeks.

56

"I'm sorry, but I didn't know what else to tell her." Rob hung his head. "Gram said when I found a good woman, her feelings would count." The words rushed from his mouth like a waterfall. "I'm not dating anybody, so there's no one else to ask, and you're always saying you'll do whatever you can to help me. This would be it."

"I don't understand the logic," Kyra muttered. "It would just be my opinion."

"But don't you see? In Gram's eyes, your opinion would mean more than hers, because she'd think we were in love. She couldn't fault me for wanting to win if you thought it was a good idea."

She met his stricken expression with a glare. "She thinks we're getting married?"

"No! No!" He shook his head. "At least, not right away. But I know she wants to see me settled before she . . . you know."

Kyra's heart shifted in her chest. How could she be angry with a man who loved his grandmother that much? "How many times would I have to meet her?"

A smile flickered across his boyish face. He held up his hand as if swearing in court. "Just once, I promise."

One time? Gazing at Rob, with his nice-guy grin and honest open attitude, made "just once" sound easy. She rested her elbows on the table. "Okay, I'll do it."

* * *

The next morning, Jake hung up the phone and leaned back to think. This last call was his third to Mr. T, and he had yet to receive an answer. Maybe the hotel mogul was still ensconced on his yacht in the Mediterranean, or staying in a suite at his casino in Monte Carlo. Wherever he was, why couldn't Mr. T respond to his messages?

He glanced fondly at the framed photo sitting on the corner of his desk. His mother had no idea he'd followed in his father's footsteps and made his living as a gambler. She thought he'd used his business degree to secure a position in Mr. T's management organization, and the job kept him traveling. If he succeeded in this quest, he'd have the position and his mom would never know he'd been lying all these years. She'd never understand that he'd done it to make up for his dad's shabby treatment and one-big-score attitude.

That he was a better gambler than his father, and capable of taking care of her in a way his dad never had.

He read over the proposed schedule for the Voice of Vegas, and checked the bio on the candidates. Each was a local unknown who worked in a hotel on the strip, exactly as the rules stated, including the participant from the Acropolis—a computer nerd named Robert Garrett.

Since there had already been a computer in his office when he arrived, and Jake had hands-on knowledge of their use, he hadn't needed to speak to the hotel's IT department, hadn't even thought to interview that sector of employees, mostly because he doubted computer geeks would have the where-withal to be involved with casino funds. He now realized it was lazy thinking. A competent hacker could break into every aspect of the system, fudge the numbers, and escape without being caught.

What was that old adage: everything happens for a reason? Was it possible being in charge of the Voice of Vegas was a step in the right direction? Maybe this Robert Garrett was someone he should get to know better, and assisting on the singing competition was one way to make that happen.

He checked his watch. Kyra Degodessa had prom-ised to phone him as soon as she reported for work, and it was after ten. He'd drifted to sleep last night with visions of the sexy events coordinator covered in whipped cream, and now he couldn't get her off his mind. But thinking of the woman as anything other than a suspect was just plain stupid. Kyra's suspi-cious habit on the casino floor was strange enough; if he discovered losses in the Wheel Deal, it would only add to her guilt factor. He had to get close to her, wedge his way into her life, and figure out her angle.

He headed across the hall to see if he could spot her on the monitors. Inside the warehouse-sized surveillance room, Jake eyed the operating system. Banks of monitors covering all public places, includ-ing the elevators, hallways, and lobby, were pictured on the wall. There were fewer cameras in the less important areas of activity, but just about every inch of the hotel was under watch.

The screens directly in front of him scanned the gambling room, including the private gaming rooms upstairs and the counting room in the basement. Because more cheating—and sometimes downright stealing—took place in those sections, a dozen men carefully scrutinized the monitors while a tape system recorded every transaction or deal.

On the final wall were the monitors for the offices, the workroom where machinery was repaired, and a few of the parking lots. These screens were usually handled by Herb or whoever was second-in-command, plus six additional guards. As the least troublesome, these sites could be left unmanned if the personnel were needed elsewhere.

"Thought I'd stop by and see how it's going," said Jake as he stepped to Herb's side. "Anything we need to discuss?"

Herb nodded to a co-worker, and he and the guard exchanged places. "It's quiet today, but I heard you and Ardmore butted heads in front of the elevators last night."

Jake sat down and kept his voice low. "What do you know about him?"

"He's okay, I guess. Mel liked him well enough."

"But . . . ?"

Herb blew out a breath. "Mel was a hands-on guy, but Ardmore never comes down here to look around.

Don't get me wrong—he sends cohorts to check, but he doesn't bother slumming in the basement himself."

"The mark of a good leader is his ability to delegate. If he trusts his workers to do their job . . ."

"It's more a gut feeling," mused Herb. "First thing Ardmore did when he took over Mel's office was order us to disable his security camera. And not for a while—permanently."

Jake had often thought about hanging a hat over the Cyclops in his own office, just to get past the feeling he was living in a fishbowl. Though tight security was vital to this business, the intrusive camera was also one of the reasons he spent so much time on the gambling floor. At least there he could walk around and stretch his legs.

"And that's his biggest sin?"

"Far as I can tell. Did he talk to you about what's planned for the Voice of Vegas?"

"We discussed it," muttered Jake.

"You got a problem with singers?"

"Nope, though it's the reason we were at odds last night. According to him, I'm officially in charge of a few areas of the competition."

Herb's eyes grew wide. "So why do you look like he asked you to clean the men's room?"

Jake shrugged. "As far as I can see, the only good thing about it is Kyra Degodessa. Seems we're supposed to work side by side on the event."

"Gee, tough assignment," said Herb with a laugh. "The woman is a goddess—just ask any of the guys."

"I'll pass on taking a poll. But I do need to know about event security. What happens to your staff when the hotel holds one of these extravaganzas? Do you go to a firm and hire extra help, or do our guards double up?"

"It can go both ways. Last big to-do we had here, we offered the overtime to our guys first and filled in with bodies from a local company. Coordinating the shifts is a pain, but once the leg work is done it goes pretty well." Herb gave a grin. "Not to belabor the point, but I caught you on camera in Kyra Degodessa's office yesterday. Is that what you were doing? Discussing the contest?"

"I was trying to talk her into an interview, especially after I watched her at work on the casino floor."

"Then you saw her do her shoulder tap thing." He raised a brow. "Did the customer win big?"

"Big enough. And Kyra missed our appointment. But since we'll be working together, I'll have time to study her technique further." Jake swiveled his head toward the monitors surveying his office. "Stay tuned if you care to watch us together."

"It's okay by me if you want an hour of privacy," Herb answered with a snort. "Happens a lot around here. Bigwig looking for a quickie brings a girl to his office, and they take their *conversation* to the couch.

62

When he gives the high sign, my men shut his camera down for one hour."

"The high sign?"

"Yeah. Just turn the lock on your door." Herb demonstrated with his fingers. "The guys will take the hint and you'll be free from prying eyes for sixty minutes."

"I don't plan on using my office for anything but business," said Jake. Uncomfortable with the tip, he changed the subject. "Is there a way for someone to shut down the camera in their office, or can it only be done from here?"

"From here, but the system is scheduled to be upgraded the first of next year. We're going big, like the Bellagio, with a bank of about fifteen hundred screens. We'll need to triple our manpower, but it'll be worth it. Until then, there won't be any cheating on my watch." The guard settled back in his chair. "You still got my permission to spend some free time with the lovely Kyra."

"No, thanks. Our meetings will be strictly on the up and up." Jake stood. "I'm taking a stroll to the machinery repair room. After that," he nodded to the viewing screen, "you know where to find me."

Chapter 5

Kyra parked in the employee lot and trotted toward the Acropolis. It wasn't her fault she was running late. She just hadn't expected Rob to move so quickly. When she promised to help him gain his grandmother's approval for the Voice of Vegas finals, she didn't know he'd expect her to do it first thing this morning.

It had required a bit of coaxing but, with a little help from Rob, she'd been able to convince Marge Garrett her grandson had real talent. Mrs. Garrett even promised to attend the grand finale. The only thing left in her crusade to aid Rob was convincing Rupert Ardmore to foot the bill for voice lessons. After Rob won, Kyra could say she'd inspired good fortune without using her powers. Even though her father had never made it clear that she and her sister muses *couldn't* call on their special gifts, it wouldn't hurt to toss a few of those success stories into the mix.

She entered the building and paid her daily tribute to Zeus. On the way to her office, she stopped at a supply closet and collected a few basics to restock what the cleaning crew had removed—pens, pencils, paperclips, notebooks—whatever she might need in her job.

Now in her private domain, she set the items on her desk and gazed around the room. A hollow space opened in the corner of her heart and she brushed away a tear. If she were a mortal, this would be the type of career in which she could excel. Now that she was on the verge of leaving, she realized working at the Acropolis, even as a lowly cocktail waitress, had been fun, mostly because she enjoyed meeting people. Several thousand years of living with the same deities day after day had grown boring and lost its sparkle. On Earth, a new adventure dawned with each sunrise.

When she returned to Mount Olympus, she would miss the friends she'd made here—Eddie, Lou, and Katie, some of the dealers and other waitresses, and Rob. In her opinion, humans weren't as foolish as the gods assumed. Even the patrons she'd helped at the casino, whether or not they believed in her good karma, kept returning just to say hello.

She checked her phone messages. Besides one from Buddy Blue, she'd received one from each of the contest judges' personal assistants.

And two from Jake Lennox.

Zeus's eyeballs, but the man was persistent. Many mortals lost patience, but Jake seemed to have been born without a shred of the trait. Worse, thinking about him only continued to make her itchy in *those* places, something she desperately wanted to forget.

She glanced at the security camera pointed directly at her desk, and remembered Jake telling her yesterday that he'd seen her leave through one of the monitors. Was he watching her now, waiting for her to lift the receiver and contact him?

Well aware the employees were under surveillance in most areas of the casino, she'd learned to accept the situation exactly as she had on Mount Olympus, where Zeus always seemed to know what type of mischief she and her sisters had created. But Zeus was the chief god and Olympus his domain. It was disconcerting to think that complete strangers were able to observe and judge her every move.

Startled from her reverie by a sharp knock, she sat straight in her chair. "Come in."

The door opened and Rob Garrett strutted in, pushing a cart laden with equipment. "Your computer, ma'am, as promised."

She stared at the monitor, keyboard, and other odds and ends sitting on top of and under the trolley. "Great. Just set it on the credenza."

Rob began unloading the cart. "Have you learned any more about operating one of these?" he asked. "I know you have the e-mail thing down pat, but what else?"

"You know how I feel about computers. E-mail is all I care to use it for."

She envisioned the bits and pieces of technology piled on her living room floor. When she returned to Olympus, the next person to lease her condo would inherit a gold mine. She didn't doubt Zeus was watching them right now, rubbing his hands in glee at the prospect of speaking with her on a daily basis.

"I thought after I'd taught you the Internet basics, you'd get curious and branch out on your own." said Rob as he disappeared under the knee hole in the credenza.

She glared at the stack of plastic rectangles and cables. "Not interested."

"Really?" came his muffled voice. "Wow."

"Wow as in good or bad?"

"A little of both, I guess. Good because some people get so wrapped up in the Internet they neglect the things they should be doing." He backed out on his hands and knees and stood. Then he set the monitor on the credenza's surface and continued to thread wires and cables behind the station. "Bad because you can use it for more than e-mail. It saves time writing letters and talking on the phone, plus you can bank online—which makes it easier to pay bills. And you can find out about stuff."

Aside from Lou, whom she saw every day, Kyra had no intimate friends but her sisters. Other than food, she had no expenses, so there were no bills to pay. And since she wasn't going to be here much longer, none of it mattered.

"Tell me again, what kind of stuff?" she asked, merely to be polite.

"Do you have any hobbies?"

"Nope."

"Favorite music?"

"Nu-uh."

Rob gave her a puzzled look. "Jeez, and here I thought you were a woman of the world. How come you never told me?"

"Told you what?"

"That you're lonely. We could have gone to a concert, or found you a hobby, or—"

"I am not lonely," she huffed. Then she realized how pathetic her "do nothing" confession must have sounded. "I go to the library and I watch television." She hesitated to tell him the shows she enjoyed most were those on ancient history, and her favorite channel was the Home Shopping Network, from which she'd never bought a thing, which would sound even more pitiful. "I take walks around town, and sometimes I visit Lou and her daughter."

"Who's Lou?"

"You know—Louise."

He shrugged.

"Smallish girl, long brown hair, big hazel eyes?" She raised a brow when his ears turned pink. "Lou serves drinks on the gaming floor. We used to work together."

Rob's cheeks flushed red.

"Oh my gosh. You have a crush on Lou." She grinned. "How come you haven't asked her out?"

"I . . . um . . . I don't know."

"It's not because you're shy, is it?"

"No," he answered a bit too quickly.

"Then if I introduce you, you'll ask her out?"

"Sure. Maybe when the contest is over or—"

"You're not getting out of it that easy. Promise me, if you're given the opportunity, you'll ask Lou for a date."

A smile graced his boyish face. "If it will make you happy."

"Trust me, it will make you a pretty happy guy too. Now let's see what you can do to get me up and running."

Rob fiddled with the wires and cables, then began muttering about broadband connections and phone lines. The screen powered on and he tapped the keyboard. Seconds later, Kyra's jaw dropped. Before her, under a clear cerulean sky, stood Olympios, the ancient temple dedicated to Zeus, in its original glory. Her father and the other deities had admired the building so much when it had first been erected, they'd created an exact replica on Mount Olympus, and Zeus lived there even today.

"Pretty cool, huh?" said Rob, who now stood behind her. "This unit belonged to Mr. Ardmore until yesterday, so I guess this was his wallpaper. Since you didn't have a requisition slip for a new machine, I checked with a supply guy and he said you could have it."

"The temple looks so real," she commented, aware the edifice had fallen to ruin over the centuries.

"It's probably been video enhanced. Which means someone took a current photo and, through the magic of digital imaging, recreated it as they thought it had once been."

The lump in Kyra's throat grew to the size of a stuffed grape leaf. She'd seen the same type of picture in the books she'd skimmed at the library, but none of the photos appeared this alive or compelling. This much like home.

Standing, she turned and hugged Rob tight to her chest.

Jake paced his office. While waiting for Kyra to call for their meeting, he collected the report on the slot machine that had given the customer she'd befriended a jackpot, and found the machine was in perfect working order. Which only made him more confused and more curious about her. He glared at the phone. Why the heck hadn't she tried to reschedule their appointment? He didn't want to believe he was getting the brush-off, but what else was he supposed to think?

He'd also run a check on the outcome of the past six months' Wheel Deal giveaways, which was about when Kyra had taken over the event. Odds on a customer hitting the big payout were a hundred to one, yet players at the Acropolis were winning at three to four times that number. He'd inspected the wheel first thing this morning. Hell, he'd spun it himself about two hundred times and never once hit the big money. What caused the wheel to halt on the jackpot so often when Kyra was in charge? What did she do to make so many customers win fifty large?

A knock on the door startled him. If this was Kyra she could damn well wait, just as she'd made him do for the past several hours. He sat behind his desk and adjusted the knot in his tie. "Come in."

Herb stuck his head around the door. "Your pigeon just flew through the lobby."

"Did she look okay? I mean—normal and all?"

"Flipped Zeus the bird, as usual, then headed upstairs. She's in her office arranging supplies while one of the IT guys sets up her computer. Maybe you should call her."

"I already left a message." The security chief didn't need to know he'd tried twice. "The ball's in her court."

Herb shook his balding head. "The woman sure is a tough nut to crack."

Jake scrubbed a hand over his face. When he finished, Herb was gone. He set aside the Voice of Vegas file, arranged a few folders on his blotter and

topped them with a legal pad. Then he buttoned
and unbuttoned his navy suit jacket. Standing, he
walked around the desk and repositioned the chairs
in the room so Kyra would face him when they
talked and . . .

Hah! Who was he kidding? She had no intention
of dropping by to see him, or phoning to arrange a
meeting. Her promise had been another ploy to get
him off her back. He had no choice but to go to her.
Again. But he wasn't about to accept a third excuse
or a plea to "catch her later."

Picking up the file, he marched to the elevator,
rode it to the mezzanine level, and skirted the door
that led to Ardmore's private suite. Kyra's office was
at the end of a long corridor, making her space quiet
and secluded.

He stopped at her door and raised a hand to
knock. Then he heard a murmur of voices. Pressing
his ear against the wooden panel, he remembered
Herb's comment. She was probably talking to the
computer technician. He pushed inside, only to find
his new partner in the arms of a very large man.

"Jake, what are you doing here?" Kyra asked as
she peered at him over a linebacker-sized shoulder.

"I thought we had an appointment." Kyra disen-
tangled herself from the man's arms as he continued.
"I see now you had something more important to do."

She ignored his jibe and took her seat. "This is
Rob Garrett," she responded in a prim voice. "Rob,
Jake Lennox."

The hulk nodded and held out his hand. "I was just seeing to Ms. Degodessa's computer. She's ready to roll."

Jake accepted the handshake, and tried to place the man's name. Then Rob smiled at Kyra. "Thanks again for helping out with my grandmother. It was great you both could finally meet."

Grandmother? Were Kyra and this computer nerd involved? If so, it didn't fit. Rob Garrett was a boy. Okay, not exactly a boy, but he couldn't be more than twenty-five. She'd struck him as someone who would be attracted to a sophisticated man, a guy who'd been around the block more than once.

Someone like him. •

"It was fun. And don't worry about the contest. We'll figure something out."

The contest? No wonder the name rang a bell. Rob Garrett was the Acropolis's Voice of Vegas representative. His mind whirling, Jake put the pieces together. He'd found Kyra and Rob in a heated embrace, which showed how much she cared. She'd met his grandmother, which meant they were more than co-workers. She was in charge of the contest, and he had easy access to all the IT data . . .

"I know I can count on you. And call me if you need help with the system. I'm always available for private lessons." Rob hustled from the room. "Nice to meet you, Mr. Lennox."

"Same here," said Jake as the door closed. He focused on Kyra, who was facing her monitor, and decided then and there that if anyone was going to give her private lessons, computer or otherwise, it would be him. "I thought you were an assistant to Ms. Simmons?"

"I was," she answered, her gaze intent on the screen.

"I would have thought there was one in here already. Wasn't computer work part of your job?"

"Hmm?"

"A computer. You know, spreadsheets, data collection, reports," he repeated more slowly. "E-mail."

Ignoring him, Kyra placed an elbow on her keyboard tray, and set her chin on her fist. Her unruly curls had broken free of their restrictive bun and now spiraled out of control. Jake couldn't help himself. He strode to her desk to see what held her in thrall.

"Have you been there?" he asked when he viewed the picture. Sitting high on elevated ground, the massive structure was impressive in size and design.

"Yes."

"And where's there?"

"Athens."

"Athens, Georgia?"

"Greece," said Kyra, her voice wistful.

"I wondered about your last name," Jake commented. "It's unusual. Is that where your family's from?"

"I have lots of sisters and a father, plenty of cousins, as well. Two of my sisters live here in the U.S., the rest are . . . wherever they're needed."

"And your dad?"

"My father is still close to Greece."

"In the country?"

"High in the mountains." She sighed. "I miss my family and my home."

"Looks to me as if you and Garrett were pretty much at home with each other," he said, trying to keep his voice calm. Business. His relationship with Kyra Degodessa was strictly business.

"That is *so* none of your concern," she said with a glare. "Rob and I are friends."

Jake almost ran his fingers through his hair, but thought better of it. He wasn't as angry about Rob Garrett as he was nervous of being alone with this obstinate yet sexy woman, which he didn't want to admit even to himself. It had been years since a female had tied him in a knot of anxious hormones, and he didn't like it. Especially when he was supposed to charm her to his side.

"Look, Ms. Degodessa—Kyra. I know you don't want to talk to me. I imagine you thought if you screwed up enough appointments, you'd wear me down and I'd stop asking."

"The idea did cross my mind," she said in a clipped tone. "But I can see you're not about to let it happen."

"I don't know why we got off on the wrong foot, but maybe we could start over." Kyra's cooperation would make getting to the bottom of things a whole lot easier. "At least, I think we should try."

75

Her eyes darkened to the color of the sky before a storm. "Why?"

Taken aback by her pointed question, he swallowed. "Why?"

"Yes, why? We've already agreed that neither of us dates co-workers. As far as I can tell, we have nothing in common, so I can't fathom why you'd want to get friendly with me, even for business."

Jake admired her ability to analyze a situation. Glancing down, he realized he still held the folder Ardmore had given him on the singing competition, which was his excuse for being here to begin with. "Because we have a project in common."

"I thought you were going to interview me."

"I was, but there's a more important reason for us to get along." He held out the file. "Rupert Ardmore expects the two of us to work side by side on the Voice of Vegas."

Her luscious lips formed an O, then flat-lined. "That is *so* not funny."

"It's not meant to be."

"Is there some concern I won't be able to do the job?"

He shrugged. "Don't ask me, ask Ardmore. I only know we're in this together, which means no more avoiding me."

Her cheeks flushed pink. Jake could almost hear her mind humming as she thought up ways to keep her distance.

"I have other things to take care of—the Wheel

Deal—the promo giveaways—and we're about to start an automobile raffle in conjunction with the contest. I can't be available whenever it suits you."

He gave her a smile of encouragement. "I'll let you set the time and place, no pressure, as long as you agree to do your part. The goal is to make the competition a success." He walked to the door and opened it. "Maybe we could have dinner tonight, to officially start our relationship."

She frowned. "I thought you were going to let me set the time and place?"

"You can, after tonight." His smile broadened. "I'm looking forward to working with you. It would be a shame to waste another day."

"Well—"

"Great. I'm in 2312. See you about six-thirty."

Kyra waited for the door to close before she sighed. Avoiding Jake Lennox was going to be harder than she'd first thought. Which gave more sense to her idea of enticing him into an *affaire*. Now that she'd gotten to know him a little better, he seemed genuine, and not as conceited as he'd been at their first few meetings.

He still had a killer smile, and a sexy body. If she learned to think like Chloe, keep her emotional distance, and take up with a mortal strictly for his looks, Jake was perfect.

Her computer gave a little ding. When a too-cheery voice announced "You've got mail," she held her head in her hands. She didn't need to log on to the Internet to know who the message was from, and why.

She glanced around the room, checked under her blotter, and opened the desk drawers. Then she parted the fresh flowers sitting in a vase on the corner of her desktop. If the chief god had sent someone to spy on her, there was no telling where that someone would hide.

Heaving a sigh, she decided to open and read the e-mail. She couldn't ignore Zeus any longer, and he was probably wise to her by now. If she ignored this message, he might do something as heinous as dooming her to the Underworld, or as demoralizing as turning her into a grain of kitty litter. And if Hera was urging him on, there was no telling how far he would go.

She connected to her e-mail, clicked on *retrieve*, and waited for a list of messages to appear. The first three missives were from Ardmore, reminding her of her new responsibilities, reiterating his threat, and informing her of her new partner, Jake Lennox. E-mails four through seventeen were from Zeus. Thinking to get right to the nitty-gritty, she erased each message but the last, and opened it.

Chapter 6

FROM: *Topgod@mounto.org*
TO: *Kdegodessa@Acropolis.com*
SUBJECT: Final warning ☹

Words cannot convey my state of mind at this moment. Suffice it to say you are skating on thin ice. If I do not receive a report within twenty-four hours, consider your mission a failure and you a slave to the citizens of Mount Olympus. The outcome is in your hands.

Sincerely,
Zeus

PS: Have a nice day.

Kyra scowled at the monitor. As if she didn't have enough trouble, Zeus expected her to write another stupid, time-wasting report on her progress. Spinning her chair to face her desk, she tallied customer names and the manner in which she'd inspired them to good fortune. Besides her latest giftee, Marie, which she'd reported for the last several months, there had been six other winners on the casino floor, and three at the Wheel Deal.

Were there enough names to satisfy him for the week, or would Zeus think she was a slacker? Did he actually check on each of the winners to make certain she'd done things in the proper manner?

Turning to her computer, she composed a pleasant if not gushing note.

FROM: Kdegodessa@Acropolis.com
TO: Topgod@mounto.org
SUBJECT: Weekly accomplishments

Father: Your magnanimous patience in my progress is much appreciated, as the week was exceptionally challenging. Marie is a continual believer in good fortune, as are Jenny Hill, Steven Soldano, Marcy Stewart, Peter Phillips, and

Her fingers stalled and she exhaled. Dealing with Zeus was ten times more difficult than handling Rupert Ardmore on his worst day. She'd say good-bye and farewell to her many friends, and try to forget them, as well as the Acropolis and these weekly reports. She had a ton of company on Mount Olympus. So what if they were self-absorbed gods and goddesses who vied for Zeus's approval? Unlike Jake Lennox, at least she knew where she stood with them.

Kyra continued to type names and positive experiences, added a kowtowing and respectful sign-off, closed her eyes, and hit the *send* key. The message should satisfy the father god for another few days, but what about Jake?

Could she have a relationship with him and still protect her heart, or was that merely a pipe dream? Was there a reason beyond his pleasant attitude other than their working together, or was her imagination running on overdrive?

One minute he looked at her as if she were a thousand-calorie dessert and he'd just come off of a month-long fast; the next he acted as if she were his own personal slave in training.

Rarely had a mortal so confused her, and she didn't enjoy Jake's torment one bit. The gods were quixotic, but she'd grown used to their overbearing manner and come to expect their quirky demands. They'd been around for thousands of years; they were full of themselves and loved to be in control—especially Zeus and Hera. From what she'd observed in her time on Earth, mortals were a simpler lot, like Louise and her daughter, or Rob and Marge: insecure and in need of constant assistance.

Which didn't apply to Jake.

No matter his reason for stalking her, she would not let it stop her from completing a successful mission. She'd do whatever it took to keep him off her back and out of her business so she could continue to inspire mortals.

Rising from her desk, Kyra headed to the casino floor. She needed to be with someone who enjoyed her company and cared about her feelings, and the first person she thought of was Lou.

If Zeus wanted more names, she would get them. Just let Jake Lennox try to stop her.

Kyra made her way to the service bar, where she found Lou sitting on a stool while she waited for Eddie to fill her latest order. Her forlorn expression had Kyra trotting to her side. "You okay?"

The cocktail waitress groaned. "Just dog tired. Katie had a bad night, my car battery died, and I got notice the new lease on my apartment is going to increase by seven percent. I'll have to hustle to pay for the replacement battery. I have no idea where I'm going to get the extra rent money."

"You sure I can't summon my mojo and bestow a little luck?" Kyra asked, half jokingly. Lou would rather starve than accept charity in any form, but Kyra continued to prod. "It seems to work for everyone else."

"You know how I feel about counting on good luck to solve problems," said Lou. Obviously exhausted, she rolled her shoulders. "But I have to admit, watching customers rely on you for help is a trip." She gave a tepid smile. "I find it hard to believe so many people think you're their own personal four-leaf clover, and they're only winning because you do that two-fingered tap thing."

Lou and Eddie had caught on to her ritual of wishing certain customers good fortune almost from the first day Kyra started work. She'd managed to convince them the tap was merely a confidence builder for those who thought they were down on their luck, and it had become a running gag. Only Zoë and Chloe knew the true strength of her positive inspiration.

"Whatever makes them happy. By the way, I'm supposed to hire hostesses to staff the VIP lounge for the Voice of Vegas. I bet the tips will be worth the extra hours. And since you have an in with the coordinator of the event . . ."

"Are you crazy? You can't hire me. Have you taken a gander at the women who work those functions? Legs up to their armpits and faces like cover models."

"Don't be silly. I'm running the show, remember?" Jake would have to go along with her on this if he wanted her cooperation. "I can hire anyone I want."

Lou sighed as her gaze dropped to her near-invisible chest. "But I don't fit the qualifications. I have no experience making small talk with the whales. Ardmore will have a fit."

Whales, a friendly term for the ultimate high rollers of Las Vegas, were the bread and butter of the casino. And they were sure to tip big at a special event like the singing competition, especially since that type of entertainment was offered to them for free, in thanks for the money they spent at the hotel.

"Ardmore doesn't have a thing to say about it, nor does my new partner," said Kyra, hoping to reassure Lou. The hotel manager would never find anyone to run the contest at this late date, and if he dared give her a hard time she'd charm him exactly as she did Zeus when he was unreasonable. Surely she could deal with a mortal blowhard as easily as she did a deity of the same ilk. As for her so-called partner . . . it wouldn't do for Lou to know how itchy she felt in his presence.

"New partner?"

"Jake Lennox. I found out about it a few hours ago."

"Wow." Lou smiled. "Lucky you."

"Luck had nothing to do with it."

"Maybe not, but he's so—so—"

"Cocky?"

"Not really."

"Repulsive?"

"Golly, no." She shook her head. "I was thinking virile. The guy exudes masculinity. Too bad I've sworn off men."

When they'd first met, Lou had told Kyra she'd given up on the opposite sex after Katie's father left her broke and pregnant. The waitress had never given her a reason to doubt that statement.

Eddie shuffled over and set down Lou's fully laden tray. "What are you girls talking about now?"

"Us? Nothing." Lou gave a little wave, then left with her drink order. Kyra was about to ask Eddie if he wanted some extra hours working the VIP lounge bar, when he spoke.

"Don't look now, but here comes one of your chickens." He rolled his eyes and hustled away.

"Hey, Kyra. Long time no see."

Kyra recognized Frank's voice immediately. He was one of the regulars who continued to beg her favor, even though he kept vowing to quit gambling.

"You got a minute?" he asked when she turned to face him.

"Frank, I thought we'd agreed you were through here. How often do I have to tell you my shoulder taps have nothing to do with your good fortune. It's just a ritual you really don't need, because you're a naturally lucky guy."

Frank licked his lips. "Aw, Kyra, I know it's just a game we play, but without your special tap my brain don't work right. This is my last freebie, honest."

"You said the same thing weeks ago." She frowned. "What is it this time?"

"Braces," he replied, his expression somber. "Two of the girls need them now, and Dina will be ready sometime next year. That fancy dental stuff isn't covered by my insurance. Cheap bastards."

"And you'll stop when you win the exact amount you need? No losing it in another casino, the way you did a couple of weeks ago?"

He raised a hand. "Swear to God."

"And this is your final request?"

"I certainly hope so."

She noted his anxious grin and knew the gods enjoyed poking fun at mortals like Frank. The deities had vices of their own but chose to ignore them, and wagered instead on the foibles of humans. The outcome of sporting events, political elections, beauty pageants, even reality show winners, all were fodder for their pleasure.

She was still debating what to do about Frank's dilemma when Art Robinson, a silver-haired man well past his prime, joined them. "You up for sharing the wealth, missy?" he asked with a flirty wink.

Art was an outrageous tease, so Kyra winked in return. She guessed his age at eighty, and even then she was probably giving him a few years. Wearing an orange and yellow striped tie, black shirt, and brown suit that looked to be twenty years out of style, he still cut a dashing figure on the casino floor.

"What do you need, Art?"

"Got a friend who lost his job and can't find work, so he's short a couple months' rent. Thought you might throw a bit of your special encouragement my way, build up my smarts so I can give him a little gift."

Because his requests were almost always for someone else, and he never won more than what it would take to achieve his goal, Kyra believed Art told the truth. Besides, Art seemed to view the taps as more of an excuse to speak with her than a dire need. Frank had gone a bit overboard the first few times she'd helped him, but when she threatened to ignore his next plea, had taken it more slowly . . . and she hoped it would stay that way.

The men stood before her, and she took care of them one at a time. "I wish you the very best of luck, Art." She did the same for Frank.

They trotted off grinning from ear to ear, and Kyra left in the direction of the main staircase. It was time to finagle an appointment with Rupert Ardmore.

Partially hidden behind a bank of slot machines, Jake pushed off the wall across from the service bar. The two men talking to Kyra appeared to be ordinary customers, and a floor manager had confirmed they were regulars. Right now, it seemed she was using the identical practice on them she'd used with Marie, only something told him these guys wouldn't be satisfied with a mere couple of hundred in winnings.

Unable to follow both men, he chose the one headed toward the craps table. Blackjack required skill and a working knowledge of the rules. Palming and other forms of cheating usually involved a group of two or three, but the dealers, pit bosses, and cameras were adept at catching those who took advantage of the system. Since succeeding at craps was pure chance, it'd be interesting to see how Kyra's wish of good luck panned out.

Frank hung back at first, observing the crowd while he edged to a position beside the shooter. Jake muscled his way to the opposite side of the table in order to get a better view of the dice as they landed. When the guy to Frank's right lost control of the play, Frank accepted the cubes with an eager smile. His initial roll set his point and earned him a cheer of encouragement from the crowd.

Six rolls later, the man was up ten thousand dollars, and the other players were in his corner. Frank shoved his chips to the line, and the bettors went into a frenzy. Everyone loved a winner, and right now their man was riding high.

Frank blew into his closed fist, shook the dice, and tossed them across the felt. Whoops of joy rang out when he made his point. After accepting his winnings—close to fifty thousand, Jake guessed, he waved to the crowd and left the exalted circle.

Jake snatched up the dice and worked his way to the croupier. "Okay with you if I take these downstairs?"

"Fine, but I didn't see anything odd about them."

"With a win that size it never hurts to check," he responded, backing out of the mob. He tucked the dice into his pocket and moved quickly toward the service bar. Maybe Kyra's bartender pal could shed some light on the situation.

"Can I get you something, Mr. Lennox?" asked Eddie the moment Jake arrived.

"How about a glass of tonic water with a twist?" Jake had learned long ago that smart men never mixed alcohol and gambling. He propped himself on a stool and nodded his thanks when the man passed him his drink.

"You a member of AA or something?"

"I never drink when I'm on duty," said Jake. Realizing how officious the remark must have come off, he tried to sound less superior. "Uncle T doesn't approve, and I'm trying to stay on his good side."

"I can't blame you, having an uncle as flush as Mr. T." Eddie swiped a rag over the bar. "Nice to know you two get along. So, what exactly are your duties around here?"

"A little of everything," Jake muttered. "The latest is handling some of the details for the Voice of Vegas competition."

The information seemed to take Eddie aback. "I thought that was Kyra's job."

"It is. She and I will be working together." The man's eyebrow quirked, and Jake asked, "Is that a problem?"

Eddie held a hand up in implied surrender. "Hey, what do I know? I only make the drinks. It's just . . . does Kyra know about this or is it a surprise?"

"She knows."

"I guess it's good for me then, you and I being buds and all. I'd love to get a shift in the VIP lounge the night of the competition. Think you could help me out?"

Jake had never considered himself Eddie's buddy, but it couldn't hurt to have a few employees on his side, especially if they were close to Kyra. "Since I'm responsible for clearing the staff, I imagine so. Go to Ms. Degodessa's office tomorrow and tell her I sent you to fill out a form. From now on, she'll be too busy to visit the floor."

He tensed at Eddie's unhappy expression. The bartender was either totally smitten, or in league with Kyra and worried about his cut of the profits if she couldn't work the casino. Right now, Jake didn't want to address either scenario, since the idea of Eddie being in love with Kyra irked him more than the thought of him being an accomplice.

"I'm gonna miss seeing her down here. She's a bright spot in my day. You can't replace a woman like Kyra with just anybody." As if embarrassed by what he said, Eddie wiped frantically at the bar. "The customers are gonna ask about her, is all I'm sayin'."

"Sounds as if the two of you are more than friends."

"Me and Kyra? Heck, no. Not that I haven't tried, of course, but she keeps to herself." His demeanor turned proprietary. "Does asking so many questions mean you got a yen for her yourself? Because as far as I know, the lady isn't interested in seeing any man after work hours. Unless you count Rob."

Rob Garrett, the would-be contest winner. "What's so special about him?"

"He lives in her building. She's the one who talked him into entering the competition, so I assume she sees him as a special kind of guy." Eddie hitched an elbow onto the bar. "Say, why are you so interested in Kyra?"

"Just curious about the people I work with. Uncle T wants me to get acquainted with everyone."

"Kyra doesn't hang out with anyone except Lou."

Kyra was involved with two men? "Do you know this Lou person well?"

"Sure do. Hold on a second."

A petite waitress who looked to have the weight of the world on her shoulders made her way to the bar. With her hair scraped back in a bun, she appeared barely the legal age to serve drinks.

The woman passed Eddie an order sheet, and he grinned. "I'll get right on this while you spend a little time with my friend here. Louise, this is Jake Lennox. Jake, meet Lou, one of the best cocktail waitresses at the Acropolis."

Relief washed over Jake as he shook the woman's hand. "Nice to know you."

Lou gazed at him through wary hazel eyes. "You hanging around to check up on the girls?"

"The girls?"

"Me and the other waitresses. You want to find out how many drinks we serve a night, or make sure the customers aren't complaining?"

91

Chapter 7

Except for her once-a-century review by Zeus, it usually took an event as momentous as the Trojan War to make Kyra nervous. Over the several thousand years of her existence, she'd learned to handle the few difficulties in her life in stride. Here on Earth, she tolerated those who considered themselves her superiors, because it was relevant to the successful completion of her mission. To her mind, speaking with Rupert Ardmore about Rob's voice lessons was as problematic as a paper cut, and no worse a challenge than some of the things she'd done while working for a perfectionist like Ms. Simmons.

Smoothing her hair, she *tsked* when she realized it was trailing in a tangled mass down her shoulders.

"I need to speak with you about Rob Garrett. Our entrant in the Voice of Vegas contest," she reminded him. "He works in the hotel's IT department."

"Ah, yes, Garrett." He set his pencil on the blotter. "What about him?"

"Rob would like to take a few singing lessons before the competition, and he asked me to get approval for the hotel to pay for them."

"The Acropolis? Pay for voice lessons?" He furrowed his brow. "Out of the question."

"But—"

"There's a budget for the event, Ms. Degodessa, with no room for incidentals or money to waste on an individual, even if he represents the hotel." He picked up a gold pen and rolled it between his fingers. "There should have been a financial statement in the folder Ms. Simmons left behind."

Kyra remembered seeing sheets of paper covered with columns of numbers but, as of yet, hadn't had time to study them or anything else having to do with the competition. "A win for Rob can only help the casino. Surely we can—"

"I doubt it, but have a look. If you find a way to pay for the lessons, you have my permission to take care of it. Just be aware, you and Lennox will be responsible if we're a cent over budget. I don't think I need to remind you what that means."

At the mention of Jake's name, Kyra's even and serene temper bubbled in her chest. "I'd like to talk

anything more than a dalliance as long as she planned to return to Mount Olympus. And she certainly didn't want the pain of having to say good-bye.

She and her sisters were unsure of how Zeus would regard their achievements when they went home, but the three muses were determined to make Zeus eat his words.

Now settled in her office, she checked her watch and realized she still had to get a hold of the judges' assistants and Buddy Blue, as well as look over the budget Ardmore insisted she follow. She phoned the coffee shop and ordered a sandwich and orange cream soda, a drink that brought to mind the taste of her favorite ambrosia. While waiting for the food to arrive, she made her first call.

Buddy Blue answered immediately.

"Blue, here. What can I do for you?"

"It's Kyra Degodessa, Mr. Blue. I've calling because I have some news."

"About you and me, doll? 'Cause the offer I made for a night on the town still stands."

In the past, Buddy had made plenty of comments about how badly the "tight-assed" Ms. Simmons was handling the event. He always ended his complaint by asking Kyra out.

"I'm afraid the answer to your invitation is still no, Mr. Blue—"

"That's Buddy to you, and why? I'm a laugh a minute and I know how to show a lady a good time . . . if you know what I mean."

"I'm sure you do." *Or not.* "I called to inform you that Ms. Simmons has moved on, and I'm now in charge of the Voice of Vegas."

"No kidding? Terrific." After waiting a beat, he said, "So, how about you and I have a private get-together? I could help you iron out the wrinkles, maybe offer some suggestions on how the gig should run. I can be a very entertaining man—with the right woman."

"Thank you, but I don't think that will be necessary. And please remember, I'll be calling shortly to give you the schedule of the final rehearsals."

"I'm lookin' forward to it. And *you* remember, I'm yours whenever you need me."

Kyra hung up and took a long drink of water, hoping to wash the nasty taste from her tongue. It was difficult being nice to a man whose brain was located behind his zipper. Buddy Blue had a hard time taking no for an answer, and she suspected she'd have to meet with him sooner or later, if only to keep him from complaining about her to Mr. Ardmore or even Mr. T.

The calls she made to Dr. Slick's and Simon Cloud's assistants were handled quickly. Each celebrity had special dietary and room requests, but it was nothing she couldn't supply. Her final call to Missy Malone's secretary was a different story.

"Missy Malone's office. You're speaking with her personal assistant, Miss Ennis."

Penelope Ennis had the voice of an Oxford graduate and an egotistical personality that would put royalty to shame. She'd treated Kyra like a peon every time they'd spoken in the past; when she learned Kyra was the replacement special event coordinator, her voice would probably take on an even haughtier tone.

"It's Kyra Degodessa, Miss Ennis."

"Oh? What is it now?"

"I just wanted to let you know I'm the new coordinator of the Voice of Vegas."

"You? What happened to Ms. Simmons?"

"Ms. Simmons had to leave. This is a courtesy call to inform you and Miss Malone of the change in leadership."

"I see." There was a long pause, punctuated by a tortured sigh. "I trust you're taking care of Miss Malone's dietary needs, as well as her special requests?"

"You're referring to the goat's milk and vegan menu?"

"The *tub* of goat's milk, and the macrobiotic menu."

"Right. I have our head chef working on it."

"I should hope so. If you have any questions, I expect a phone call. We wouldn't want to arrive and find an ugly surprise waiting, now would we?"

The royal *we* set Kyra's teeth on edge. The woman was as bad as Hera. "No, we wouldn't. I'll be calling again to coordinate your arrival. In the meantime, if you think of anything that will make Miss Malone's stay here more pleasant, please give me a ring."

Kyra heard a dismissive click and glared at the receiver. The celebrity judges, she decided, were very much like the gods in their demands and expectations, but Miss Ennis was the worst.

She spent the afternoon going over the budget, adding numbers and reading cost estimates. In the end, she decided that not only was there no room for Rob's voice lessons, she'd be lucky to meet their monetary constraints in any area.

Resting her head in her hands, she chastised herself for making the event such an important goal. As the Muse of Good Fortune, what she needed was to inspire mortals to believe in luck. So what if things didn't work out and Ardmore fired her? She was going home to Mount Olympus on the evening of the competition and had no plans to look back.

When she left, someone else would handle the special events, interface with promotions, and have fun meeting the customers. Another person would give mortals a chance to win money and prizes to better their lives. So what if she had to give up a position that gave purpose to her existence and made her feel useful for the first time in thousands of years?

Her phone rang and the front desk clerk reminded her it was after four. The line for the daily Wheel Deal had already snaked around to the elevators.

"I'll be right there," Kyra answered, reminding herself Mount Olympus was a paradise anyone would be grateful to have as a home.

No daily deals, giveaways, or challenging contests. No friendly customers who relied on her shoulder taps. No Eddie, Lou, or Rob to chat with. Just empty days of idle gossip and endless nights of decadence and pleasure.

What wasn't there to like?

Sighing, she left her office, but her mind was on her job. Where in the world was she going to find enough goat's milk to fill a bathtub each morning for three days, and still stay under budget?

Jake checked his watch as he paced. He'd already called the bell stand and been told the Wheel Deal was running late. He'd give Kyra five more minutes, then find her and drag her back to his suite. She was going to meet with him, and they were going to work together as professionals, whether she agreed to it or not.

He glanced around his living area to make sure everything was in order. Whenever he was in the money, he stayed in places very much like the Acropolis, a luxury hotel with the finest food, service, and appointments. When he was off his game, well, any hole in the wall would do. He'd been riding a six-week high when he met Socrates Themopolis in Monte Carlo, but he was smart enough to know that what went up had to come down. Over the years, he'd honed his skills at blackjack and poker, the only games where a man had a chance to earn a living. The job offer from Mr. T had been just what he needed to help him untangle the lie he'd been living where his mother was concerned.

It had been a month since he'd seen his mom, and it was time to at least get in touch. Aside from seeing to his own basic needs, he used his winnings to make certain she had an easier life and a home in good repair. She'd gone through hell while married to his father. These days, she shared the two-bedroom cottage he'd grown up in with a live-in companion. Once Jake snared the position of casino manager, he'd buy her a house in Tahoe where the cool mountain air was similar to that of the Adirondacks where she now lived. She'd be close enough to visit whenever he wanted, instead of the infrequent trips he now made.

A knock at the door drew him back to the present. He ran a hand through his hair and exhaled, preparing to meet Kyra on his turf. But when he opened the door, the sight of her took his breath away as fast as a kick in his solar plexus.

"Sorry I'm late. I was going over the budget for the contest, then the Wheel Deal ran behind and I—" She shrugged as she brushed past him into the suite. "Can we get started?"

Jake's gaze rested on her rounded hips swaying in a knee-length red skirt, then trailed downward to her long legs encased in sheer, seamed black stockings that traced the curve of her legs the way he'd imagined his fingers one day doing, and further to her three-inch sling-back heels. Kyra Degodessa acted if she had no idea how beguiling she looked, a fact Jake found amazing. In a town where women regularly flaunted their faces and figures, it made the special events coordinator even more appealing.

He pulled out a chair at his dining table and indicated she take a seat. "We should probably order room service before we get to work. Do you need a menu?"

"No, thanks." Kyra set her folder on the table. "I'll have a Greek salad, no onions, extra feta cheese. And an orange cream soda."

He smiled at the interesting combination, and placed their orders, then took the seat opposite her and waited while she flipped through the file. "So, you've studied the budget?"

"All afternoon. Ardmore told me if we went a penny over I'd be responsible—and so would you. I took it to mean we'd be fired if we screwed things up."

"That won't happen," he said without thinking.

"Going over budget or being fired?"

Jake cringed inwardly. Kyra would be fired if she were the one responsible for the hotel's missing money. If not, there was no way he would let her leave the Acropolis when he was in charge. But he couldn't reveal that until after he had the position of manager. "Going over budget," he said instead. "I'm an expert at handling money."

"I'm glad one of us is." Her lips quirked into a smile. "So I can concentrate on other matters."

"We should probably divvy up the tasks," he suggested. "Once we know our individual responsibilities, we can get to work without stepping on each other's toes."

He spread out the pages he'd been perusing, intent on ignoring Kyra's honey-sweet scent. "I'll take crowd control, security, and the hiring of hostesses and bartenders for the VIP lounge. They'll need security clearance and I'm already familiar with the hotel's system."

"Then I need a favor. I want you to hire Lou to work the lounge. She could use the tips and the extra hours."

The comment took him by surprise. Was Lou part of Kyra's money-skimming contingent? Surely she wasn't planning to run a scam on the VIPs.

"She's not exactly the type of woman you'd expect to find in a VIP lounge," he said, referring to Lou's slight figure and demure attitude.

Kyra's cheeks colored pink. "She may not resemble the Barbie dolls who cater to the high rollers, but she'll work hard and do a good job. That's what's important."

"Okay, okay. I didn't mean to push a hot button."

"Lou is important to me, as are all my friends."

"Then I suppose you'd also approve of Eddie tending bar in the lounge the night of the event?"

She raised a brow. "Is that your idea or are you asking just to placate me?"

Loyalty was definitely one of Kyra's strong points, unless of course the bartender was also a part of her gang, which was a possibility. "Actually, he asked me if he could have the job. I told him to see you in the morning for an application. After he fills it out, tell him to bring it to me so I can slot him in. The same goes for Lou."

"Thank you."

She twirled a finger around a spiral of hair and a vision of Kyra lounging across his bed with those russet curls in tumbling disarray overwhelmed him. "Eddie's competent. There's no reason he can't have the gig," he said, bluffing past the wayward thought.

They discussed a few minor details. Kyra told him responses to the RSVPs she'd sent out for Ms. Simmons a few weeks ago were beginning to trickle in. Jake informed her he was working with Herb on hiring extra security. They talked about the number of employees needed to work the VIP lounge, as well as the food and other amenities.

"I'd like to supervise the singers' wardrobes. I think they should color-coordinate with the set. Women in evening wear and men in tuxes," she said decisively.

105

Impressed with her ideas, Jake was about to tell her so when a knock brought him to his feet. "Must be dinner."

Kyra exhaled a sigh of relief. Instead of his usual brash confidence and cocky manner, Jake was being pleasant and considerate. So pleasant, she could almost breathe. Problem was, the itch that assailed her whenever he was near was growing stronger by the minute. The ongoing assessment he gave her through his navy dark eyes had her melting from the inside out, a reaction she hadn't experienced in hundreds of years.

He led a waiter pushing a trolley to the table, and she cleared the files while the young man served their food. When he finished, Jake signed the tab, took out his wallet, and gave the waiter a handsome tip. Sitting down, his eyes narrowed when she smiled.

"What?"

"That was very generous of you."

"People in the service industry depend on tips for their living. The men and women at this hotel deserve it."

"Then you understand why I want to give Lou a break."

He cut into his steak, then smiled in return. "Yeah, I guess I do."

Over the next two hours they divided the responsibilities, discussed the budget, and prepared a timeline for the duties leading up to the event. The task had been so simple and Jake so agreeable, Kyra could hardly believe he was the same man she'd first met.

And darn if that didn't make her itch all the more.

After they finished dinner, she stacked her paperwork and slid it into the folder. A few more minutes of pretending to pay attention to his words instead of the way his deep voice resonated throughout her body, and she wouldn't be responsible for her actions.

"Did anyone win the jackpot on the Wheel Deal?" he asked.

Though his tone had been casual, the hairs on Kyra's nape prickled. "No."

"Good to hear it. I've done a few percentage comparisons, and the game payout has me worried. When it comes to wheels of chance, this hotel has an unusually high incidence of loss. More than triple the odds."

"I wasn't aware that was your job," she said as she stood. After slipping into her jacket, she sidled to the door, hoping to show him how little she cared about facts and figures.

"My uncle asked me to look into it. The Acropolis seems to be on the losing end of all its wheel games." He shrugged into a leather jacket and followed her out the door. "Why do you suppose that is?"

"Maybe the Acropolis attracts only the lucky gamblers." Kyra made her way to the elevator and pressed the button. "I can get to my car without an escort."

"Maybe so, but my mom taught me to be a gentleman. I'll walk you out."

Zeus's eyeballs, but the man made her crazy. First he gave her an itch that wouldn't be relieved with any amount of scratching. Then he questioned the Wheel Deal. Now he was following her to the parking lot. Could he possibly know what she'd been doing all these months?

"My car is just a few rows from the exit," she said, still trying to dissuade him.

"Not a problem. The fresh air will do me good."

He fell in step beside her, letting her go first when they threaded their way between vehicles. When she neared her BMW, Kyra reached into her bag and pressed the automatic lock on the key ring. Before she could open the door, Jake grasped her arm. She glanced up, unprepared for the way he moved closer and pulled her near.

"I had a good time tonight. Working with you is going to keep me on my toes."

"Why—why do you say that?" she stuttered.

"Because you have definite ideas and opinions." His gaze roamed her face and settled on her lips. "I like that in my women."

She opened her mouth to let him know she wasn't his *anything* and he took full advantage. Stepping forward, Jake pulled her against him and brought his hands to her throat.

Chapter 8

Kyra hadn't realized she'd been driving at NASCAR speed until her car bumped the curb in front of her apartment. Jolted to attention, she was amazed she hadn't been stopped by the police. In the months she'd resided on Earth, she'd been able to keep her mind on her goal of returning in splendor to Mount Olympus.

Until she met Jake Lennox.

From the moment she'd awakened in her apartment, she'd instructed herself to resist personal involvement with mortal men—yet she was attracted to Jake in a very personal way.

A smattering of goosebumps danced along her arms at the mere sound of his name. No doubt about

"Not a chance," Kyra answered.

A few seconds later, the three muses were on the line. After a round of pleasantries, Kyra and Zoë waited for Chloe to begin her usual litany of complaints about life among mortals. A natural blonde, Chloe embodied every earthly hair-color joke Kyra had ever heard. Of course, neither she nor Zoë mentioned it, because Chloe was also intelligent enough to recognize her eccentricities and use them to her advantage. To put it plainly, the word *diva* fit her like a hand-knit cashmere sweater. It was much easier to let her get everything off her chest before they spoke.

"I've sworn off men for the remainder of my stay. With only a few days left, it'll be too much trouble to find another man worthy of my attention."

"I'm sure Miss Belle will be thrilled to learn your revolving-door policy with men has been shelved," said Zoë with a snort. "You are shameless. How many has it been?"

"Twelve, but who's counting, and Miss Belle thinks a woman should sample a bushel of fruit before she picks a favorite orchard. It's not my fault mortal men are so easy."

Knowing Chloe as Kyra did, she ignored the outrageous remarks, made mostly, she was certain, for their shock value. But she didn't doubt her sister used a calendar to X off the days she started and stopped a relationship.

"Is there something you don't want to tell us?"

"It's just been a couple of interesting days."

"Explain interesting," said Zoë.

"I'm finding it difficult to leave the friends I've made here, that's all."

"I know what you mean," said Chloe. "Miss Belle is a sweetheart."

"I've got some good friends, too," added Zoë. "This assignment wasn't as easy as I first thought it might be."

"And I met a man . . ." Kyra began. Since they were being so honest, she figured she might as well tell them the rest.

"I don't like the sound of that," said Zoë.

"Me neither," agreed Chloe. "What did you do?"

Kyra took a deep breath. "I kissed him."

"Kissed him!" Chloe shrieked. "Why didn't you say so?"

"Well, actually, he kissed me. I didn't plan on it, and I don't think he did either. It just happened. But it's been so long, I couldn't help myself. I had to respond."

"See what I mean. Absence does only make it worse. If you'd enjoyed a couple of *healthy* relationships, as Zoë and I have done—"

"Don't compare my two encounters with mortal men to your dozen," said Zoë in a clipped tone. "And this is about Kyra. You know her heart takes a hit whenever she gets involved. It's the reason she decided to keep her distance from humans and concentrate on inspiring good fortune. You should have done the same, instead of having twelve *affaires*."

"And I wouldn't have had any fun, either. Besides, not having sex for a year is unnatural for a healthy citizen of Mount Olympus." Chloe *tsked*. "Can you at least give us the details? Was it passable? Stupendous?"

"It was better than I remembered." Kyra had never lied to her sisters, and wouldn't start now. "It was . . . Jake was . . ."

"Please give it the kiss-o-meter evaluation," prodded Chloe, using her personal rating system for a man's osculatory expertise.

Kyra toed off her shoes and tucked her legs underneath her. "An eleven . . . maybe a twelve."

After several audible gasps, the line went silent. Since it was rare for any of them to be at a loss for words, she steeled herself for what she hoped would be helpful comments. "Will someone please say something?"

"Tell us it isn't so," whispered Zoë.

"What are you talking about? It was just a kiss."

"It didn't sound like *just a kiss* to me. Did it sound that way to you, Chloe?"

"Nu-uh. Not in the least."

So much for helpful comments. "You two are talking in circles. Spit out what you're trying to say."

"You're in love," pronounced Zoë, her tone dour. "Or very close to it."

"Don't be silly. I hardly know Jake."

Or was it?

Without warning, her lips tingled with the memory of Jake's kiss. No, positively, she did not think or want it to be true.

"I do not, repeat, do not love Jake Lennox."

"Tell that to Zeus," chorused her sisters.

"Zeus might spy on us at random, but he's so busy ruling his empire he doesn't have time to snoop into our lives after hours. I highly doubt Jake will be brought into this, and the two of you won't say anything, so who's to know what I feel?"

"Then you admit you have feelings." Zoë turned the question into a statement of fact.

Kyra closed her eyes. "Maybe, but only because I've been lonely. I thought about it on the way home and decided I might be able to scratch that itch and still keep everything impersonal, if I put my mind to it."

"I guess it's worth a try . . . if you keep your head straight," said Zoë. "It will be so satisfying to see Zeus humbled when we succeed."

"And don't forget Hera," reminded Chloe. "The witch."

"I think you've got the first letter in the last word wrong," said Zoë with a chuckle. "I believe it should start with a capital B."

The girls giggled, then Kyra yawned. "I have to go to sleep before I pass out."

"We'll talk next week," said Chloe. "And remember, I love you both very much."

the second floor as a warmup, entered with his key card, and went straight to the rowing machine. Thirty minutes later, he was dripping perspiration, but he was also able to assess more calmly the puzzle named Kyra.

He'd cracked into her bank records, so he knew she didn't make enough money to afford the fancy clothes she wore, or much of anything besides frugal living. She didn't make a car or rent payment, never mind pay a utility bill. There were no unusual transactions and no deposits from an outside source except her weekly paycheck. Because she withdrew just enough for essentials, she'd accumulated a tidy sum, but it was minuscule compared to the casino's losses.

Considering the heat radiating from her body when he held her, there was no doubt the woman had enjoyed their kiss, yet she'd acted as if it were a mere handshake when it was over. Did she have a *benefactor?* And would she cheat on the guy if he provided her with a comfy lifestyle?

The thought only made everything more confusing. Why would she work if she was a kept woman? Unless the man was also her boss, and she was running the scheme at his direction . . .

He could connect the dots from Eddie and Louise to Marie, the dapper old blackjack player, and the craps shooter, but he hadn't found a link between Kyra and the Wheel Deal winners. What purpose would there be for her to manipulate the giveaways

right now she was trouble. And he'd already navigated a river of that in his life. He didn't need any more.

The next morning, Jake walked from the repair room to his office to mull over the technician's report. The dice Frank rolled had shown up clean as a whistle when put through the usual battery of tests. Since this was his second request for an equipment check with negative results, the exchange had caused him more than a bit of embarrassment.

The tech guy had grinned as if Jake was operating one bar shy of a jackpot. "Did we provide these dice?"

"It looked that way," Jake had answered.

"Then they'll be clean. The Acropolis follows the regs. Nobody cheats here we don't know about."

Jake had excellent instincts and a good eye, but he wasn't infallible and neither was the technician. Even though he'd scooped the dice from the table himself and taken them away before Frank touched them again, there was always a chance they'd missed something.

He checked his watch. He still had to go over the day's itinerary, and he was supposed to meet with Kyra this morning. According to their schedule, they had a lot of ground to cover before the competition.

But the more time he spent with Kyra, the more he liked her as a person. Besides being beautiful, she was efficient, incisive, and loyal to her friends, traits he admired. There had to be a way to find out what she was up to without compromising their relationship, especially if he wanted to move to the next plane.

Before entering his office, Jake detoured to the security room. Herb, an expert in evaluating surveillance tapes, might be able to review Frank's play, and find a logical explanation for the guy's win. The senior guard wasn't in, so he left a message outlining his request and trotted into the hall, where he practically plowed into Kyra.

"Jeez, I'm sorry." He grabbed her by the elbows to keep her upright. "Are you okay?"

Her eyes widened as she gazed into his face. Stepping back, he took in her black jacket, pink slacks, and matching sweater. She had a folder in one hand and carried a leather bag over her shoulder. With her abundant red hair knotted at the nape of her neck, she appeared the epitome of a professional, and very sexy, special events coordinator.

"I thought you were going to call when you were ready to meet me?"

Her lips twitched as she said, "I did, but you didn't answer your phone, so I decided it was my turn to come to you." She glanced down the unassuming corridor. "This place is a lot different from the upstairs offices."

Jake tried to imagine the lower level from her perspective. Everything above ground was loud, glitzy,

and larger than life. This floor held about as much
charisma as a prison: cement walls, dim lighting,
and a dingy black and white checked linoleum floor.
"When I got here, Ardmore told me this was the
only space available."

"Where's your office?"

He opened his door and swept out an arm in a
gesture of entry. "After you."

Kyra's lip twitch turned into a frown as she inspected the colorless, sparsely decorated room furnished in early reject. "This place is depressing. No
wonder you're always prowling the casino floor."

Compared to some of the places Jake had worked
in when he was out of the money, this was a palace,
but she didn't need to know that. "I'm only down
here when I have to talk on the phone or be on the
computer. I spend most of my time upstairs."

"Then you're a gambler?" she asked, her tone casual.

Jake believed the closer he stuck to the truth in a
cover story, the better chance it had of passing
muster. "In a manner of speaking."

"Because of your uncle?"

"I spent a lot of time with Uncle T after my fa . . .
er . . . after he married my aunt."

"I see. And when was that?"

Jake hadn't contrived much of a past, because
Themopolis told him his second wife rarely visited
any of his casinos. He picked a date out of thin air

and hoped to heaven he got the woman's name right. "Uncle T and Bianca married in 1990. I tagged after him here for a few summers and stayed with them in the south of France for a couple of years after I graduated college. Aunt Bianca loved Monte Carlo, so he opened a hotel there. Unfortunately, it didn't help their marriage."

"So you know the Mediterranean well?" Kyra's expression turned almost dreamlike, just as it had when she'd stared at her computer wallpaper. "Turquoise-colored water, clear bright sky, white sandy beaches . . . It's a beautiful part of Earth."

Though it sounded as if she were an alien describing a foreign planet, Jake didn't comment. Since she was being so chatty, now might be a good time to ask a few questions of his own. "If you like the water so much, what brought you to the desert?"

She thought about her answer before she spoke. "I was at loose ends and my father decided we . . . I needed a chal . . . er . . . change. Getting a job at a casino just seemed the right thing to do."

"And before you came to work here?"

"I did whatever my father wanted, of course."

"Funny, but you strike me as too independent a woman to be under any man's thumb."

"Not under his thumb, but there were rules to follow, as in any family." She wandered to his desk and her gaze rested on his mother's picture. "Nice-looking lady. Is she a relative?"

"My mother," Jake answered.

For a moment, Kyra's expression softened, then she continued her inspection. "What's this?" she asked, pointing to the drawing on his blotter.

Yesterday, before he and Kyra were scheduled to meet, Jake had dug through the hotel archives for an overview of the building. "A schematic of the arena where the Voice of Vegas will be held." He came around the desk and brushed her shoulder with his own, rewarded when she didn't draw away. "Have you ever been to the pavilion?"

"The Dionysos? I've been to a few shows. I enjoy the magic act and wild animal revue playing there now, but I've never been backstage to get the full effect."

"Want to take a walk with me? I have to check out the entrances and exits."

"Good idea. I probably should inspect the judges' private rooms, VIP lounge, and dressing area for the contestants."

She raised her head and their gazes locked. Jake stared into her eyes and her face flushed a becoming shade of pink. Nearly toe to toe, Kyra licked her full lips and his groin tightened. Without thinking, he stepped closer.

"Kyra, about last night," he began. Held in place by her mesmerizing gray eyes, he continued with his apology. "I didn't mean for it to happen."

"It?"

"The kiss. It was presumptuous of me, and I'm sorry."

When she furrowed her brow, he edged away and banged into his desk chair. She backed up, and they danced in place until he again caught her elbows.

Tugging from his grip, she took a step of retreat. "Let me guess. You want to keep things strictly business. I'm a co-worker, nothing more."

"No—yes—not exactly—" He raked his fingers through his hair. "I didn't plan to take advantage—it just happened. It was wrong to make you uncomfortable or act like a jerk."

"You didn't, not really." Her expression remained thoughtful. "I found the kiss to be rather . . . stimulating."

"I apologize if I came off as—" Jake blinked. "Stimulating?"

"Yes." She tucked a strand of hair behind her ear, then resumed her business stance. "And I've decided to forgive you. There's no need to discuss it further."

He stifled a grin, rolled up the schematic, and stuck it under his arm. "I know I said I didn't date co-workers but . . ."

"We can talk about it later . . . provided you want to," she said hesitantly.

Could it be he was starting to grow on her?

Kyra headed out the door, and he fell in step beside her. "We'll take the elevator to the first floor. From there, we can walk to the pavilion."

Chapter 9

Kyra digested Jake's apology on the elevator ride. He'd sounded sincere, had actually hinted he wanted them to go beyond a professional relationship. He hadn't said he was sorry he kissed her, but he did regret that he might have offended her. Instead of being obnoxious, as she'd thought, he showed every sign of being a nice guy, right down to the picture of his mother proudly displayed on the corner of his desk.

When she added in his capable business persona, and the fact that he was a twelve on the kiss-o-meter, it was inevitable she at least toy with the idea of a relationship.

Apparently still in gentleman mode, Jake held the elevator door and motioned her ahead of him. They walked in the opposite direction of the casino, through an archway supported by massive marble columns, and into a corridor lined with more larger-than-life statues of what she assumed were gods and goddesses.

Kyra recalled her wonder when she'd first visited the pavilion, a replica of the Theater of Dionysos built in fourth century Athens. She'd seen two different shows in the pavilion before its familiar architecture made her so homesick she decided to simply stay away.

"We'll cross the stone bridge and enter through the market area. I'd like to take stock of what a customer intent on making trouble might see. That'll help me figure out how many guards we need and where to station them."

They dodged patrons strolling one of the hotel's three shopping areas. The agora, a recreation of the open air market of ancient Greece, was set up between walls that arched high overhead, and were painted with designs echoing a long-ago era. Vendors dressed in semi-authentic costume hawked household goods, jewelry, clothing, food and drink, music, even DVDs of plays performed in today's refurbished Theater of Dionysos. The nostalgic scene drew Kyra back to Greece's golden age—a time no one in the modern world remembered.

When they reached the ramp leading to the main entrance of the pavilion, Jake nodded to the guard stationed at the doors. "I phoned earlier," he said, pulling out his ID, as did Kyra. "Ms. Degodessa and I are in charge of the Voice of Vegas. We'll be here for routine checks as we near the competition, so get used to our faces."

The guard gave their badges a once over, then unlocked a door. Jake took Kyra's arm as they entered. Though the lighting was dim, the grandeur of the auditorium was evident. The stage's semicircular apron thrust ten rows into the seating area. Far behind it were three viewing screens, each twenty feet tall.

He gave a low whistle. "This is some palace. Anyone sitting up this high is going to think they're watching a string of performing ants."

"It's no wonder they need the viewing screens," added Kyra.

"We'll use ushers to make sure nobody tries to jockey for a better seat."

"I'm going backstage to find the dressing rooms." Kyra started down the steps. "You want to come along?"

"May as well. They'll need security in the back, too."

They continued in the direction of the stage, until they found a door marked "principals only." Assuming it was an entrance for the actors and extras,

Jake let Kyra go ahead of him. Enveloped by darkness, he searched for a light.

"It's creepy back here," she said in a whisper.

Jake took her hand in a protective gesture. "I'm glad I decided to follow you. Never know who might be lurking in the dark."

"Or in a parking lot," Kyra quipped, subtly bringing up last night.

"Ha-ha. Very funny," he answered in an amused tone as he groped the wall.

She smiled as the itch that usually plagued her whenever she was in Jake's presence turned to a warm fuzzy feeling in the middle of her chest. He led her into another hall and flipped on a light switch, but didn't release her hand. As one, they inspected several rooms, each outfitted with dressing and makeup stations, and space for a dozen performers to sit and prepare for a show.

"I have to make notes," she said, reluctantly tugging from Jake's grip. "I need to look everything over in my office."

Kyra jotted down her thoughts and they continued to explore. He again clasped her hand, and they settled into an easy pace. Several more rooms held racks of glittery headwear, feathered boas, slinky dresses, and spike-heeled shoes. Some of the outfits were so small they were barely strings of fabric, which brought to mind the few scantily clad showgirls she'd seen in the lobby who sometimes escorted the whales to their limos.

Jake held up a hanger holding three strips of red sequins. "This would be illegal anywhere but here."

Even on Mount Olympus, she thought, taking a look at the bits of fabric. How in Hades would you cover the right parts? "Or a nude beach."

"Ever been to one?" Jake asked.

Kyra felt her cheeks heat. "No."

"Well, I have." He grinned. "Maybe you'd like to take a trip with me when this function is over. Cannes is nice this time of year."

Only if Zeus allows me to return for a visit. "I'll have to think about it."

They continued checking rooms until she found the perfect space for the competitors and guest stars. Since three men and three women were in the finale, she decided they could share two rooms while each of the three judges would have their own private suite.

Adding to her list, she wrote "signage for doors" and "staff to handle details." She also had to confer with the contestants on their wardrobe choices. Even though she hoped to be gone by the end of the show, she wanted it to be a success.

Jake stayed by her side, moving furniture or costume racks when she asked. The itch that had settled in her chest continued to build, reminding her of the conversation she'd had with Zoë and Chloe. Her sisters had warned her to be careful when she dealt with him, but both of them had already enjoyed sexual fulfillment on Earth. Since Jake was a twelve on the kiss-o-meter, what was the harm in using him to get a little TLC of her own?

The more time she spent with him, the more she believed she could handle a mindless fling with Jake Lennox, the single mortal who had everything she looked for in a god—er—man.

As long as she guarded her heart.

When they returned to the stage entrance, Jake asked, "Ready to see the lounge?"

Kyra nodded. Still holding his hand, she followed willingly as he led her to the elevator.

Jake gazed out the Plexiglas window of the thirty-by-fifty-foot gallery suspended high above the auditorium. He'd found the control panel operating the overheads and decided to keep them low. Even in the dim light, the lounge was impressive, with a panoramic view of the stage that also took in a goodly amount of the audience.

Two rows of plush chairs were staggered at the front of the box, with twenty seats to each row. Long tables graced the rear wall, while richly appointed portable bars sat at both ends of the suite. Twin butter-soft sofas covered in black leather took up the center area, creating a perfect spot for seduction.

After placing the schematic on a table, he walked behind one of the two bars to inspect the contents. A bottle of cognac, probably left over from the last show, sat on a shelf. He glanced at Kyra, who was staring down onto the stage. Would she accept a

hoping the cool liquid would put out the fire his intimate perusal ignited in her belly. He set his glass on the counter, then took hers and did the same.

Zeus's eyebrows! How had their interaction gone from adversarial to warm and friendly to steamier than a sauna so quickly?

Without speaking, Jake led her to one of the huge sofas facing the window. After guiding her down, he settled beside her and inched forward. Then he raised his hand and gently stroked her cheek, much as he'd done in the parking lot. His fingers edged downward, brushed her throat, and wrapped the nape of her neck. Ever so slowly, he drew her near and let his lips nuzzle hers, sipping, tasting, teasing . . .

The kiss was gentle as a zephyr, warm as the July sun, and as breathtaking as the turquoise waters of the Aegean. She clasped his wrist, and he pulled away to rest his forehead against hers.

"You drive me crazy. You have since the moment I watched you flip off the statue in the hotel lobby."

"You saw me do that?" Kyra asked, confused.

"I was in the surveillance room a few days ago when you entered the building. Herb Molinari thought it was funny. Said you'd done it from the first day you started working here."

"I had no idea I've been on display in such a manner."

"Not on display. But the guards gravitate toward beautiful women, especially when there isn't much going on in the casino."

"Damn, but you're fine," he whispered, bending to suckle a distended bud.

Kyra threaded her fingers through his hair and lost herself in the sensation of his teeth scraping her flesh. He groaned as he sucked her throbbing nipple deeper into his mouth. Her legs opened wide and welcomed his rigid length to her center, lifting and thrusting in rhythm to the stroking of his tongue.

In a burst of desire, she made her decision. If she was to have only one fling with a mortal, she wanted it to be Jake. But not here, in a darkened yet public place where anyone could surprise them. And definitely not on a cold leather couch.

As if sensing her unease, he pulled away. "What's wrong?"

Sitting up, Kyra reached underneath and fastened her bra, then straightened her sweater. "I don't want it to be like this."

He drew back further, his expression one of concern. "Was it something I did?"

"It wasn't you. But if we're going to move to the next step in our friendship, I'd like it to be . . ."

"More romantic?" He grinned. "No problem. I can do romance."

She smiled. "Romance is good, but I was hoping things wouldn't get too serious. I'm not in a posi— er—ready to get seriously involved with anyone right now."

her breast. His promise of things to come made her itch in every important place on her body.

There was no doubt the man could overshoot Chloe's silly kiss-o-meter by a dozen points or more. The fact that he, too, was looking for a no-strings relationship only made the offer of an *affaire* more tempting. Because of him, she hadn't completed a single item on her list that had to do with the Voice of Vegas, and she was late for the Wheel Deal. Again.

Gathering her bag and folder on the competition, she rushed from the room. When she rounded the corner, she ran into Rob, who she guessed had been heading to her office.

"Sorry, I didn't mean to give you heart failure, but we have to talk." He picked her file off the floor and held it out to her. "I just came from the Dionysos Pavilion. I told the guard I was our competitor, so he let me inside. I went on stage and took a gander at the audience seating—" He swallowed. "The place is as big as a football stadium."

"Not quite, but it is impressive." At the sight of Rob's pale face, Kyra's right temple began to throb. She had no time to hold his hand just because the venue was daunting. "You must have been there before; you've worked here for a while."

"I've gone as a spectator, but I never thought I'd be on that stage." He tugged on his shirt collar. "It's hard to imagine standing up there in front of a dozen television cameras with about a bazillion people watching . . ." If possible, his complexion grew even whiter. "I . . . it's . . ."

"Look, Rob, this competition will be exactly like the others, and you made it through them, didn't you?"

"This is different. It's for all the marbles. And Gram will be there."

The photo she'd seen sitting on the corner of Jake's desk flashed through her mind and Kyra straightened. Her tendency to hold a soft spot for men who loved their mothers, or in Rob's case, grandmother, was becoming a roadblock to her common sense. "I'm late for the daily contest. Walk with me and tell me what I can do to help."

"Have you talked to Ardmore about singing lessons?"

She stopped at the landing. "I did, and I'm sorry, but he said no. There's not enough money in the budget." It wouldn't help Rob's stage fright if he knew the top man didn't give a fig about who won the prestigious competition. "I've tried finding a way to cut corners and take care of the fee, but so far . . ."

"I never did like that guy." Rob confessed. "You think he'd want me to win to add prestige to the hotel."

"I agree, but I'm not sure—"

"The blonde from the Luxor sounds like Alicia Keyes. And the guy from the Bellagio could be Pavarotti's twin. It's tough trying to see myself as anything more than a lounge singer . . . and not a very good one."

They reached the lobby and Kyra took a look at the day's lineup of players—close to eighty eager winners, each hoping to make it big at the wheel.

"Maybe I should drop out."

She whirled in Rob's direction. "What?"

"Quit. Now. I hate to be a chicken, but—"

"You'll do no such thing." Kyra had thought of something that might work, but the idea was a little far-fetched. Since Rob was threatening to walk away from the contest, she had no choice. Tucking her hand in the crook of his elbow, she dragged him beside her as she spoke. "I have a friend, someone I know very well, and I'm sure she'll take you on at no charge. Now stop being such a wuss and go find an empty room with a piano. Then call the front desk, and leave a note telling me where you are. I'll meet you there after the Wheel Deal, with or without my friend."

"You know a voice teacher? Why didn't you say so?"

Kyra crossed her mental fingers. "It slipped my mind until two seconds ago."

"And she's in Vegas?"

"She could be." *If she and I connect, and she's not inspiring another singer or dancer. And she's feeling magnanimous.* "It depends."

Rob raised a brow. "Where does she live?"

"She moves around a lot." That much was true. "I'm not sure where she is right now, but I'll do my best to find her."

"And she's good?"

"She's the greatest voice instructor in the world. She can also show you a few moves, if you know what I mean. Just phone the desk when you find a room."

Rob grinned, then grabbed her and gave her a drawn-out and exaggerated kiss. Kyra sighed as she watched him strut down the hall with newfound confidence. Too bad she wasn't attracted to Rob in anything more than a brotherly way, because it would be a lot safer to have a no-strings *affaire* with a simple guy than with a dangerous man like Jake.

And she did know the world's greatest vocal coach. She just wasn't certain she could convince her to come to Las Vegas merely to inspire a single mortal. Last she'd heard, her sister muse stuck strictly to rock stars, and that was only because Zeus had reassigned her to modern music. Still, it wouldn't hurt to ask . . . or wheedle.

Or beg.

Chapter 10

Jake ran a hand across his jaw as he stared at the monitor. From the moment he'd said good-bye to Kyra, he hadn't been able to stop thinking about her. He'd spent the afternoon going through employment applications and studying the pavilion schematic, but none of it made sense. Not when their interlude kept intruding, painting pictures far more enticing than mere blueprints.

So far, he had no concrete evidence that she was the reason the hotel was losing buckets of money. Even though she was his only positive lead, the more time he spent with her, the more he believed he'd been wrong.

When his mind had wandered again and again to their hot and heavy session in the VIP box, he'd come to the surveillance room, where he hoped to pass the time talking to Herb about the film of the guy with the suspicious dice. That idea had fallen through the moment he'd seen what the older security guard was studying on the viewing screen.

Herb gave a shake of his balding head, then glanced at Jake with a smirk on his face. "Woo-ee, that was some lip-lock."

Jake scanned the screen, saw Rob sweep Kyra in his arms and bend her backward in a movie-style kiss. He tamped back a rush of jealousy. If the touch of Kyra's lips affected Garrett the same way they affected him, it was a wonder the poor schmuck could walk. It had taken him the entire afternoon to erase the taste of her from his mouth. Seeing her in a lip-lock with the computer nerd–star singer wanna-be brought everything back in vivid technicolor.

"Why do you think he planted one on her?" asked Herb, his expression puzzled. "I mean, Garrett doesn't look her type, and I've never seen them do it before, so why do you suppose—"

"I don't know," said Jake, keeping his voice even and in control. "Maybe they're in love."

"Hah!" barked the security guard. "No way in hell would the gorgeous goddess waste her time with a boy like Garrett. Not when there are dozens of real men ready, willing, and able to tend to her needs."

"What men?" asked Jake, annoyed the statement made his gut churn with the green-eyed monster.

"You mean besides the ones who've already hit on her? For starters, there's Big Fred, one of the bouncers at the all-girl review. Then there's Bill Phelps, the pit boss who could double for that George Clooney fella, Phil Reardon, senior night-shift supervisor, a dozen bartenders and dealers, and just about every man in the security department." Studying Jake's face, his smile stretched wide. "Looks like I can add a certain guy who's working here undercover as Mr. T's nephew to the list."

Jake refused to meet Herb's smug gaze, noting that Kyra now sat at her old desk in the lobby, registering customers for the Wheel Deal. Damn, but she had him twitchy when she perched behind that tiny writing table so prim and proper. Made him wish he was back in high school with an hour-long detention, and she was the teacher in charge.

"Okay, so ignore me. But you might wanna wipe the sweat from your upper lip and rearrange the family jewels before you leave," warned Herb. "Because it looks like she's got you by the—"

"I'm going to my suite," said Jake, cutting him off with a growl. "I have to get ready for a dinner date."

"With Kyra?"

"Never mind with who."

The security guard snorted. "Take a cold shower when you get there. Maybe it will help."

Jake doubted even a soak in a tub full of ice cubes would cure what ailed him, but he had to do something while he waited for seven o'clock to arrive. It was near five and he had yet to plan a menu. He'd even thought about ordering flowers for his suite. Would Kyra prefer roses, or an orchid, or some other type of exotic bloom . . .

He took the elevator to the main floor, where he decided to stop at the hotel florist and check out their selection firsthand. Maybe something would strike his fancy, like a flower the color of her fiery hair mixed with a few of the same creamy hue as her skin. He had no idea where Rob Garrett had gone, but if he ran into the would-be singing star, a serious talk about the status of Garrett and Kyra's relationship might be just the thing to cool the embers of jealousy that burned in his gut.

He exited the elevator, turned his back on the lobby, and followed the outer walkway around the casino, passing two gift shops, an upscale women's boutique, a high-end leather dealer, a men's apparel shop, and two famous-name jewelry stores. Bells, whistles, and buzzers rang in the distance, the familiar clatter an anchor to his senses.

Kyra had him in knots—not good for his job or his emotions. He had to concentrate, remember a successful ending to this investigation would secure his future, as well as garner a slice of respectability for himself.

He took the corridor leading to the outdoor market they'd passed that morning and strolled into the florist shop. A multitude of roses, loose or in ready-made bouquets, filled vases in one cold case; lilies and a variety of unfamiliar flowers occupied another; a third case held carnations, daisies, and more common blossoms. The center of the store featured a display of orchids, while the shelves were covered with greenery both natural and made of silk.

He chose a mixed bouquet, stood in line, and overheard the conversation of the two men in front of him.

"I lost about five hundred this afternoon," said an older gentleman holding a dozen red roses. "These are for the wife, in case she freaks out."

"You've lost more than that here before," said his pal. "She'll understand."

"Maybe, but she expects us to come back in a couple of days for the big singing contest, and be settled in one of the penthouse suites. When I asked the concierge about an upgrade, he told me the Sky Tower was closed for remodeling. It's the same story they gave me three months ago. How the hell long does it take to paper and carpet a couple of rooms? When the wife finds out, this may be our last trip here."

"I know where she's coming from," said the friend, pulling out his wallet to pay for his flowers. "You can take your business elsewhere, and get their big suites for the amount of money you spend."

"I guess, but I like this place. The architecture and design are different, and the décor and atmosphere are top notch. Ditto the food." He sighed. "We'll see what the wife says after the singing competition. Maybe the job will be done by the next time we visit."

Since Jake was taller than both men, it wasn't difficult for him to inch closer and catch a glimpse of the name on the man's credit card right before he tucked it away. It was odd to hear that a customer who usually got special treatment was being ignored. Free rooms and meals, complimentary limo rides, or other fancy upgrades were a given; if the patron was used to being ensconced in the Sky Tower, they were definitely whales. When the man mentioned five hundred, it was "whale speak" for *thousand*, which meant the guy had dropped a half million dollars in an afternoon. It would be stupid of the Acropolis not to have a classy suite for his use.

Of course, the complainer might be exaggerating the situation. There was no way to tell until he scanned the guy's playing record and checked the type of accommodations he was normally given. Unfortunately, Jake had no time to bother with it now. He made a mental note to check the man's history as soon as he got an extra minute.

He paid for his purchase, and asked that the bouquet be delivered to his room, in case Kyra spotted him on his way to the elevator. On his return, he passed the lobby and eyed the action at the Wheel Deal station.

As if on cue, Kyra tapped the next person in line on the shoulder. The gesture brought him up short;

curious, he watched the man give the wheel a mighty spin. Raucous music filled the air, bells and whistles sounded, lights flashed, and a contingent of clowns began to dance around the lucky contestant. Kyra beamed at the winner, and they chatted as they walked to the front desk.

Damn.

Kyra's simple yet suspicious ritual did an encore in his mind. Though she hadn't touched the wheel, things just didn't look right, but why?

On the way to his room, he composed a menu for seduction. Kyra often spoke of the Mediterranean and how much she enjoyed the water, so he assumed she liked seafood. Visions of lobster, dripping in melted butter, seared scallops resting on a bed of greens, or raw oysters on the half shell filled his thoughts. And for dessert, he'd ask the kitchen to send up a half dozen of their signature dark chocolate truffles.

How could she resist him after a meal made for love?

Kyra waited for the crowd to clear, then checked for a message at the front desk. The clerk handed her a note from Rob saying he'd found an empty room at the end of the corridor hosting the complimentary shows performed by less famous entertainers. She had some time before her date, so she went to the employee lounge, where she smoothed her hair and reapplied her lip gloss.

Then she stepped into a stall and locked the door. Taking a deep breath, she closed her eyes and concentrated on a vision of her sister as she uttered a chant the muses used when they tried to reach each other.

"Terpsichore, if you hear my plea, this I beg, come now to me. I need your guidance, your inspiration too, so here I wait until I meet you."

Seconds passed before Kyra opened her eyes and peered about the stall. She sat on the commode and sighed. This wasn't going as well as she'd hoped.

She repeated the poem, putting a bit more emphasis on the words. Shoulders hunched, she opened one eye and saw that she was still alone. "Terpsichore, it's me, Kyra," she whispered. "Where the heck are you?"

The bathroom door opened and footsteps tapped across the tile floor. She peeked under the door and spotted a pair of dainty feet covered in familiar sandals. Bursting from the stall, Kyra grinned when she saw curling tresses of black trail to the visitor's tiny waist. Raising her gaze, she met her sister's smiling reflection in the mirror.

"Hey, girl. What's shakin'?"

Kyra hugged Terpsichore tight. "I thought you'd never get here." Then she drew back and said, "I hope I didn't take you away from anything important."

With her rosebud lips twitching, Terpsichore shrugged. "Just my latest attempt to inspire a new wave, retro-grunge group that spends a lot of time

149

thinking about their next big hit." She gave an unladylike snort. "As if that will ever happen."

"You haven't had any success with them?"

"I'm the one who inspired their first chart-topper, and believe me it was a challenge. Since then, they've been *boor-ring*. I need to move on, so this is the perfect time to take a break and start a new project."

"What I have in mind for you won't exactly be a project, but I do need your help. I'm just happy you didn't mind coming here."

The muse of song and dance gave a knowing grin. "To Sin City? Are you kidding? Besides, you haven't asked for a favor in a couple of hundred years. I figured it was important. What's up?"

"I have a friend who needs some serious inspiration, and not the kind I'm able to give."

Terpsichore narrowed her eyes. "Male or female?"

"Male."

"Young or old?"

"Young."

"Is he cute?"

"Very, but not your type."

"Honey, these days any man who isn't sporting a tattoo or a nipple ring is my type."

Kyra giggled, and Terpsichore frowned. "Please don't tell me he has a tongue stud. Those things give me the creeps."

"No pierced body parts that I know of. He's more an all-American boy."

"Big, brawny, and dumb?"

"Actually, Rob is intelligent. He's a computer nerd."

"Ack! I'm not sure I can work with someone who's into technology á la Zeus. Ever since the old fart discovered the Internet there's been no stopping him."

Kyra inched forward. "Shh, he might hear you."

"Since Hera's returned to Olympus, I doubt it. I don't have to tell you what that means."

It definitely explained the reason she hadn't received a pestering e-mail all morning. When Hera was in their mountain home, she demanded every second of her husband's time—and made each citizen of their paradise miserable while doing so.

"Rob is nothing like Zeus. He's just a really nice guy competing in a singing contest, and he needs a healthy dose of confidence-building. I told him I knew the world's greatest vocal coach, and he can't wait to meet you."

"A contest? I love contests." Terpsichore's baby blue eyes danced with delight. "Do we get to kick butt?"

"In a manner of speaking. I'll fill you in."

Terpsichore took in Kyra's black blazer, and pale pink sweater and slacks. "Hang on. I can't go out there dressed in this old thing with you wearing designer duds." She snapped her fingers, and her diaphanous white gown melted into a form-fitting sky-blue silk suit the exact color of her eyes. Then she ran her fingers through her coal black hair, and it magically turned into a short and sassy bob.

She spun in place on matching three-inch pumps. "What's the verdict? Will I fit in?"

"Terrific," said Kyra. "Very chic."

"Judging by your clothes, I guess this trial isn't exactly a hardship," said Terpsichore, striding alongside Kyra.

"Up until the last couple of days it was a lot of fun."

"Uh-oh. That doesn't sound good. How are Chloe and Zoë doing?" the muse asked as they hurried from the lounge, down a long corridor and into the casino area.

"Better than me, I think. You know how Chloe can be."

"Still pulling the dumb-little-diva act and driving men to dri—" Terpsichore stopped in her tracks. The casino grew busy after 6 P.M. and was now crammed with customers. Men in designer tuxedos and women in glamorous evening gowns mixed with people in jeans and sweatshirts. The action at two of the three craps tables was fast and furious, and the cheers from the roulette wheels could be heard from across the room. Many of the slot machines were in use, their lights blinking while coins jingled gaily in the troughs.

Her eyes wide, the muse of song and dance took in the flash and dazzle of the gaming floor. "This place is rockin'. Is it always this exciting?"

"Most evenings," said Kyra, trying to move Terpsichore along. She checked her watch and noted it was a few minutes before seven. "I can show you around later—tomorrow night, maybe?"

Glancing at her sister, she did a double take. The muse now wore a blue evening gown with a plunging bodice covered in diamonds so sparkly Kyra was certain they were real. "Terpsichore!" she said with a shriek. "People are watching."

The muse gazed at the dozens of customers who walked past as if they hadn't witnessed a thing. "Now one is paying us a bit of attention," she said with a giggle. "Now that I see what the players are wearing, I want to fit in. Besides, I have to be ready in case I meet a shark or a walrus or a—a—you know, one of those high rollers named after a fish."

Kyra blew out a breath. "They're referred to as whales. And I might be able to introduce you to a few, after you take care of Rob."

"You'd do that for me?"

"If the ones I know are playing tonight. If not, I'll bring you to the upstairs gaming rooms and see if a friend will let you mingle."

"A demi-goddess does not *mingle*." Terpsichore fluffed her shining ebony hair. "I'm perfectly capable of finding someone with whom to party on my own."

"After you see to Rob. Please?"

Kyra grabbed her elbow, and the muse nodded, though she gazed longingly at the cluster of well-dressed men playing craps. Passing a bank of slot machines, they turned into the entertainment corridor and walked by a typical bar area with its singer du jour, another with a dance floor and a band preparing for their nightly gig, a room with a female comedian doing stand-up, and another with television monitors hosting a variety of sporting events. The last set of double doors was closed, and Kyra assumed it was the room where they'd find Rob.

Before she could knock, the door swung open. A hand clutched her arm and reeled her inside. Then Rob released her and began to pace.

"I didn't think you'd ever get here. And where's your . . ." His gaze centered over Kyra's shoulder, and he gulped. ". . . friend?"

Kyra turned and found Terpsichore smiling sweetly. "Rob, this is Terp . . . ah . . . Trixie. The voice coach I told you about."

Terpsichore held out her hand. "It's a pleasure."

Rob wiped a palm on his shirt front and took the tip of Terpsichore's slim fingers in his meaty paw. "Uh . . . yeah . . . it's my pleasure too. I mean, the pleasure is all mi—" His face colored red. "Happy to meet you."

"Kyra tells me you're in a singing contest, and you need some help."

"I could use a few pointers."

"Then let's get started, shall we?" She took his hand and led him to the piano.

Before she was seated, Kyra waggled a finger. "Trixie dear, could I speak with you for a moment?"

Terpsichore gave Rob a blinding smile. "I'll be right back." She reached Kyra's side wearing a toned-down grin. "You said cute, when you should have said gorgeous. And honestly—*Trixie?* You might as well have said Bambi or Boom Boom. Why can't I just be me?"

"Because *you* are too much woman for a nice man like Rob. Besides, he has a crush on a friend of mine, and I was hoping to get them together before I left."

"Oh, pooh." At Kyra's grimace, Terpsichore scrunched her lips into a pout. "I'll try to behave."

"*Try* isn't good enough. Promise me you won't put the moves on Rob."

"If you promise to take me on a tour tonight."

The dire words told Kyra she could say good-bye to her romantic evening with Jake. "Okay, I promise."

"Great. I don't think this will take long." Terpsichore sashayed to the piano, settled on the bench, and played a string of scales. "Okay, big guy, show me what you've got."

Kyra heaved a breath. It was probably for the best that she stuck around, if for nothing else than Rob's protection. She wouldn't put it past her good buddy *Trixie* to accidentally forget her half-hearted promise and make a move on the poor guy.

She walked to the house phone, dialed the hotel operator, and asked to be put through to Jake's suite.

Chapter 11

Jake hung up the phone and speared his fingers through his hair. He'd already straightened his picture-perfect suite and added the special bouquet of flowers to the dining table. Then he'd shaved, showered, and changed his clothes. When it became obvious Kyra would be late, he'd started to pace. Good thing he hadn't ordered food, because he'd lost his appetite when he answered his phone and learned she'd be a no-show.

What was it Kyra had said? "I'm sorry, something's come up. I won't be able to make our appointment."

Appointment, hell! He thought they had a lover's tryst, a rendezvous, a date—call it any of the above, but he certainly hadn't labeled their upcoming evening a business meeting. What the heck was so freakin' earth-shattering she couldn't have dinner with him?

He remembered their short phone conversation. There'd been little background chatter, but he had heard a piano playing . . . not a song, exactly, but a riff of notes more like a scale . . . and maybe a man's voice.

It was too late to ask Kyra for the details, so Jake put on his tie, slipped into a sport jacket, and headed for the basement. Opening the surveillance room door, he took stock. With every camera in use during evening hours, double the manpower of the day shift was necessary to watch over the tables in play. Engrossed in canvassing the action-packed casino, the night crew paid him no mind.

He nodded to the supervisor and sat at a bank of monitors keeping tabs on the less security-sensitive areas of the hotel. Curious to see what would pop up, he clicked on the search grid, typed in the word "piano," and hit go. After several seconds, every location in the hotel that held a piano appeared on his screens.

Giving the rooms a quick scan, he zeroed in on one showcasing Rob Garrett singing while an attractive woman in formalwear accompanied him on a baby grand. And in the corner, stood Kyra, gazing with a look of rapture on her lovely face.

Unfortunately, there was no way Jake could compete with the younger man in the musical department. He'd heard his off-key voice echo in the shower, and recalled his mother had once jokingly commented that he sounded like an outboard motor badly in need of a tune-up whenever he tried to sing.

Shoving away from the desk, he stood and crammed his hands in his pockets. Kyra had melted in his arms this morning, then canceled tonight's dinner, apparently to be with the boy crooner. Was she in love with Garrett, Jake wondered, and just stringing him along?

Jake had never been a quitter, and he wasn't about to start now. A realist, he knew he came across as an experienced man with enough money to live comfortably, a fair sense of humor, and a way of handling himself many ladies enjoyed. Batting triple zero with a woman that had him tied in knots was damned hard to swallow. The computer geek might be able to vocalize, but Garrett was a minor league player in the man-woman game. Besides his boyish appeal and puppy-dog personality, the guy had zip going for him.

Jake didn't realize he was pacing until he bumped into the shift supervisor, who was on his way out the door. "Sorry."

"Something on your mind?" asked the guard.

"Do you know how I'd find that room?" Jake asked, pointing to the monitor.

The supervisor peered at the screen, then flipped through papers in the folder he carried. "It's in the cheap seats. You know, the wing with the complimentary entertainment. Besides the pavilion, those lounges are the only place with a piano, and there are usually one or two free each week." The supervisor eyed the screen. "Chart placement says it's the room on the right, end of the corridor marked 'This Week's Headliners.'"

"Thanks." Jake left for the elevator, and took a couple of deep breaths on the ride. No sense showing up with an attitude, something he was certain Kyra would disapprove of. Better he acted as if he was worried about her and longed to be in her company, so she'd start taking him seriously as a man.

On the lobby level, he tugged at his jacket and made sure his tie was straight before he located the room. Pausing at the door, he inched close and heard a man belt out a popular song from a few years back. And darn if the guy didn't sound . . . better than average. At least as good as a couple of recording artists who'd hit it big and were now a mainstay in the contemporary scene.

Vowing to keep his cool, he opened the door and peeked inside. The cutie he'd seen earlier on the monitor had finished playing and was now lecturing as if she were in front of a classroom.

"The only thing you need to improve is your delivery, and by that I don't mean facial expression or body movement. Your voice may come from here." She tapped her diaphragm with two fingers. "But here," she placed the fingers above her left breast, "is the most important."

"I think you sounded fabulous," said Kyra, smiling at Garrett from the other side of the baby grand. "You've improved already. I can't imagine anyone beating you if you continue to do the exercises Trixie taught you."

Trixie? Were there still women under the age of sixty-five who used that name? Jake took stock of the stranger's glamorous appearance and classical features. Though she wasn't a knockout like Kyra, she definitely had babe potential. But Trixie?

He stepped into the room and applauded. "From what I heard, the ladies are right. Keep it up, and you'll win the Voice of Vegas hands down. In fact, if the odds makers heard you now, I'd lay two to one they'd name you as the favorite."

"Thanks," said Rob with a grin.

Kyra seemed surprised to see him, then quickly composed herself. "Jake. How did you find me—us?"

He sauntered toward the trio. "After you canceled, I figured I'd come downstairs and catch a show. When I heard singing coming from this room, I didn't know it was Garrett. Imagine my surprise at finding you tucked away back here."

The dark haired, doe-eyed woman rose from the bench, her arm outstretched, her smile inviting. "I'm Trixie. It's nice to meet you."

"Jake Lennox," he answered with a polite shake. "You new here?"

"Trixie's my sis—a friend," Kyra interjected. "When Mr. Ardmore informed me he wouldn't pay for Rob's voice lessons, I asked her to take him on. She's inspired some of the world's most famous singers and dancers."

"Is that so?" asked Jake. Trixie didn't appear old enough to have inspired a vocal group before the Backstreet Boys. "Anybody I might have heard of?"

"The last was a band out of Seattle—the Gutter Rats. And about a few thousand more," said Trixie. As if sensing the electricity arcing between him and Kyra, she asked, "How do you two know each other?"

"We're co-workers," said Jake before Kyra could answer.

Trixie's eyes widened. "Really? How interesting."

"Didn't Kyra tell you? We're running the singing competition together."

"Hmmm . . . I guess she managed to forget that tiny detail. Though I can't imagine why."

Kyra shot her friend a glare and grabbed Jake's hand. "Trixie, why don't you and Rob have a final practice run, while I talk to Jake? Then we can take the tour I promised."

The voice coach gave him a flirty grin, waggled her fingers, and took her seat. Kyra dragged him into a far corner. "What are you doing here?"

"I wanted to find out what was so important it would cause you to cancel our date," he said simply. "I don't appreciate being stood up."

"I called, so you weren't stood up, and I had a good reason," she countered.

"You expect me to believe helping a friend give Garrett a voice lesson is excuse enough to change our plans?" He snorted his disbelief. "I was looking forward to tonight. I thought you were, too."

"I am . . . I was," she said with a sigh. "But Rob came to me for help and I couldn't disappoint him."

"What if I wait around and take you and Trixie on the tour? Then you can tell her good night, and we can have a midnight supper . . . or something."

Kyra eyed him dubiously. "I promised to introduce her to a high roller."

"I'll go to the front office and check the hotel guest list. There's got to be someone here I know who'd like to entertain a beautiful woman. If not, I'll take a walk through the upstairs game rooms and find her a decent companion."

Kyra's expression brightened. "You'd go to that much trouble just to be alone with me?"

"Sweetheart, right now, I'd do just about anything to have you to myself. Provided Garrett doesn't enter the picture."

Was he jealous of Rob? "Enter the picture? We're friends."

"Lovers?"

She folded her arms and arched a brow. "How can you ask such a thing after you and I—did what we did in the pavilion?"

Jake's expression morphed from curious to relieved. Their eyes locked and he ran a hand across his jaw. "I heard a few rumors and I saw you in a clinch the day he installed your computer, so I just assumed—"

"You assumed I would sleep with two men at the same time? You are such a jerk."

"Hold on a second—"

"Oops, excuse me. Make that an insensitive jerk."

She turned to storm away, but Jake grabbed her and swung her around to face him.

"Kyra, wait. I didn't mean to insult you." His grip gentled as he steered her into a half-filled coat closet off the main hall. Maneuvering her into a hidden corner, he propped his hands on the wall and caged her in. "I'm sorry. But you should know I play to win. If we're going to take the next step and sleep together, I won't accept a third person in the bed."

Leaning close, he breathed against her lips, sending a shiver down her spine. "Forgive me?"

Kyra's insides fluttered. Even though he wasn't playing fair, the warmth flooding her stomach made her ache with longing. "I'm not sure I can."

"Just say you'll try." Jake bent and kissed her, softly at first, then with a more searing intensity. Drawing her to his chest, he lifted her up, molding

163

her to him so they were eye to eye. "Say you'll stay with me tonight."

"No—"

He pressed his mouth to hers in another steamy kiss, then pulled back. "Yes."

"I don't—"

He kissed her again, teasing her lips apart and sucking at her tongue. Kyra sighed with pleasure and gave herself up to his tender demand. It was fruitless to resist. Jake's torturous persistence was a drug to her senses, making her so addled she hadn't the strength to fight.

Summoning a last bit of bluster, she said, "I'll need a few essentials if I'm going to spend the night."

He nuzzled her neck, nipped at her earlobe. "The hotel boutiques are open twenty-four hours. Buy whatever you need and bring it to my room."

The tempting idea made her answer so easy it was frightening. "Then I guess I'd better go shopping before Trixie finishes with Rob."

Jake eased her down his body and held her hand as they walked to the curving staircase and followed it to the lobby. Then they turned right and took the busy outer walkway that led to the specialty stores.

At the exact moment they passed a bank of slot machines, three men broke from the throng, shoving customers out of the way as they ran. One went into the shop-filled hall, while the other two shot toward the front exit.

Seconds later, the crowd parted again and one of the senior guards, with a handful of other hotel personnel, flew toward them. Jake pulled her out of the way and called to the guard. "Herb, what's going on?"

Herb skidded to a stop. "This could be the break you're waiting for. We'll go after the pair heading outside. You and Nesbitt take the other guy."

The guard named Nesbitt raced toward the concourse. Kyra wasn't sure why chasing cheats had anything to do with Jake, but she could tell by the look on his face it was important.

"Go ahead. I'll wait here," she said, stepping aside.

He opened his mouth as if to speak, then shook his head, broke into a jog, and disappeared after Nesbitt.

Chapter 12

FROM: Topgod@mounto.org
TO: Kdegodessa@Acropolis.com
SUBJECT: TRIXIE ☹

Permission to receive aid from another muse was
not granted. Terpsichore has more than her share
of tasks to handle without coming to your rescue.
Mortals need inspiration, not meddling.

For clarification, see corporate document No.
4907, subsection 3B, paragraph 12.

I am not amused, and I expect an immediate
explanation.

Sincerely (and still Top God),
Zeus

Kyra was ready to explode. First, she'd summoned the muse of song and dance in order to help Rob, not inspire good luck, which caused her to miss her special date with Jake. Then Jake had disappeared and she'd left the hotel alone. Once home, she remembered she had yet to do a thing about getting Rob and Lou together. Now this.

Sitting at her desk mid-morning, she read Zeus's unpleasant e-mail for the third time. Corporate document No. 4907? What in Hades was the father god talking about?

And how had he found out so quickly that she'd gotten a hold of Terpsichore for assistance?

Simple, you idiot. Zeus has spies everywhere. He could have ordered any of a dozen minions to check up on you, Zoë, or Chloe.

Or Hera had sent spies, and snitched to her husband after receiving an update on the trio's progress. The chief goddess had always been jealous of the muses, especially since Zeus had created them with Mnemosyne and not her. Sadly, as a minor goddess, Mnemosyne held little power on Mount Olympus.

Thanks to Hera's envy and interference, Mnemosyne had been prohibited from interacting with her daughters, so the muses had matured without a woman's guidance. Their lack of parental advice—Zeus never did anything but shout, threaten, and demand—was one of the reasons Kyra had a soft spot in her heart for anyone, male or female, who was thoughtful of their mother.

She resisted the urge to pick up her computer monitor and toss it in the trash. She never should have learned how to use the cursed machine. She did better dealing with live bodies. She could have swayed any messenger sent by her father until the year was over. At worst, he would have summoned her home for a tongue lashing.

If only she'd received some feedback from Zeus these past months, just to let her know she'd been on the right track. Problem was, even though her father strived to run his kingdom like a Fortune 500 company, he was still a god. He'd never outgrown his temperamental and quixotic nature. One moment he could compliment her on a job well done, the next he might chastise her for being a disappointing do-nothing of a daughter.

Though it was interesting dealing intimately with humans, this past year had been uncomfortable. Zoë and Chloe were right. She should have had an *affaire* or two by now. Surely she was strong enough to resist the useless emotion called love, have an enjoyable romp with a mortal, and still accomplish her goal. Avoiding male companionship just because she feared for her heart had left her . . . empty.

Until Jake.

Last night, before he'd disappeared, he'd done as he promised and found Terpsichore a pleasant man who guaranteed he would entertain her for as long as she wanted. They'd found Richard Gale in one of the upstairs gaming rooms, which meant he had a credit line of at least one million dollars. There was no doubt he was a whale, exactly what Terpsichore had hoped for, when he offered to take her dancing at Rio Rio, a spot renowned as a playground for the wealthy and sometimes famous. He'd even offered her a limo ride in the desert if dancing didn't appeal. Her sister muse's flirtatious manner had been over the top, but Mr. Gale's attitude made it clear he could handle a spirited woman.

When Jake had taken off after the card cheat, she again wondered about his position at the Acropolis. From the senior security guard's comment, it sounded as if he was on the hunt for a specific felon, much like a private investigator instead of Mr. T's nephew.

This morning, she'd not heard from either Terpsichore or Jake. It wasn't unusual for the muse of song and dance to disappear without a good-bye, but Jake seemed to enjoy following her around and sticking his nose in her business. It was odd that, after making such a production of wanting to be with her, he had yet to contact her.

Enough daydreaming, Kyra told herself. She had things to take care of. Answering Zeus's e-mail had to wait until after she'd seen to Lou and Rob. She tapped a finger to her chin. What could she do to bring them together that wouldn't be too obvious or over the top?

A computer emergency would work for Rob, but not Lou. And a stroll on the casino floor would get her to Lou, but not Rob. How could she mix the two?

"Well, you certainly look lost in thought."

Kyra's head whipped up at the sound of Terpsichore's dulcet tone. "I wasn't sure I'd see you again on Earth. Did you have a good time last night?"

The muse gave a feline grin. "Actually, I had a ball. For a mortal, Rick's a fun guy. Did you know he has his own island somewhere near the Fijis? He wants to take me there for a mid-winter vacation." She finger-combed the ebony curls fringing her forehead. "He might be good for a few days of carefree fun in the sun."

"How nice," said Kyra. Obviously, Terpsichore had no problem guarding her heart. "Will you go?"

The muse buffed her fingernails on the bodice of her flowing, double-girdled chiton. "I told him I'd let him know."

Kyra didn't fault Terpsichore for her blasé attitude. The self-important muse had always expected the best from life and in turn had always received it. To Kyra's knowledge, Zeus had never given her or the other eight muses the "no falling in love" rule. Terpsichore had taken her job seriously over the past several centuries, which meant she deserved the perks and freedom that rewarded a task well done.

"Why so glum, sister dear?" the muse asked. "Didn't your hot night with the delectable Jake turn out to your liking?"

"Um . . . not exactly. Something came up and I never went to his room."

"What a pity, especially since I stopped by to hear the juicy details."

Kyra sat up straight and ignored the comment. "Right now, I have a more pressing matter on my mind."

Terpsichore dragged a chair to the front of Kyra's desk and plopped down. "I've got a few minutes before I'm due back in dullsville. Tell me about it."

"I need to figure a way to get Rob together with a friend, and it has to look completely innocent, or my friend will be angry."

"Hmm." The muse closed her baby blues. After a few seconds, she blinked open her eyes and snapped her fingers. "I've got it."

"Fast work," muttered Kyra, a tad puzzled by how quickly the demi-goddess was able to come up with an answer. So what if Zeus disapproved of her receiving help? This second visit was Terpsichore's idea, not hers.

Her sister leaned closer. "Just see if she can . . ."

"Hey, Mom. To what do I owe the honor of this phone call?" Jake leaned back in his chair and gazed at the photograph of Laura Marie Lennox propped on the corner of his desk. A petite woman with few wrinkles, curling light brown hair, and twinkling blue eyes, she looked younger than her fifty-five years.

Judi McCoy

"It's been a while since I've seen you, Jacob. I miss you," said his mother. "Any chance you'll be coming east for a visit soon?"

He hadn't spoken to his mom in a couple of weeks, ever since he'd left this number on her answering machine, and suddenly realized it was a long time for them not to have talked. "I'm involved in something for Mr. Themopolis here at the Acropolis, and it's kept me busy. Are things okay at home?"

"Things are fine. Cilla's gone to a family celebration of sorts, so I'm at loose ends. She may be with her folks a while."

Cilla, her companion, was a decade younger than his mother and a fun-loving lady. He always saw to it she was included on the vacations he arranged for his mom or gave her the time off with pay.

"What's the happy occasion?"

"Her youngest sister had her third baby, so Cilla's playing the doting aunt. When I insisted she visit, she jumped at the chance."

"Which was very nice of you." Jake tried to remember the last time his mom had gone on a trip. "If you want to take another spa break, I bet Aunt Doris would love to join you. Tell her it's on me."

His mom's sigh came across the wire loud and clear. "That's very generous, Jacob, but you know how I feel. You do too much for me. All I really want is to see more of my only child."

They'd spent Christmas together in the Adirondacks just four weeks ago. Right now, there was no way he could arrange a trip home. "Mom—"

"I know, I know. Socrates needs you. But you are staying in Las Vegas for a while, correct, instead of traipsing the globe?"

"Yes, and I can't leave. Things at the casino are . . . difficult."

"I swear, I respect the man, but he's wearing you out, sending you from city to city to tend to his hotels, and now chaining you to a desk. Maybe I should have a talk with him—"

"No! I mean, that's not a good idea." Especially since Mr. T had never returned any of the messages Jake had left over the past week. Themopolis was probably up to his ears in a multi-million-dollar business deal. "He's really under the gun right now. If things go well, I should be able to get free in a few weeks. Then I'll be on the first plane east. I promise."

"Oh, all right. But I'm thinking of you. Take care, and let me know when you can visit."

Jake hung up the phone, his eyes still focused on his mom's photo. The woman was a saint, putting up with her husband's gallivanting and irresponsible behavior. In plain English, his father had been a prick. Edward Lennox had expected his wife to work two jobs to pay the mortgage and see to their son's needs whenever he was on one of his many gambling jags. His mother had been a rock, taking care of them whenever his father had a run of bad luck, which in Jake's mind translated to inept play and mismanagement of funds.

Their life had been a roller-coaster ride of highs and lows. Sometimes his dad would come home flush from a week's junket in Atlantic City, Vegas, or Reno. Other times, he'd wire for the cash to buy a plane ticket home. Either way, Jake remembered hearing his mother cry behind her closed bedroom door many a night as he'd grown up.

She'd never complained, but he knew the erratic lifestyle had drained her. He'd made a vow after his dad's funeral that he'd never let her work herself to exhaustion or want for anything again. And in the ten years Jake had been a professional gambler, he'd succeeded in keeping that vow.

Even though he'd lied to her to do it.

Which brought him back to his dead end of an evening. Three men had worked a scam at the black-jack table. It was a tired game that had been played a thousand times before. One guy acted the novice and distracted the dealer by asking questions, while the other two exchanged the cards they'd been dealt to make the best hand. If their fingers were agile, they could even raise or lower their bets. Usually the would-be novice was a woman. Last night they'd used an older, but very fit, man in his sixties.

The gent was spry, so it had taken Jake and Nesbitt a while to snare the fellow and bring him to the downstairs surveillance room, where they'd met the two cons Herb and his men had corralled. They'd called the gaming authorities, answered questions, sworn out a complaint, and turned over the tapes with the evidence.

By the time he realized he'd left Kyra high and dry, it was too late to reach her at home.

To make matters worse, the three creeps they'd captured didn't have anything to do with the hotel's consistent loss of revenue. He'd reviewed a few past tapes with Herb this morning, and hadn't been able to find the men on any of them. Which meant, as the cheats had insisted, they had never run a scam in the Acropolis before.

Pushing from his desk, he decided he had to get back in Kyra's good graces. He trotted to the elevator and rode it to his floor, grabbed the vase of flowers he'd bought for their dinner, and headed to her office with the peace offering. Maybe it would be enough to soothe her into forgiving him.

He reached her door in time to see Lou leaving the office. "Is she in?" he asked the waitress.

"Yes, but she seems very busy," Lou answered, her gaze on the bouquet.

Too busy to accept his apology? Lord, he hoped not.

"I've been meaning to ask—Kyra said you might be interested in a hostess position in the VIP lounge the night of the competition."

Lou chewed her lower lip. "I guess so—I mean yes. I'm interested. If you're willing to hire me."

"Why wouldn't I hire you?"

The woman glanced down at her less-than-bountiful bodice. "Because I'm not exactly hostess material."

Jake smiled, and Lou followed suit. When her lips turned up at the corners, he noted her lovely hazel eyes and attractive, even features. Most women enjoyed a compliment, and he imagined she was no different.

"Not a problem. You have an engaging personality, which is the most important requirement of the job. The hotel's seamstress can alter any gown in to . . . um . . . play up your assets."

Lou's smile grew from ear to ear. "That's what Kyra said. I just wasn't sure you'd want me, seeing as you're . . . a man and all." She went back to chewing her lip. "Sorry, the words didn't come out quite the way I intended."

"Don't worry about it. If you're as good in the lounge as you are on the floor, things will be fine. I'm sure Kyra can help locate a flattering gown and do your makeup. You'll fit right in."

Lou clutched her fingers to her waist. For a second, Jake thought she was going to shake his hand, but the moment passed.

"Thanks again, and if those flowers are for Kyra, she's a lucky girl."

Jake waited for her to walk away before he listened at the partially open office door. When he heard Kyra's lilting voice, he guessed she was on the phone.

"Trixie's left town, but this is something she told me you needed to do . . . that's right, three o'clock in the same room we met in last night."

Damn! She'd said there was nothing going on between her and Garrett. Had she lied to him again?

Kyra hung up with Rob and patted herself on the back. Terpsichore had given her the idea, but she'd thought up the details on her own. The plan was a sound one, provided she was able to stretch her powers.

Men, she thought with a shrug. Women often had to do the silliest, most outrageous things to get their attention. Rob had a crush on Lou, but was too shy to do a thing about it. Lou was too bitter to be receptive to a man, but needed a nice guy in her life. Bringing them together was the least she could do to thank them for their friendship.

Her mind again turned to Jake, and she admitted one of the reasons she was so attracted to him was simple. He wasn't afraid to go after whatever he felt passionate about. What she'd first thought was a cocky and self-absorbed attitude was really the mark of a confident man. Instead of making suggestive comments and playing games, as so many of the men she'd met had done, he'd come right out and said he was attracted to her, and wanted to engage in an *affaire* for however long it lasted. And he'd done it without a single leer or sleazy comment.

If things had worked out, she might still be upstairs in his suite, lying in his arms while he tantalized and teased her from head to toe . . .

There was a knock at her door, then it opened and a hand holding a vase filled with an assortment of flowers appeared, followed by Jake. "I hope you're not too busy to give me a few minutes."

At the sight of him, Kyra's heart stuttered in her chest. "Lou just left. Did you see her?"

"I did. We made arrangements for her to work the VIP lounge on the night of the competition. She's going to need help choosing a gown, and I told her you'd take care of it."

"I will, and I appreciate that you're giving her a chance. She needs the money one night of working in the lounge will bring."

"I told you I didn't have a problem using her or Eddie." He sat in the chair vacated by Terpsichore and Lou and held the vase in his lap. "By the way, Eddie already handed in an application."

"Good." Kyra waited for him to mention the bouquet. When he didn't, she said, "Nice flowers."

"They're for you. A peace offering to make up for the disappearing act I pulled last night." He set the vase on her desk. "Actually, I bought them yesterday to spruce up my suite. Since I managed to ruin our plans, I figured you could enjoy them here in your office."

"Is this an apology?" Kyra asked, secretly pleased by the romantic gesture.

"It is if it'll get me out of the dog house. What do you think? Can we start again?"

Tempted to make him squirm, Kyra's lips twitched. "I'll have to think about it. I'm not used to being stood up," she said, echoing the words he'd said to her.

"How about I take you to lunch? I can have the kitchen pack a picnic and I'll hire a limo to take us on a drive in the desert. I promise I'll have you back by four." He raised a brow. "Unless you have other plans."

"Nope, won't work." Especially since she had a three o'clock appointment with Rob and Lou. "I have a—a prior engagement."

"Does it have anything to do with the competition?"

Confused by the darker tone his voice had taken, she said, "In a way, but I'm free after the Wheel Deal."

Jake rose and ambled to the door, then turned. "Okay, seven o'clock, in my suite. I'm looking forward to it."

Her phone rang and Kyra waited for the door to close before answering. What had put a damper on Jake's upbeat attitude? For a second there, it almost sounded as if he didn't believe she was booked for the afternoon. Or was she imagining it?

Filing the thought for later, she picked up the phone. "Kyra Degodessa. May I help you?"

"Hey, doll face, how you doin'?"

Kyra cringed. A conversation with Buddy Blue,

lounge lizard extraordinaire, was not the way she wanted to spend her afternoon.

"Hello, Mr. Blue. What can I do for you?"

"How many times do I have to tell you, the name's Buddy. Isn't it about time we got together and talked about the Voice of Vegas."

"What is it you need to discuss?"

"What kind of shtick do you want me to use the night of the competition? I kept the elimination rounds light and breezy, but this is the grand finale with national television coverage. Are we goin' highbrow and ritzy-titzy, or can I be myself and run the gig the way I do my act?"

No way could she imagine Buddy ever doing anything highbrow or ritzy-titzy. "Well, since I've never seen your act—"

"You've never seen me perform in person? How the heck can that be?"

Because I don't enjoy off-color stand-up routines? "Um, I've been busy at the Acropolis. I never seem to have a free moment to enjoy the entertainment this town has to offer."

"Then you got to come to the Sis Boom Bah. It's the hottest club on the strip. I'll send over a couple of tickets for the seven o'clock show. Bring a girlfriend—someone as good lookin' as you—and come backstage when I'm through. We can have a few drinks while we go over how you want me to play the competition after you watch me in my element." He chuckled. "I'm a very entertaining guy."

"But—"

"No buts. See ya tonight."

Kyra sighed as she hung up the phone. So much for spending time with Jake. Now what was she supposed to do? Buddy's attitude during the show could make or break the competition. If she got on his bad side, he might be so unbearable everything would fall apart.

She drummed her fingers on her desktop. Why was she worrying about the contest, when it didn't matter a hill of beans? If she were smart, she'd do the minimal work required on the competition, and not give a moment's thought to the way it turned out.

Making it a success wasn't part of her challenge from Zeus. What did it matter if the show was a hit and the Acropolis gained notoriety and prestige? She'd be gone by the time it was over and, if everything went according to plan, Zeus would make Eddie, Lou, and anyone she'd befriended on earth forget about her.

So what if she let them down?

Kyra held her head in her hands. Even Terpsichore, who was self-centered and vain, was honorable. Her sisters were equally conscientious, though each had a distinct personality. Zoë was a perfectionist and Chloe a diva. Polyhymnia was a weeper, Thalia saw the good side in everything, and Clio, though serious and subdued, was still dedicated to her work, as were the others. Kyra had been imbued with a strong sense of loyalty, and the cursed virtue could be a darned pain in the neck.

She phoned Jake's office extension and was relieved to get his voicemail, because she couldn't think of a thing to say. How could she tell him she had to cancel their date, when she'd insinuated this was *his* last chance?

Opening her folder on the contest judges, she began calling those she'd failed to reach yesterday. Maybe getting lost in her work would take her mind off tonight. She'd simply have to tell Jake the truth and hope he understood.

Chapter 13

Why had she lied?

Jake took the stairs to the lobby, nursing his wounded ego. Why was it that just when he thought that Kyra started to play it straight and be honest with him, she did something to smack him down a peg? When he made his feelings clear regarding her relationship with Garrett, she'd assured him he had no worries. If there was nothing going on between her and the boy wonder, why had she kept him in the dark about this second meeting?

Don't act like the wounded party, buddy. What about you? his conscience whispered. *Your interest isn't strictly social, either.*

Jake chastised himself at the admission. Yes, he was attracted to Kyra. What red-blooded male with active hormones wouldn't want to make time with a beautiful redhead with snapping eyes, a body to die for, and a breezy attitude? Getting under her skin, the way she'd gotten under his, was a big part of his nice guy attitude and gentlemanly manner. Time and again, he found himself apologizing to her or saying things a woman might consider *sweet*, yet no one but his mom had ever thought of him that way, and it didn't count because everyone knew how mothers felt about their only sons.

Which might be the problem. Instead of acting like an ordinary guy with a yen for a beautiful woman, he'd been acting too much the perfect gentleman.

Maybe it was time to pull out the stops and go the caveman route. Instead of romantic gestures or teasing words of coercion, he should throw her over his shoulder, bring her to his suite, and show her what he wanted. Plain old mind-blowing sex, performed in a variety of ways . . .

As often as possible.

From the moment he'd seen Kyra Degodessa, he'd envisioned her moaning with pleasure in his bed. The image of her curling red tresses spread on his pillow while she rocked in passion beneath him had intruded on his days, haunted his nights, and made it damned near impossible to concentrate on his job.

The honest admission had him stiff as the handle on a slot machine. And he wanted her to pull the lever so they could hit the jackpot together.

He shook his head. Holy crap! What a god-awful analogy. Now he was thinking like an idiot.

Unfortunately, as much as he wanted her, and as much as he'd like it to be otherwise, Kyra was still his best link to the Acropolis's lost revenue. Though the money she gave away didn't come from the hotel, she might have managed to fiddle with those funds as well. The Wheel Deal losses had quadrupled since she'd taken charge, and the facts and figures of her finances and personal life were disturbing. None of it made sense, yet there was zero to connect her to anything illegal.

Tired of obsessing, Jake decided to check another lead that had piqued his interest over the past several days. Last night, Rick Gale mentioned a problem with the complimentary suites he'd been given on his last few visits. If Jake added the complaint to what he'd overheard from the guy in the flower shop, there could be something fishy going on in an area of the hotel he had yet to investigate. He'd kick himself all the way out of town if he left a single stone unturned that might solve the mystery.

After walking to the registration desk, he spoke to a clerk. "I need access to the program that keeps records of our clients' spending habits. Can you point me in the right direction?"

"Go to the IT department and ask Rob Garrett for the information. He's the man in charge of the data."

Freakin' great. Not only was Garrett screwing up his plans for Kyra, now he had to ask the boy crooner for help with his job.

He took the corridor that wound behind the main desk and led to the inner workings of the hotel. The computer department housed reservations, ticket sales, comps, and banquets in a single room. Jake had been there only once when he first arrived and wanted to get acquainted with each area of the Acropolis. He remembered the section as huge, humming with the clatter of keyboards and printers in the background.

Each day, about fifty percent of the casino guests used their Acropolis card, which was similar to a credit card, whenever they played a game. The card was swiped by a pit boss or floor manager when they exchanged money for chips or tokens. Each transaction was automatically fed into a program, enabling the computer to track their spending habits. The dollar amount was used to dole out rewards for the cash they spent in the casino.

Rick Gale gave the hotel hundreds of thousands of dollars in business a year. James Bannon probably did the same. Both men should be receiving the premium suites, complimentary chef and valet services, and a whole lot more.

He spotted Rob in a far corner, his back to the

entrance, working in a fairly large cubicle. Before Jake got the man's attention, the phone rang and Rob answered.

"Garrett here. Nope. Sorry, I won't be able to get to it today. Tell the secretary you're the regular trouble-shooter, and you're the one to fix it."

Rob hung up and turned at Jake's knock on the cubicle wall. "Mr. Lennox. What can I do for you?"

How about telling me what's really going on between you and Kyra Degodessa?

"I received a complaint from a customer regarding his comp situation and thought I'd look into it. Mandy at the front desk told me you were in charge of the records."

"I tailored the current program to meet our specs. It runs like clockwork, or at least it should. What's the customer's name?"

"Richard Gale," said Jake, dropping into a chair.

Rob logged out of his program, tapped into a new one, and typed in the name. "Here he is," he said, scrolling down the roster of Rick's activity. "The guy's a big player, by the look of it."

"Go to the comp section. I want to see his list of freebies."

After a few keystrokes, data appeared on the screen. The long and involved columns of numbers made Jake's head swim. He'd need to study the report with a magnifying glass to make heads or tails of the information.

"Can you run a printout, say for the last six months, and do the same for a customer named James Bannon?"

"No problem." Rob sent the data to a printer. "Anything else I can help you with?"

"I might need to go over a few accounting records. Would I have to speak to someone in that department, or can you get me the info?"

"I'd be happy to requisition the exact data you want. Just tell me what you need."

"Right now, I'm curious about the Sky Tower suites."

"The ones going for five thousand a night?"

"The very same."

"I think they're being remodeled. You'd have to check with maintenance."

It would explain why Gale and Bannon hadn't been offered a top-of-the-line luxury suite for a while. "Do you know when the job's supposed to finish?"

"Sorry, but I don't know a thing." Sheets spewed from the printer next to Rob's desk. He handed the dozen pages to Jake with a smile. "Rumor has it you took part in a little excitement last night—a threesome cheating at blackjack."

"Yeah. The guys are in custody." Jake raised a brow. "How did you hear about it?"

"Kyra told me this morning. She was bummed because it caused the two of you to miss dinner."

Kyra had talked to Garrett about *him?* "What else did she say?"

"Nothing. She mentioned it when she called and asked if I could meet her in the practice room today." Rob glanced at his watch. "It's almost time. Guess I'd better get moving."

Okay, this was too weird. Kyra didn't want him to know she was seeing Rob, but the crooner didn't have a problem with it? Maybe she'd told the truth, and she truly was doing nothing more than giving Garrett a hand with his act.

"Do you want to come along? I'm supposed to see someone Trixie recommended."

"Can't." Jake raised the comp data. "But tell Kyra I said hello. Remind her I'll be waiting for her at seven . . . in my room."

"Will do," said Rob, ambling away.

Jake's lips turned up in a grin. He wished he could be there to see the look on her face when Kyra got his message. Especially delivered by Garrett. Maybe it was time she learned he was wise to her game and playing to win.

"I'm really rusty, Kyra. I doubt this is going to work," said Lou, staring through narrowed eyes at the baby grand piano.

"You don't have to be in concert mode. Just play well enough to carry the tune, tell Rob what you did or didn't enjoy about his rendition of the song, and share a few thoughts on how he can make it better."

Kyra smiled inside at her clever idea. Terpsichore had suggested Lou get involved in Rob's practice sessions. When Kyra remembered Lou once telling her she'd taken piano lessons as a child, the idea for getting them together fell into place. Once she worked a bit of magic, she was positive nature would take its course.

"Did you warn him it's been years since I did anything more than tap out 'Chopsticks' or 'Heart and Soul'?" said Lou, sitting on the bench.

"It's not important. Playing the number he'll perform in the competition is what matters." Kyra opened the file she'd been holding, pulled out two pieces of sheet music, and placed them one behind the other in front of Lou. "This is the one he's singing."

" 'I Can't Help Falling in Love With You'? Why did he pick an old Elvis classic?"

"He didn't pick it, I did," said Kyra. "And I had my reasons. For starters, other than Wayne Newton, who's a better representative of Las Vegas than Elvis? The melody has a lovely bluesy tone and heartwarming lyrics. Rob can pretend he's singing to one special girl, and every woman within earshot will think it's her. He'll captivate both the judges and the crowd. Go ahead, try a few bars."

Lou began fiddling with the keys. She'd removed her makeup and changed from her waitress costume into a pair of snug-fitting jeans and a sweater the color of cognac. The rich amber of the textured wool complemented her hazel eyes and light brown hair to perfection, while the lack of cosmetics emphasized her natural beauty.

Walking behind Lou, Kyra raised her arms and chanted her wish internally, while at the same time outlining the young woman's slim silhouette. In seconds, Lou's fingers traversed the keyboard in a confident and practiced manner, and she finished the piece with a flourish.

"That was wonderful," said Kyra, returning to Lou's side. "Very professional."

"I don't think I ever sounded so good." Lou gazed at her hands, then at Kyra with a dazed expression. "It must be the piano."

"Piano or not, it was fabulous. Rob will love it. Be encouraging and tell him he's going to knock the judges' socks off." Kyra rested her forearms on the baby grand. "You won't be lying. He does sound great."

"I know." Lou's cheeks turned a becoming shade of pink. "I heard him at one of the elimination contests, but he sang a different song. And won't he be expected to perform the *big* number if he wins? You know, the one they'll be taping for a CD and television commercials?"

"The contestants will sing it for their second number. The music is right here." Kyra lifted the Elvis song and revealed "Las Vegas Rhapsody." "Have a go at this one, too, so Rob will know it as well as the Elvis song."

Kyra sidled to the door while the waitress practiced the second tune. If all went well with her special good luck wish, Lou's fingers would connect smoothly with her brain and she would continue to play the baby grand like a veteran until Rob no longer needed her help. By then, he'd be on his way to a successful career and Lou wouldn't have to worry about tip money or single parenthood any longer. She and Rob would fall in love and live happily ever after.

Opening the door to check for Rob, she found him standing outside. "What are you doing out here?"

"Listening. Whoever's playing sounds better than Trixie."

"She's a real doll, too." Kyra locked onto his elbow and tugged him inside. "You ready to get started?"

"Sure am, but first I have a message for you."

"Oh?"

"Jake Lennox came to the IT department hunting for information and I mentioned I was on my way here. He said to say hello and remind you about meeting him in his room at seven." Rob grinned. "He's an okay guy."

Well, wasn't that dandy? Jake knew she was here again with Rob, because Rob had spilled the beans. Just wait until he found out she had to beg off their special night due to her appointment with Buddy Blue.

"Is that my vocal coach?"

She turned to see Rob gazing at Lou's back as the waitress continued playing "Las Vegas Rhapsody." "Isn't she great? She's not a vocal coach, exactly, but she does have a good ear. Trixie and I thought she'd be perfect for you."

"She looks familiar. Do I know her?" Rob asked, following Kyra to the piano.

The second he saw Lou's face, Rob's eyes opened wide, and his cheeks grew red. Before Kyra could speak, Lou stopped playing, stood, and held out her hand.

"Hi, I'm Lou. Kyra's told me so much about you. I heard you perform at one of the elimination contests, and you were wonderful."

He accepted the gesture. "It's nice to meet you, too. You sound really good, by the way."

"Glad you like it. I'm out of practice, but it's coming back to me." She smiled tentatively. "I guess."

Kyra felt like a third wheel, and she knew immediately things would work out between her two best mortal friends. Lou seemed more relaxed with Rob than any of the men she served on the casino floor, and Rob, well, if the dopey grin on his face was any indication, he looked as if he was already in love.

"I have to take care of the Wheel Deal but I'll be back to check in around six-thirty," she said, but neither appeared to hear her. Lou fingered a trill of scales as if she were a prodigy while Rob gazed at her from cloud nine.

Kyra cleared her throat. "You might want to start with the singing."

"Hm? Oh, yeah." Still staring at Lou, Rob seemed to float back to Earth. "I'm ready if you are."

Lou nodded and they began the session. Kyra wandered to the door, checked her watch, and realized she had a few minutes before she was expected in the lobby. She couldn't put it off any longer.

She had to tell Jake about her meeting with Buddy Blue.

Jake stared at the comp list and rubbed his eyes. He was computer savvy, but he wasn't a number cruncher. Over the years, he'd been a model citizen when it came to keeping records for the IRS, especially because of his profession. But he'd left the technicalities of a profit and loss sheet to his accountant.

It appeared as if the number of comps both men received had held steady in all areas except their accommodations. Neither one had been given a Sky Tower luxury suite for over a year. That jived with what Rob had told him, but it was still odd. For one thing, he hadn't heard word one about the remodeling job, a chore he'd rectify in the morning. Unfortunately, he couldn't afford to alert more people than necessary. Sooner or later, word of his snooping would get back to Ardmore, and the manager wanna-be would want to know why Jake was poking his nose in that type of casino business.

He thought about his original assessment of Rob Garrett. If the computer nerd was having an affair with Kyra or helping her run a scam, he wouldn't have been so eager to open the records to Jake's scrutiny or reveal his and Kyra's meeting. He'd given Jake what he asked for and offered more. It stood to reason the guy was innocent of whatever accusations Jake had thought him guilty.

An idea that had been playing over in his mind for the past day or so rose to the forefront. There was no such thing as serendipity. He'd learned that from his father years ago. A gambler was only as good as his level of play. He had to know when to up the ante, bluff, pass the hand, or simply quit. The evidence he had against Kyra was nothing more than a hunch.

And a hunch wasn't admissible in a court of law.

If the only thing he had to incriminate her was a few taps on the shoulder and a couple of extra wins, he'd look like a fool to Mr. T, Ardmore, and the authorities. Someone else had to be scamming the Acropolis. But who?

A knock pulled Jake from his reverie. "Come on in."

Kyra edged inside and closed the door behind her. "Hi. Do you have a minute?"

He leaned back and appraised her through narrowed lids, hoping to calm the turmoil in his gut. Her all-business mode of attire, a one-piece hunter-green sweater dress, played up her voluptuous curves, just as her tumbled curls accentuated the beauty of her heart-shaped face and storm-gray eyes. From her flustered expression, Jake knew Rob had given Kyra the message.

"Do you need something?"

She squared her shoulders, as if whatever she'd come to say was difficult. Would she confess to an *affaire* with Garrett—or something more?

"I . . . um . . . I have to cancel tonight's date."

He'd prepared himself for an excuse, but the words still filled him with disappointment. "Is Trixie back in town, or did someone else show with a better offer?"

"Trixie's gone, for good I think, and no, it isn't because of another friend."

"Then it sounds as if I'm being stood up again."

"I'm not standing you up, I have a date with Buddy Blue."

The lounge lizard? "The clown hosting the Voice of Vegas?"

"The one and only." As if regretting the words, she leaned back against the door. "Believe me, it's not the way I want to spend my evening."

Jake braced his palms on the desktop and rose to his feet, his gaze locked on Kyra's. Judging by her unhappy demeanor, she was telling the truth. He walked to her and caged her between his arms. "Then why go?"

"It's for the competition," she said, meeting his eyes. "He wants me to see his act, in person, so I can advise him on how to best emcee the contest. He's sending over two tickets for the seven o'clock show."

"You're going to the Sis Boom Bah?" Jake had visited the small, smoky dive once, and that was plenty. The club served overpriced, watered-down drinks to noisy out-of-towners who came to see Buddy, a Don Rickles–type comedian, because he'd appeared on Leno and Letterman a few times. He'd made a name for himself by playing heckler to the crowd and, strangely enough, the tourists loved him.

Kyra grabbed onto his wrists as if they were a lifeline. "I don't see I have a choice. He can make or break the show and I really want the contest to be a success for the good of the Acropolis, and for Rob."

Damned tired of playing second fiddle to the computer nerd, Jake cupped her jaw with his hands. "Does Garrett mean that much to you?"

"As a friend, yes. I set him up with Lou—she plays the piano—and they're rehearsing right now. I'd like to see them together before I—" She licked at her lower lip. "Before the show is over."

Stepping into her, he asked, "And what about you? What do you want for yourself?"

She focused on his mouth. "I want—"

He bent forward and nuzzled her nose with his. "You want . . . ?"

She sighed. "To be with you."

Jake's chest swelled with relief. Moving his lips to hers, he teased her mouth. When she opened for him, he took full advantage, seeking out her moist heat, and was rewarded with the taste of oranges and mint, and a heady dose of passion.

Kyra wound her arms around his neck and threaded her fingers through his hair. He nestled against her hips and molded her to his chest. The kiss took on a life of its own, drawing them together until they were one. Long moments passed while they explored, tantalized . . .

Breathing hard, Jake pulled back when he remembered the Cyclops that continually scanned his office. Kyra rested her forehead on his chin as he spied the intrusive device. Inspecting the camera's angle, he realized they were standing directly under its probing eye. Something to be grateful for.

"I'm going with you," he said, speaking before he thought the words through. He hated comedy clubs, especially raucous, smoke-laden ones like the Sis Boom Bah. Still, he couldn't—wouldn't—let her go alone.

"Buddy told me to bring a girlfriend," she whispered, gazing at him. "I think he's a pervert."

Jake held back a snort. "No kidding. And what was your first clue?"

Kyra grinned, the only time she'd done so since entering the office. "I don't appreciate the way he leers at me, as if I were a bimbo."

"A bimbo? God forbid," he said with a smile. "I can't imagine why."

"Very funny." She gave a wounded sniff. "I hate being treated like a sex object."

"Then I'd better not tell you what goes on in my head whenever I think about you, huh?"

"I don't think you're a pervert." Her lips twitched into a full-blown smile. "At least not yet."

"Baby, if you could read my mind . . ." He inclined his head toward the couch on the wall opposite his desk. "It's taking every ounce of my self-control not to drag you over to that sofa and show you how I feel," he confessed.

She raised a brow. "You seem to have a thing for couches."

"Where you're concerned, I do."

She opened her mouth to comment, and her gaze latched onto the watch at her wrist. "Oh my gosh. I'm late."

"Late?" He held both her hands. "For what?"

"The Wheel Deal. I can't ever seem to get there on time these days."

"Then I won't keep you." He pulled her to his chest. "But promise me something."

"I'll try." Kyra gave him a naughty grin. "Provided it's not too perverted."

"Cute." He nibbled at her earlobe. "Don't go to the Sis Boom Bah without me. I'll meet you and we'll cab to the club. Buddy won't dare act anything but the perfect gentleman if I'm your escort."

Judi McCoy

She settled in his arms. "I told Rob I'd come to the practice room when he and Lou were through. How about you get there around six-forty-five?"

He let her go and opened the door. "It's a date."

Kyra tucked a stray curl behind her ear. "See you then." She gave him a wave and headed down the hall.

Jake waited until she disappeared into the elevator, then closed his office door. Giving the one-eyed monster a scowl, he shook his head. The last thing he needed was for Herb or any of the surveillance crew to have seen him and Kyra in a clinch on his sofa. It was bad enough the senior security guard knew he lusted after her like every other guy at the Acropolis.

And lust after her, he did.

He walked back to his desk and took a seat. It was obvious Kyra wanted him as much as he wanted her, and he was positive she was telling the truth about her interest in Rob. Should he come clean and confess the real reason he was at the Acropolis?

Pondering his next move, Jake shifted his attention to the sheets on Rick and Bannon. Maybe it was a good idea to take Garrett up on his offer, and go over the accounts in the main computer. Rob had access to data, and data was fact. Fact wasn't serendipity or good fortune, or anything too crazy to believe in. Fact was something he could count on.

And right now, he needed a dose of fact to counter the way he'd begun to feel about Kyra Degodessa.

Chapter 14

Kyra floated to the practice room, tote bag slung over a shoulder, and her head—no, her entire body—in the clouds. The two hours she'd spent supervising the Wheel Deal had passed in a blur of giddy anticipation. Jake had understood when she'd told him she had to cancel their date in order to visit the Sis Boom Bah. He even seemed to accept the fact that she'd seen Rob again, especially after she explained why.

And when she confessed that she'd agreed to meet Buddy Blue, he'd shown a protective, almost jealous side she found sweet and appealing.

The kiss they'd shared in Jake's office was everything a kiss should be. Her lips still tingled from the exquisite pressure of his mouth as it had plundered her own. His gentle hands had cupped her face, coaxed her to respond, and drawn her so close she thought she would be absorbed through his clothing and molded to his skin.

Every inch of his body had been hard and demanding, including his impressive erection. The simple thought of having him inside her, stroking her to a climax, caused her to shudder. It had been so long since she'd been touched, cared for, or wanted by a man.

Throughout the ages, the gods hadn't changed their sexual habits one iota. Most remained cavalier in their treatment of the opposite sex, taking whatever they wanted as if it was their right. It didn't matter if there was no commitment in the couplings. Self-gratification and a fast, pleasurable interlude were their only goals.

Kyra craved pleasure, too, but after a few dozen centuries, it was nice to think of something more. Too bad that *thing* couldn't be Jake.

She stopped at the practice room door and took a breath, forcing herself to examine her feelings from the practical side. Jake was but a mortal with a limited life span, while she was a demi-goddess, created by Zeus to live forever. She had to focus on her goal of returning in splendor to Mount Olympus, because Jake would never believe what she was, even if she told him.

And since telling him wouldn't matter, she was prepared to accept all he could give her for as long as she was here. Eternal glory was better than a forever love, wasn't it?

She edged closer to the door, but didn't hear a note of music or syllable of song from inside. Maybe Rob and Lou had finished early and left. Better yet, they'd gone somewhere to share an intimate moment. Rob had already revealed his attraction to Lou, and Lou had hinted that she admired Rob and his singing. If Kyra couldn't experience true love for herself, the knowledge that she'd taken part in bringing these two mortals to fulfillment would have to satisfy her.

Inching open the door, she peered inside. Lou sat on the piano bench while Rob stood with his arms propped on top of the baby grand, his gaze like that of an adoring puppy. They were speaking softly, and Kyra didn't have the heart to interrupt.

Just then, Rob raised his head. "Hey, Kyra. Lou and I were . . . um . . . discussing my number." He nodded to Lou. "Isn't that right?"

Lou swiveled on the bench, her expression one of embarrassment. "I didn't realize it was so late. I guess I'd better phone my mother and let her know I'm on my way."

"Do you need a ride?" Rob asked.

Bravo, thought Kyra. At last he was taking the initiative by letting Lou know he wanted to spend private time with her.

"Uh, no. I have a car."

Wrong answer, Lou.

"Oh."

Ask to see her again, you silly man, maybe for lunch or dinner later in the week.

"I was thinking . . ." Rob drew himself up straight. "How about sharing your lunch break with me tomorrow?"

Lou hesitated, her eyes suddenly clouded with suspicion. "I get thirty minutes, and I usually bring something from home."

"Then don't bring anything tomorrow," said Rob, grinning. "We'll go to a restaurant in the casino, so it won't take long. Ring my extension and let me know what time's good for you." He paused, turning toward Kyra. "You're invited, too. It's my treat for everything the two of you have done to help with my career."

Kyra shook her head. It was obvious he wanted her company as much as he'd appreciate a swarm of ants at a picnic. "I'm busy. You two have fun without me."

Lou rose from the bench. "But—"

"I think we can handle it." Rob's smile stretched from ear to ear as he stopped in the doorway. "I'll be waiting for your call." He ducked out before the waitress said another word.

"So, what did you think?" Kyra asked, sidling to the piano. "Isn't he a great guy?"

Lou plopped back down and closed the keyboard cover, her mood somber. "Don't get any ideas. You know how I feel about men." She gave a disapproving sniff. "Besides, he was pushy."

"Not pushy—focused. Not every man is like the idiot who fathered Katie and left you flat, Lou. Some are very nice."

Lou raised her head, her lips pursed. "Do you seriously expect me to accept advice about men from a woman who hasn't had a single date in the entire time I've known her?"

Kyra ground her back molars. "Yes, I do. Just because I've decided not to—"

There was a knock on the door, then Jake walked in.

"Oops." Lou smiled knowingly. "Looks as if you're in the process of rectifying my observation." Standing, she made a beeline for the exit. "Thanks again for giving me a hostess position, Jake. I've got to run."

Kyra's heart skittered in her chest as her eyes met Jake's. Dressed in light gray slacks, a pristine, open-necked shirt, and a navy sport jacket, he looked casual yet elegant. At her side in three strides, he reached for her hand.

"I asked the doorman to hold a cab. We'll make the show on time if we leave now." He led her to the door. "Do you have the tickets?"

She patted her bag. "In here, but . . ."

"But what?"

"Are you sure you want to go? I got the impression you don't enjoy this type of establishment."

205

Jake tucked her hand in the crook of his arm. "Trust me, sweetheart, there is no way in hell I'd send you off alone to the Sis Boom Bah or any other club in town. Especially with a guy like Buddy waiting for you."

The statement caressed her from the inside out. A few months, even a week ago, she would have snapped out a comeback on a female's right to independence. Instead, Jake's possessive tone touched a chord in her heart.

"I'm used to taking care of myself." *But it would be nice if you did the job for a while.*

"I don't doubt it, but not when I'm around." He led her into the hall. "And tonight's one night I'm not letting you out of my sight."

Jake walked with Kyra at his side, his jacket warming her shoulders, her hand firmly in his. Their experience at the Sis Boom Bah had been pretty much what he'd expected—loud, raucous, and downright uncomfortable.

Buddy Blue's brand of humor was rude, off-color and tasteless. He'd made suggestive comments to just about every woman seated at the first row of tables and shot barbs at all the men. Yet the audience hooted throughout the act and applauded at the end. No wonder the city's Division of Travel and Tourism had signed him to emcee the competition. He gave the crowd exactly what they expected from Sin City.

When they met Buddy after the show, the comedian had made clear his disappointment over Kyra's choice of companion, which justified Jake's decision to come along. He wanted to cheer when Buddy asked Kyra what she thought of his act, and she explained that his quips during the show had to be less raunchy and more sophisticated. If not, she'd have him yanked from the stage during a commercial.

No doubt about it, Kyra Degodessa could handle herself in an awkward situation.

He had suggested a walk in the fresh air after the stifling atmosphere in the club, and they were now strolling the bright-as-day strip in silence. It amazed Jake that the aerial view of this town featured on brochures and television shows always seemed to be basking in the sun. Mile-high neon signs, huge hotels and casinos, lavish advertisements of larger-than-life entertainment, were showcased in a waterfall of breathtaking brilliance.

In truth, the streets were little better than the Sis Boom Bah for air quality, but it gave him a chance to spend more time with Kyra. He found that he enjoyed watching her reaction to the limos and various luxury cars clogging the road; he even enjoyed the way she scanned the hordes of visitors that took to the sidewalk, dressed in everything from spandex to attire more appropriate for an evening at the Met. The crowds and bright lights made it easy to imagine a TV crew on the sidelines filming a Travel Channel special or weekly television show.

As a teenager, Jake had learned to accept this city when he accompanied his father during summer vacations. As he'd gone out on his own, he'd learned to take the glamour and excitement for what it was worth. His mother, on the other hand, made no secret of her dislike of Vegas and every other town that sported over-the-top spectacles. It was the reason he planned to find her a home in Tahoe, far enough away from the neon racket to be peaceful, yet close enough for him to visit whenever he wanted.

They crossed Spring Mountain Road and headed for their hotel, surrounded by spectacles from the various casinos, each trying to outdo the other for the attention of those on the street. One hotel had a life-sized pirate ship sitting out front complete with an act from Cirque du Soliel. Another had jets of light-illuminated water spewing forty feet high in time to piped music.

And set high above street level with man-made mist pumping from around the structure stood the Acropolis. As if resting among the clouds, its huge white pillars and templelike façade echoed the look of a monument straight out of Greek mythology.

When they neared the building, Kyra stopped and stared, her sigh wistful.

"Long evening?" he asked.

"Long day," she answered, still gazing at the hotel. "It's tough playing matchmaker when one of the two people doesn't want to be paired up."

"I take it that would be Lou?"

"Yes, though she has good reason for her reticence."

"You said she had a daughter. Was it a bad divorce?"

"There was never any marriage," said Kyra. "The stupid, selfish man left her high and dry, and she's had it rough ever since. Especially with finances."

Which gave reason to Lou's being so distrusting, thought Jake. "Then it's good she'll get some experience as a hostess. She'll earn extra money and, if it works out, will be used again. By the way, did anyone win the Wheel Deal this afternoon?"

"Hm?" she asked, still concentrating on the Acropolis.

"The Wheel Deal. You didn't say how it turned out."

Kyra blinked as if waking from a dream. "Oh, no. I didn't remember to—I mean, no. No one was lucky today."

Jake blew out a breath, pleased he could file his doubts away for awhile and move to a more important topic. "Still plan on spending the night?"

She smiled up at him as they strode into the hotel lobby. "I wouldn't think of doing anything else."

He flashed her a grin. "I was hoping you'd say that."

Kyra slipped Jake's jacket from her shoulders and straightened. "I still need to visit a boutique for a few of those essentials we talked about."

209

"Can you do it without me, so I can go up and order dinner?"

"Sounds great, mainly because I'm starving."

"For anything in particular?"

You, she almost blurted out loud. "I'm sure whatever you decide on will be fine."

Jake escorted her to the wing leading to the stores and drew her out of the flow of pedestrians. Gazing into her eyes, he ran the back of his hand gently down her cheek. "I'll see you in a few minutes." Hooking his jacket with an index finger, he swung it over his shoulder, and sauntered away.

A jolt of heat rose from Kyra's belly and settled in her chest when she saw the ripple of muscles play along his broad back. Soon, she'd be able to run her hands across his firm skin, wrap her fingers around the part of him she wanted most to touch . . .

Then she recalled his statement about Lou. She probably should have asked him what he had to do with future hirings and firings at the hotel. Did he plan on working here permanently? If he'd been a gambler, but wasn't one now, how did he make his living?

As fast as the questions arose she pushed them to the back of her mind. It didn't matter how Jake made money, or what he planned to do with his life. They only had a few days left in their time together, and she was going to make them count.

Turning to enter the shop, she bumped into someone. As she struggled to right herself, she recognized a familiar figure dressed in his signature colors of lavender and white.

"Hermes?" Her voice squeaked with surprise. "What are you doing here?"

The vice president of Internet technology frowned. "I've been sent by Zeus, you foolish girl. He's furious you haven't answered his last e-mail, and I don't blame him. Do you realize this is the first official trip to Earth he's ordered me on since the invention of the telephone?"

Uh-oh, thought Kyra, retreating a step. Maybe she should have seen to the father god's missive before she launched her plan to aid Rob and Lou. "I would have gotten around to it," she said with a hint of annoyance. "Zeus needs to chill out."

Hermes raised a brow. "Surely that's not the answer you want me to take to Olympus?"

"No," Kyra bit out. "But you can tell him I'll send my report tomorrow. I've been busy."

Dressed in trousers and a pale purple golf shirt, the officious god peered down the corridor in the direction Jake had taken. "So I noticed."

"Just tell him I'll see to it, please. I'm headed for a big finale here, and things are going great."

"Uh-huh."

She resisted the urge to stomp her foot. *"They are."*

"If you say so," Hermes answered, his full lips twitching. "Just get on the computer first thing in the morning and do a goodly amount of sandal-kissing, or I won't be responsible for what happens."

211

Judi McCoy

He leaned toward her and whispered, "And be fore-warned, Hera has again left the mountain. We're positive she's up to no good where you, Chloe, and Zoë are concerned, so it might be wise if you warned them." He then disappeared in a snowstorm of fluffy feathers.

Kyra glanced around to see if anyone had noticed the messenger's too-long slacks or flurry of white. Instead, everyone was going about their business as if a visit by a god was a daily occurrence. She bent and picked up one of the small white feathers that must have fallen from his winged sandals.

Served him right, she snorted in disgust. If his sandals were molting, it was probably from disuse. Both he and Zeus had neglected the older, tried and true ways and become slaves to modern technology, but that didn't mean she had to conform to their ridiculous thinking.

Sighing, Kyra made a mental note to do as she'd promised as soon as she arrived in her office. Tomorrow night was her official talk with Chloe and Zoë, soon enough to give them the news about Hera. The head goddess enjoyed dabbling in various earthly shenanigans. It wouldn't hurt to give the news to her sisters, just in case the shenanigans involved them.

Still in a dither, she entered the first boutique in the fashion corridor and began to shop. Jake was waiting.

Carrying her tote and a small shopping bag, Kyra stepped off the elevator and strode to Jake's suite.

With plenty of cash available in her checking account, she'd purchased a change of undergarments and an outrageously expensive, crème-colored nightie as sheer as tissue paper and as soft as a caress. Tomorrow, she'd handle a change of clothing the same way Terpsichore had when she'd slipped into her diamond-studded dress, and hope Jake acted in typical male fashion, ignoring the day-to-day clothing women wore.

The entire experience had taken more time than she wanted, but it had given her the opportunity to think about Hermes's visit. To stand even half a chance of returning to Mount Olympus in triumph, she'd have to include a major suck-up to Zeus in her morning e-mail. And she still might fail to placate him if the father god was in a sour mood.

She arrived at Jake's suite, and before she could knock, the door swung open, and he stepped aside to let her enter.

"You didn't buy much," he commented, flipping the security latch on the door after it slammed shut. "Didn't the stores have what you wanted?"

"I think so. You can let me know later," she answered, noting he'd shaved, removed his jacket, and smelled of a light citrus scent that reminded her of sunshine.

"Much later." He took the tiny bag from her hand and set it on the coffee table. "Right now, all I need is you."

Judi McCoy

Kyra's heart did a rapid tap dance in her chest. She glanced at the table set with a fresh bouquet of flowers, and the bottle of champagne chilling in a stand next to a chair. The silver domes covering the china plates gleamed in the soft candlelight. "What about dinner?"

Stepping closer, he brought her hands to his lips. "I ordered cold lobster salad. It'll keep . . . unless you want a glass of champagne?"

"You've thought of everything." But the bubbly liquid could wait until after she'd satisfied a different kind of hunger.

Jake cupped her jaw with his fingers. "Being with you tonight is the only thing I've thought about for a week. Your face, your lips . . ." His hand moved to her nape and threaded upward. "I've imagined your glorious hair spread across my pillow since the day I first saw you. In fact, you've haunted my every waking moment."

He leaned forward and captured her mouth with his. Kyra opened for him and his tongue slid inside, tasting her as if she were the finest nectar of the gods.

Moving her hands to his back, she caressed the play of muscles she'd admired earlier. He tensed under her palms and scooped her into his arms. Thrilled by his strength, Kyra nestled her head on his shoulder as he carried her into the bedroom.

This room, too, was filled with lighted candles, their shimmering glow reflecting in the mirror over the dresser. Stopping next to the bed, he set her on her feet, reached behind her, and tugged at the zipper of her dress. She undid the buttons on his shirt, then dropped her arms and let the dress slide to the floor.

Jake shrugged the shirt from his shoulders and undid his belt and zipper. His slacks fell to his ankles and she sucked in a breath at the bulge straining the front of his boxers. He grinned and ran a finger over the mounds of flesh spilling from the top of her bra.

"So far, so good," he said, his voice a rasp. With nimble fingers, he unclasped the front of the undergarment and sent it streaming to the carpet.

Kyra basked in his approving gaze as he stared through narrowed eyes.

"You are my greatest fantasy." Inching closer, he palmed a breast, then rolled the nipple between his thumb and forefinger. "I just pray I don't disappoint you."

Trembling at his searing touch, she inspected his well-defined pecs, rigid abdomen, and the line of curling dark hair disappearing into the waistband of his shorts. "I don't think that's possible."

"Sweetheart, you have no idea how badly I could botch this if I don't exert a little self-control. You're a goddess come to life."

She smiled at the endearing phrase. If only he knew . . .

Jake took another step, nudging her backward, and Kyra dropped to the bed. Lying back, she moved to make room, and he climbed beside her. Grasping her hands, he raised them over her head and took her lips in another burning kiss. When his tongue left her mouth and trailed to her collarbone, she thought she might faint before anything more passed between them. His body scalded her skin, awakened her senses, and filled her with desire.

Then he moved to her breast and scraped his teeth across her turgid nipple. Drawing it into his mouth, he pulled the bud deep inside.

Kyra arched from the mattress, and he slipped a knee between her legs, pushing his thigh tight to her core. She rubbed against him and electricity sizzled along every nerve ending in her body, causing her to cry out her delight.

Jake let go of her wrists and she grasped his head, guiding him to her other breast. He flicked with his tongue, then suckled hard as he pulled her panties down and inserted a finger inside her. Writhing beneath him, Kyra let herself ride the tempo of his hand, keening her approval. It had been so long . . . too long since she'd been pleasured in such an arousing manner.

"That's it, sweetheart. Let me hear you. Tell me what you want."

At his whisper, she whimpered an incoherent response, and he pressed the button of her desire, circling it in a demanding rhythm. He whispered endearments as she clenched around his fingers and clasped his throbbing erection. Lights flashed behind her eyelids and before she could do more than caress his steely length, a tremor overtook her and she shattered under his hands. Rocking in place, she rode a wave of completion, moaning when she found her release.

Moments passed while Jake slowly kissed her back to reality. His lips tickled her skin as he nuzzled her shoulder, her neck, her mouth.

He pulled away and she clutched him to her chest. "Don't go."

"I'm not going anywhere, but I need protection— unless you're on the pill?"

When immortals coupled, birth control was unnecessary as Zeus controlled every aspect of procreation, but he had no say over reproduction when the act was performed between a mortal and a god. She fastened her gaze on his midnight-blue eyes and shook her head. "I haven't been with a man in a while—"

"Somehow I find that hard to believe, but it does leave me grateful," he said with a smile.

"It was my choice, Jake."

"Then I'm honored you chose me to be next." He reached for the nightstand and opened the top drawer. Ripping into a foil packet, he removed the condom. "How about you do the honors?"

"How many of those do you have?"

"I bought a box this morning, in anticipation of . . . whatever happened between us." He continued to grin. "I hope it's enough to get us through the night."

Kyra echoed his smile of satisfaction. Grasping the sheath of latex, she inched down and kissed the head of his pulsing shaft, then unrolled the condom over his erection.

Lying back, she let Jake settle between her thighs. Then she opened for him. Guiding him inside her body, she tightened around him, shuddering when she heard him groan.

"You feel so good, so tight, so perfect." He pushed deeper into her. "I don't ever want to leave."

"Please, again," she said, clutching his shoulders.

His next stroke was long and slow and achingly sweet. Then he increased the tempo, urging her to follow.

But she needed no encouragement. As if she'd waited a hundred lifetimes, she met him thrust for thrust. Jake bit at her breast, laved with his tongue, and drove her crazy with need. In exact synchronization, they rose and fell as if they'd joined this way a thousand times before.

Sensations flared, and Kyra gave herself to the exquisite torture, letting the orgasm take her to the clouds. When Jake tensed, then stiffened above her, telling her he, too, was complete, she held him tight and let her mind and body sink into oblivion.

* * *

His arms aching, Jake counted out strokes on the rowing machine. When he reached two hundred, he glanced around the gym. At this ungodly hour of the morning, the facility was empty and eerily silent, with neither a trainer nor attendant present to see to the needs of the guests.

And it suited him just fine. The quiet gave him time to think about Kyra and everything that had transpired during the night. All night . . .

He couldn't remember the last time he'd gone through more than two condoms in a single session of sex. With Kyra, it was tough to stay in control and not use up the entire box as he'd jokingly hinted they might. Instead of exhaustion, he'd awakened invigorated, and more alive than he'd felt in years.

He'd left her sleeping soundly, determined not to touch her again until he knew she had enough rest to survive the day. If his plans materialized, they would spend another evening in his bed or his oversized whirlpool tub . . . anywhere they could be alone to do it again.

Wiping down, he tossed his towel in the hamper and left for his room. First, he'd take a long hot shower, then rouse Kyra. If she showed any resistance to an encore performance, he wouldn't push. He'd order breakfast while she got ready, and they would share a meal before going to work.

On the elevator ride, he went over every suspicion he'd originally had about her, and realized that none of them had any teeth. A woman out to scam a major hotel and casino would never give herself so completely to a man she knew was intimately involved in its inner workings. In fact, she could have used him to find out a few things about the hotel, but not once had any of her questions pertained to the Acropolis, even after he'd joined the chase for those cheats.

With nothing but a list of quirky facts on her, he was now certain he'd been playing the wrong angle where she was concerned. She hadn't mingled with the guests all week, and she said there'd been no winner in the latest Wheel Deal. Belief in good luck was a superstition, not a crime. As far as he knew, she was guilty of nothing more than feeding the hopes of a few of the Acropolis's more desperate customers.

Unless he caught her red-handed in something incriminating, he was prepared to write her off as a suspect and move on in his investigation. He definitely needed to check the casino's accounting files, and take a look at the Sky Tower remodeling project. He and Kyra would have a serious discussion on their relationship after he'd been officially named manager.

In the bedroom, he found her bundled under the covers, fast asleep. The mere sight of her russet hair, billowing across his pillow exactly as he'd imagined in his fantasies, made his penis throb to life. Ignoring the temptation to wake her, he tiptoed to the bath. He'd let her catch a couple more minutes of sleep before he coaxed her back into his arms.

Kyra heard the droning of the shower through a sleepy haze. Rolling over, she opened her eyes and took in the room's high ceiling, ornate furniture, and blue velvet draperies drawn closed to block the morning light. The white candles that had flickered so beautifully last night were mere stubs of wax puddled on the nightstand and dresser.

Jake's room, she reminded herself. A place where she'd been both cared for and tormented in the best way possible. He'd been the fulfillment of her every desire, the lover of her dreams . . . the man her beleaguered spirit had been waiting for.

Hugging the pillow to her chest, she frowned. No, no, no. Absolutely not! She would not romanticize the experience or blow it out of proportion. It had been an evening of mutual pleasure. A night spent with a man who could use three, or had it been four, condoms without working up a sweat or complaining of fatigue. Jake was nothing more than an enjoyment, a reward she chose to give herself for spending a year of celibacy while inspiring mortals.

If she could have, she would have dressed and left the room before he was out of the shower, but the idea was totally impractical. She envisioned her unruly hair, smeared makeup, and smelly breath. Her body was always perfect on Olympus, but when a god or goddess inhabited Earth for a prolonged period, they had to attend to the same grooming habits as would any mortal. And after last night's

221

intensely physical exertion . . . well, she could only guess how horrible she looked.

When the shower grew quiet, she turned to her stomach and pulled the pillow over her head. Maybe if she lay still as a board, Jake would believe her asleep and go about his business.

Seconds passed. Then came the sound of muffled footsteps. When her side of the bed sagged, she squeezed her eyes tight and held her breath. Something—Jake's hand?—stroked her derriere.

"Hey, sleepyhead. You awake?"

"Mmnnmm."

The covers slipped from her shoulders, warm lips brushed her skin. Searching fingers tripped down her spine and rested at the dip above her still-covered fanny. His hands grew bold, sliding beneath the sheet and stroking her bottom. His firm lips found their way from her back to the side of her breast, where they teased and tickled.

Jake's mouth tormented the sensitive spot behind her ear. "I'm up for another session, if you are."

When she didn't answer, the nightstand drawer slid open and she heard the tearing of foil. Then he climbed on the bed and slid his palms between her breasts and the mattress.

With her head still under the pillow, she raised up and let her breasts fill his hands. He plucked at her nipples and she moaned. He nudged her bottom and the pillow slipped from her head as he drew her to her hands and knees. Unable to resist, Kyra

222

spread her legs and welcomed him between her trembling thighs.

He continued to massage a breast, while he ran his other hand into her slick folds and found her swelling bud. Positioning himself at her center, he entered her in a single stroke and began to rock.

Kyra hummed her appreciation of the exquisite sensation. The fire that had dwindled to embers with the dawn burst into flames inside her, and she matched his pounding rhythm.

Jake raised her up and held her spine tight against his chest. She rose and fell as he throbbed in her very core. He caught her hands and pressed them to her breasts, urging her to fondle herself so they could experience the erotic sensation together. When he snared her nipples between their fingers and squeezed, she muttered her approval.

The bed seemed to rotate beneath her as they clung together, his front to her back. Once again, he slid a palm to her ribcage and over her stomach. Delving into her woman's mound, he circled the heart of her passion as he whispered erotic words of encouragement, urging her to find her release and take them both over the edge.

Kyra stiffened as he thrust once, twice, hard and deliberately. Her body turned rigid when colors as brilliant as the neon signs on the strip again danced in her brain. His ragged breath brushed her earlobe as he caressed her breasts and tugged on her peaked nipples.

Judi McCoy

Finally, Jake ground into her, shouting his completion as they crested. Panting, he lowered her gently onto his thighs and cuddled her until she returned to sanity.

"Hungry?"

"Mmnnmm."

He snorted out a laugh. "Me, too. How about I call for breakfast? French toast with warm maple syrup and fresh blueberries? Eggs Benedict?"

Unable to form a simple, one syllable answer, she sighed.

"Okay, I'll order a little of everything, and you can eat what you like. The bathroom is free, by the way."

Boneless, Kyra crumpled to the mattress and burrowed under the pillow, unable to look him in the eye. Drawers opened and closed, followed by the sound of clothing brushing across skin. Then the door clicked shut.

Still quivering, she ducked from beneath the pillow and breathed deeply. Never had she shared such an experience with another being, either god or mortal. Was it Jake who made her ache this way, or was it the year-long lack of contact with a male that gave her this feeling of wonder and contentment?

She was not looking forward to tonight's weekly gabfest with Chloe and Zoë. She doubted she'd be able to stand up to a second intense interrogation, especially if they asked her to give Jake another rating on the kiss-o-meter.

224

It was impossible to explain her tangled emotions. She only knew she was in danger of destroying her very existence.

For that's exactly what would happen if she allowed herself to fall in love with Jake Lennox.

Chapter 15

FROM: *Kdegodessa@Acropolis.com*
TO: *Topgod@mounto.org*
SUBJECT: TRIXIE

Mighty lord of Olympus: I had no idea seeking
assistance from another muse was not allowed.
Terpsichore is my sister, I was homesick, and
needed a friendly ear. Please accept my humble
apology, and be advised it will not happen
again.

Sincerely,
Your obedient daughter
Kyra

Kyra hit the send key, forwarding her message complete with another groveling apology to Zeus. Then she gave a sniff of good riddance and pushed from her credenza in disgust. She'd done her job to the best of her ability for fifty-one weeks. Wasn't that enough?

Things would be so much easier if Jake had shown up in the first or second month she'd arrived to serve her sentence. She would have had plenty of time to enjoy his company and get him out of her system. With just days left, her biggest fear was that she wouldn't grow tired of him before she journeyed home. Returning to Mount Olympus without getting her fill of the man would leave her with no closure to their relationship, something she always had to do to move on.

If Zeus deemed her year here a failure, she would be demoted to servant status, with no chance of regaining entry to Earth where she would at least have her friends. It would be even worse if he suspected a mortal had carved a permanent place in her heart. She might be remanded to Earth forever, where she would have her friends, but would live and die a mortal's existence, forced to give up an eternity of triumph for a man who wanted nothing more than a no-strings *affaire*.

She glared at the stack of messages she'd jotted down from her voicemail and the to-do list for the competition. Her phone rang, and she ignored it.

Then the computer's smarmy voice rang out its usual too-cheery "You've got mail."

Turning back to the cursed contraption, she tapped her fingers on the keys, hoping to send the program into cyberspace or Hades—either place was fine with her.

A page popped into view, one she'd never seen before, peppered with rows of small number-and-date-filled boxes. She slapped her hands on the keyboard, intent on making everything disappear. Stubbornly, the document remained on the screen.

Blinking, she peered at the monitor. Rob said he'd given her someone else's machine. Perhaps this file belonged to him. Maybe it was important, and needed to be transferred to his new system. Using various keystrokes, she attempted to store the document—without success.

Frustrated, Kyra dialed Rob's extension, and left a message asking him to rescue her from the intrusive document. Still ignoring the screen, she made phone calls to the hotel's catering service and florist to co-ordinate what they'd be supplying for the VIP lounge and judges' dressing rooms during the competition.

There was a knock at her door, then Jake walked in, wearing a grin of satisfaction. Suspicious of his smug smile, she bristled. How dare he be so happy about their *affaire*, when she wasn't even sure it should continue?

"I tried your line a few minutes ago, but you

didn't answer. Were you on the casino floor?" he asked, his mood shifting to one of curiosity.

"I've been here all morning. My computer chose today to spring one of those . . . those glitch things and be completely uncooperative." Hah! As if it co-operated on *any* day. "I got so involved I didn't hear the phone."

He strolled to the front of her desk and took a seat. "I called to see if you were free for lunch or din-ner. Or both."

Both? "Lunch is a possibility, but dinner's out of the question, unless we're through early. I have to be home by nine," she explained, intimating there'd be no sex tonight.

He raised a brow, and his smile morphed into that *come here, baby* grin, hitting her dead center in the middle of her chest. "I could buy takeout and bring it to your place."

"Not a good idea. I have to feed my cat." *Jeesh, could she sound any dumber?*

"You have a cat?"

"Are you allergic to cats?"

"Not a bit. You've just never mentioned owning a pet. What kind of cat?"

Kyra's brain went on overdrive and her mouth raced to catch up. If they were to continue their trysts, it would be on her terms. "I don't know . . . it's a stray . . . lives out back, near the Dumpsters and I . . . I bring it food and . . . and things every couple of days."

"Not a problem. I can help you carry out the kibble."

"No . . . I mean . . . that won't work. The cat is frightened of everyone but me."

Jake leaned forward and rested his elbows on his knees. "Are you trying to get rid of me for tonight?"

"Get rid of you? Don't be silly." She squirmed in her seat. Zeus's eyeballs, but she hated this dishonesty. Besides, Jake's knowing expression told her he saw right through her idiotic excuses. "Why would I want to do such a thing?"

He stood, sauntered to her side of the desk, and stationed himself behind her chair. His warm breath tickled her ear, sending an entire flock of goosebumps marching down her arms.

"I don't know. You tell me."

"I have nothing to tell," she lied again. "Did you want anything else?"

"Lunch? We could order sandwiches, take a ride in the desert or someplace equally quiet, and talk."

"Maybe, but I have phone messages to return, then I'm supposed to go over the color scheme for the hostess gowns. And I'm scheduled to help Lou choose a dress and go with her to the hotel seamstress."

"You have to eat and so do I." He pressed a kiss to the nape of her neck. "Why don't we do it together?"

Kyra jumped to her feet and backed away. "I asked Rob to come over and take a look at my computer. I must have hit a wrong key"—*or a dozen*—

"and pulled up a file that doesn't belong on my machine."

Jake pivoted to face her and their gazes locked for a long moment. As if drawn by an invisible thread, they moved slowly toward each other. Their lips met, and Kyra grabbed his wrists to keep from swaying into the solid wall of his chest. But it didn't matter. In less than the blink of an eye, she was cocooned in his strength and warmed to her marrow by his firm, persuasive mouth.

The embrace seemed to last an eternity. When they broke away she sensed a deep loss, as if she were floating on a cloud adrift without an anchor. Jake looked surprised, as if he felt the same, and she wished she could give a name to whatever had overtaken them.

He continued to hold her upper arms and stare, as if seeing her for the first time. A ripple of anticipation skittered through Kyra's stomach, rising to catch in her throat. What was happening to her . . . to them?

As if coming to his senses, he focused on her computer. "Maybe I can help."

She stepped back as if burned. "I'll give you some room. Have a seat."

Jake settled in the chair, blinking to clear his fuddled brain. He'd come to Kyra's office with the intention of keeping things cool and calm, while still letting her know he expected her to spend tonight and a host of other nights in his bed. What the hell was going on? Just being near her made his gut tremble, the way it did when he'd ridden the tilt-a-whirl at the carnival as a kid, or he doubled down and hit twenty-one. It was a frightening, yet damned good feeling, even if he couldn't name it.

He concentrated on her computer screen, hoping to heaven he didn't look as stupid as he felt. Rob strolled in at the same moment Jake realized he was staring at a spreadsheet.

"Rob, I'm so glad you're here," said Kyra. "We . . . Jake . . . I need your help. I got into a disagreement with my computer, and it pulled a dirty trick— opened a file I have no recollection of working on."

Rob walked behind the desk and gazed over Jake's shoulder. "You got it, or do you need my help?"

"Where did this PC come from before you gave it to Kyra?" asked Jake, still studying the monitor.

"There was a snafu with the paperwork, and someone removed Ms. Simmons's computer without a work order. Kyra needed a replacement ASAP, and I'd spent the day installing a new system for Ardmore, so I brought his old unit up from the graveyard and gave it to her. Why?"

"You're saying this was Ardmore's PC?"

"Yeah. Standard procedure when someone gets a new system is to wipe the hard drive and recycle it or use it as a slave, but this one was in good shape and fairly new. I could get it to Kyra faster than if she requisitioned a new one. Guess I snagged it be-

fore maintenance got a chance to run the erase."
Rob shrugged. "It's not a big deal. I can wipe the
drive this afternoon."

"Not just yet," said Jake. "I want to study this
spreadsheet, and the file it came from, for a while."

"Besides being dishonest, it's against hotel policy
for anyone to tamper with another employee's computer. Since this one belonged to Ardmore, I can't let
you do that."

Impressed by Rob's company loyalty, Jake said,
"I'm allowed to inspect whatever aspect of the
Acropolis I deem necessary, so I have the authority
to read it. If it's personal, he shouldn't have used a
hotel machine."

Before Rob made another comment, Jake pulled
open a side drawer in the credenza and found a
blank disk. After he slid the new disk in and hit a
few keys, the computer began to hum as it transferred the data. "Kyra, I'm afraid I have to take back
my offer of lunch. Rob and I are going to be busy for
a while."

"We are?" asked Rob.

Jake knew his way around a computer, but he
wasn't a geek. He needed an expert opinion and,
considering his remarks about honesty, Rob seemed
the most logical choice. "We are. And cancel any
other plans you have, because it might take a while."

When the transfer finished, he removed the disk,
returned the spreadsheet to its folder, and said to
Kyra, "What's your password?"

"My what?"

"Password. You know, the code you use to gain entry to your files."

"She doesn't have a password," said Rob. "I told her she needed one, even offered to set it up for her but—"

From the comments Kyra had made about computers, Jake knew it was useless wasting breath on a lecture. "Your data needs to be protected. You don't want to chance a break-in."

Her gaze bounced from one man to the next. "Why would anyone want to break into my system? There's nothing on file but some letters and e-mail . . . and that spreadsheet."

Jake raised a brow.

"Oh."

"I won't know until we investigate, so just think of a password. Something important, so you won't forget it."

Her brows knotted. Then she smiled. "I have it."

"Reconfigure her log-on, let her type in the word, and teach her how to use it," Jake said to Rob. He stepped to Kyra's side while Rob fiddled with the keys. "Whenever you leave the office, I want you to lock the door. And don't say a word to anyone about what you found or that we copied the data." He stroked the side of her cheek with the back of his fingers. "I'll see you after the Wheel Deal. We can discuss your cat over dinner."

At the door, he turned. "Rob, as soon as you're through here, meet me in your office."

For the next several hours, Kyra tried to concentrate on the Voice of Vegas, but her thoughts kept returning to the computer file she'd happened upon and Jake's insistence on secrecy. Though Rob had been patient when he'd explained how to use her password, and she'd written down the instructions just in case she forgot the order of commands, the ordeal reinforced her dislike of the contrary machines.

Jake was always a bit vague about the job he held with the Acropolis, but his reaction to the file had confused her. It almost sounded as if he held more power at the hotel than Rupert Ardmore. Strange.

Around one o'clock, Lou strolled into Kyra's office and plopped down in the chair in front of her desk.

"You're early," said Kyra, noting the waitress had arrived ahead of schedule for their appointment with wardrobe and the seamstress.

"You owe me lunch," Lou grumped. "It's your fault I got dumped."

"Dumped?" Kyra frowned. "Oh, Rob."

"Don't 'oh Rob' me. You're the one who encouraged me to give him a chance, and what happened? He came onto the floor and canceled our date. I should have gone with my gut and just said no, like I wanted."

"Rob didn't have a choice. He was under orders from Jake Lennox to lend his expertise with something," Kyra said, replaying in her mind the conversation in her office.

"It figures you'd stick up for him." Lou sighed. "Silly me, thinking there was one good guy still left on the planet."

"You're being too sensitive. At least Rob came to see you in person."

"So?"

"I bet he tried to talk you into another date."

Lou shrugged. "What's your point?"

"My point is that he didn't simply ignore you. He saw you personally, explained the problem, and asked you out again." Kyra bent down and retrieved her tote. "You told him yes, didn't you?"

"I said maybe."

"And will you?"

Lou's shoulders slumped. "Against my better judgment. I've traveled this road too often, friend. And it sucks."

Kyra recalled the many discussions she and Lou had held on the foibles of the opposite sex. According to Lou, she'd never had a single positive experience. Her last man had been exactly that. Her last.

Kyra stood, and they walked to the door, where she locked it as Jake had instructed. "We'll go to the coffee shop first. I'll buy you a sandwich, then we'll head to the pavilion."

Kyra continued to lecture as they took the stairs, sincere in her hope that Lou and Rob got together. "You're too young to take care of your mother and Katie alone, or go through life solo."

"The last part pertains to you, too," Lou offered. "Then again, you had a date with Jake last night, didn't you?"

"I did," said Kyra as they were seated at a table.

"And?"

She perused the menu until the waitress took their order. When the woman left, Kyra said, "We had dinner."

"Was that all?"

Unwilling to confess they'd eaten the lobster after their first round of sex, or drunk the champagne after the second, she sighed. "End of story."

Lou's brows rose to her hairline. "Really?"

"Sort of."

Instead of commenting, Lou trailed a finger down her water glass. Moments passed before Kyra said, "What? No words of wisdom?"

"Just two," Lou answered, her expression wary. "And they apply to both of us."

"Don't keep me in suspense."

Lou's hazel eyes darkened. "Be careful."

"This has to remain between the two of us," said Jake, stacking the spreadsheet Rob had printed. Though the racket in the IT department was enough to muffle most conversations, he kept his voice low. "Not a word to anyone, especially Ardmore."

The computer expert ran a hand over his chin. "Like I said in Kyra's office, that's not exactly kosher . . . unless you're hiding something I should know about."

Jake kept his eyes on the folder. Themopolis had told him to stay undercover, but Rob worked for the company and had made it known he was loyal. He had every right to question any suspicious activity, so it was up to Jake to convince Rob his main interest was the good of the Acropolis.

"Let's just say I'm here at Mr. T's request. He asked me to look into a few financial abnormalities taking place at the hotel, but it doesn't concern you."

"Everything here concerns me," Rob stated. "I planned on building my IT career around the Acropolis, so I want it to continue to do well."

"That's my intention, too."

"And what about Kyra?"

"She doesn't have a clue about the real reason I'm here."

"But you are going to tell her."

"When the time is right; meanwhile . . ."

"Who else knows?"

"Chief security guard, Herb Molinari. Themopolis asked us to work together on the problem, but no one else. Since I've clued you in—"

"I'll keep my lips zipped. But what about accounting? The auditors? The state gaming board—?"

"No one else, until I get to the bottom of the casino's money woes. Mr. T is afraid if word hits the street, people will think he's in financial trouble, and the competition will go for the jugular. Definitely bad for business."

"This explains all the time you spend in the surveillance room, and the reason you interviewed some of the employees." Rob hitched his hip and sat on a corner of Jake's desk, his expression intense. "Is that why you're seeing Kyra? Because you think she has something to do with the missing cash?"

"I did at first," Jake said, embarrassed to admit Rob had him pegged. "When I heard about the good luck taps she gave certain customers—"

Rob gave a snort of laughter. "You mean those goofy 'best of luck' pats?"

"Yes. And they were the only things I could find to explain the losses. I had hoped to gain her trust and convince her to let me in on the scam."

"But you didn't find anything to incriminate her."

"Correct. After studying it rationally, I realized the payouts she appeared to encourage were chump change compared to the millions Themopolis says are missing. Though I still have an issue with the overabundance of Wheel Deal wins, and there's no explanation for the customers she taps who suddenly hit it big at the slots or tables, I can't find any proof of manipulation on her part. Without concrete evidence—"

"I could have told you Kyra was innocent," Rob said, his voice protective. "She was only being nice, letting people use her for good luck the way they would a rabbit's foot or a four-leaf clover."

"There is no such thing as luck," Jake insisted. "It takes knowledge, determination, and an exceptional amount of betting savvy to win at the only games a smart player has a chance of winning—blackjack, baccarat, and poker. Gambling is an art form not to be taken lightly. The smart amateurs are the ones who come here for fun with no expectation of a win."

"Sounds as if you're well acquainted with the profession." Rob's eyes narrowed when Jake stayed mum. "I'll be darned . . . you're a pro."

"Yeah, but I'm not here to gamble. Themopolis believes I have the business acumen and working knowledge of a casino's ins and outs to figure who's doing the dirty work without contacting the authorities."

"I'm glad you decided you were wrong about Kyra, but if you hurt her I'll make it a point to stake you out in the desert and applaud when the buzzards circle." Rob clenched his hands into fists. "You clear on that?"

Jake smiled at Rob's go-to-hell stance and kick-ass attitude. To his credit, the boy crooner was turning out to be a stand-up guy with a lot more moxie than he'd given him credit for. "Might as well confess, at first I thought there was something personal going on between the two of you—"

"There is. She's a good friend."

"I got the picture," said Jake. "So if you don't mind, I'd just as soon you hold off smashing my face in. It would ruin my debonair, man-of-the-world image." He stuffed the papers into the manila folder. "I'll go over these and get back to you in the morning. Meanwhile, you compare those accounting figures—"

"I should warn you, I'm not an accountant."

"You can add and subtract can't you? And something tells me you can put your own spin on a spreadsheet. Just point out anything you think is out of the ordinary, and I'll take it from there, especially if it concerns the Sky Tower remodeling job."

"Okay, I can do that." Rob glanced at his watch. "Crap, I'm late for my session with Lou. Thanks to you, I've already got one strike against me."

Jake stood, only half listening. Kyra was going to ask about the file at their next meeting, and he wasn't sure how much to reveal. "What did I do?"

"Ordered me to work with you on this project, which meant I had to cancel our lunch date. From the mutinous glare she gave me when I begged off, she's not a happy camper."

"Cut her some slack. Kyra says the lady's had to overcome her fair share of problems."

"What kind of problems?" asked Rob, walking alongside Jake as they left the room.

"It's for Lou to explain. Besides, I'm not privy to the details." They parted at the front desk. "Have a good practice. I'll see you in the morning."

Kyra grinned as Lou gazed with open-mouthed shock at her reflection in the mirror. Wearing a figure-hugging dress of mahogany silk scattered with gold sequins, the gown played up the highlights in the young woman's hair and showcased her large hazel eyes. "I knew this dress would be perfect the second I saw it. You look great."

"Correction, I *will* look great," said Lou, nodding to the seamstress kneeling in front of her while pinning the hem. "As soon as Consuelo works her magic. But even without enhancements, I have to admit I'm . . . passable."

The older woman stood and clucked her tongue. "Forget passable. Once I give you more shape here," she tugged at the gaping bodice, "and a little contour here," her hands ran over Lou's narrow hips, "you will be every man's fantasy."

"Go easy on the shaping and contouring," warned Lou. "I don't want to be accused of false advertising."

"Not false," offered Kyra. "Just new and improved. You'll knock Rob's socks off."

"Do you ever listen to a word I say? Rob is *persona non grata* as far as I'm concerned."

"Really? I thought you were scheduled to play another practice session today?"

Lou blinked, checked the time on her watch, and rolled her eyes. Reaching for the zipper, she ran it halfway down her back. "I'm late. Consuelo, get me out of this thing."

The seamstress undid the zipper and gave Lou a hand stepping from the gown, then draped the garment on a padded hanger. "I'll take care of everything. People will think you are a princess," Consuelo said over her shoulder as she trundled from the room.

"You have fifteen minutes before it's time to meet Rob," said Kyra, handing Lou her jeans. "Take it easy. Men expect women to be late."

"I have this thing about punctuality. Being punctual is a virtue I take seriously, as well as keeping my word." After buttoning her jeans, Lou pulled a bright red sweater over her head and slipped her feet into a pair of black leather flats. "Don't get me wrong. I'm still ticked with Rob, but I don't want him to think—"

"So you are going to help with his number?"

"Of course. I promised."

"Then what's the hurry? A little insecurity is good for a guy's ego. It'll make him appreciate you all the more when you show up."

"I don't believe in playing games, Kyra. If Rob and I are going to have a friendship—"

"Then you decided to go out with him?"

Sighing, Lou gave a half-shrug. "You convinced me he had a believable excuse, and I'd expect him to understand if I were the one who'd canceled. Everybody deserves a second chance." She dumped her high heels into her bag, stuffed the waitress uniform on top, and hoisted the tote over her shoulder. "It's the least I can do."

"Now you're talking," said Kyra.

"How about escorting me to the practice room while you list Rob's superman qualities for the tenth time? Just in case I've forgotten one or two."

"Not a problem. I have to head in that direction anyway. I'm sure the Wheel Deal contestants are waiting for the big drum roll as we speak."

The women remained silent as they rushed through the indoor-outdoor market, into the casino, and lobby. Viewing the long line of hopeful players, Kyra exhaled. So many people . . . and just one big winner. If only there were some way to inspire a thousand mortals at once, Zeus would have to agree she'd earned a promotion to go along with her five-star review.

"How do I look?" asked Lou, tucking a strand of hair behind her ear.

"Like a competent and attractive woman," said Kyra, giving her a quick once-over. "Not that it matters. Rob already thinks you're special, and it's his opinion that counts. By the way, did you take my suggestion and ride the bus today?"

Lou's cheeks glowed pink. "Yes. But not so Rob would give me a lift home. My mother offered to do the grocery shopping."

"Uh-huh."

"She did," Lou insisted. "It'll save me the trouble of spending a Saturday at the food store."

"Just remember to say yes when Rob offers to

bring you home. In fact, you could ask him for the favor. Men enjoy feeling useful."

"Here I go again, taking advice from a dateless shut-in. Unless you're going out with Jake again?"

"In a manner of speaking," said Kyra. If one chose to count a fast dinner while they discussed a make-believe cat as a date. There wouldn't be time for more because of her scheduled conversation with Chloe and Zoë. "But this isn't about me. You're the one with the possibility of a hot night. Go be your adorable self and say yes to whatever Rob suggests."

"Okay, okay," muttered Lou, heading in the direction of the practice room. "I can take a hint."

Chapter 16

When Jake finished meeting with Rob, he took refuge in Herb's office. "What can you tell me about the remodeling that's taking place on the top floors of the Sky Tower?" he asked the senior security guard.

"The luxury suites have been closed for renovation for the past year, per Ardmore's orders. The only people allowed there are workmen from the company who won the bid. They were instructed to enter via a service elevator, take it to the twenty-third floor and climb a flight of stairs reserved for maintenance to get to the top tiers." Herb rifled through his desk drawer. "Far as I know, it's Ardmore's baby."

He pulled out a shoebox, found what he'd been searching for, and passed it to Jake. "Here you go. This is the only elevator key that's still free. I had to surrender the others when the project was announced, because Ardmore claimed he didn't want anyone going up there and interrupting the work. A little birdie talked me into keeping one for myself, just in case, if you get my drift."

The Acropolis was comprised of three towers positioned in a triangle from the rear of the hotel lobby. *Up there* were the twenty-fourth and twenty-fifth floors of the tallest of the trio. Jake had taken a tour as a teenager, and knew the Sky Tower housed the most luxurious rooms in the hotel; four suites per floor, each comprised of thirty-five hundred square feet of opulence and over-the-top customer services. The only way to reach the suites was in a private express elevator that ran directly to those floors and no others.

Though the suites could be booked for upwards of five thousand a night, they were normally reserved for the most loyal and moneyed customers, and usually given as a thank you for their high-dollar play. Besides the complimentary use of a private chef, masseuse, and live-in maid, the fixtures in each of their three full baths were twenty-four-karat gold-plated, their furnishings genuine period pieces worth a small fortune.

"I'm going up to take a look around," said Jake.
"Because . . . ?"

"Because a year is too long for renovations, especially when the suites are a source of bonus income."

"And what makes you think the remodel of those penthouses has anything to do with the missing money?"

Jake didn't want to reveal the spreadsheet data just yet, in case the renovation order was legit. "Doesn't it seem odd the upgrades aren't finished?"

The guard shrugged. "Beats me. I just do what I'm told. But I do remember hearing something about delays with the suppliers." He scratched his stubbled chin. "Come to think of it, that was months ago."

Jake quirked a brow. "See what I mean."

"Yeah, I do." Herb stuffed his hands in his pockets. "Come to think about it, it does sound hinky. Sure you don't want some company?"

"No, thanks," Jake said, backing from the room. "I'll let you know tomorrow if my suspicion has legs."

Now, two hours later, he was still prowling the twenty-fifth floor of the Sky Tower, puzzled by what he'd found. He'd run into his first problem when he'd arrived on the top floor, realized the door to every suite was locked, and had to return to Herb's office, where it took the senior guard another half hour to locate individual room keys.

After walking through the eight richly appointed penthouses, Jake was surprised to discover the suites were in the exact same condition as pictured in the hotel's year-old brochure. In fact, the dust on the tables and furnishings was so thick it appeared that no one had been in any of the suites since they'd been closed off.

He inspected every storage closet and utility area for signs of workmen. The result? Aside from some drop cloths and paint cans, nada, zilch, zip. Not a single thing to support a renovation venture in any way, shape, or form.

Were Rob and Herb misinformed? Had he misread the information on the spreadsheet that showed money being funneled to an account to pay for the units' extensive makeovers?

What in the hell was going on?

He took the elevator to the lobby, then switched cars and rode down to the surveillance room, where a quick glance conveyed Herb had left for the day. Jake decided to go to his office and reread the data. He must have misinterpreted the numbers or confused the statistics on the expenditures.

Before he opened the folder, he checked the wall clock and noted the time. *Well, hell.* He'd been so involved in snooping he hadn't stopped in the lobby to watch the progress of the Wheel Deal which, by his calculation, had ended several hours ago. He ran a hand over his face. Kyra probably thought he'd stood her up a second, or was it third, time.

Without Rob's accounting figures, he had no way to ascertain the exact cost of the renovations. Tomorrow, he'd ask Herb to confirm the security clearance for Fast Track Design and Restoration. He'd also have Rob dig around accounting for more in-depth numbers and the actual contracts. Until then, he had to tread carefully, and tiptoe around the idea that the interim manager was involved in anything shady.

It was too late to go further tonight.

Hoping to get his mind off the nagging questions, he tried Kyra's office line. Of course, she wasn't there. Why would she wait for him to escort her to dinner when they had no special arrangement, no promise of exclusivity or even a hint of future involvement?

Hadn't they both agreed to keep things casual, no strings and no commitment?

Unfortunately, ever since he'd spent an entire night with her, he realized it would be impossible to continue the pretense of a so-what relationship. He wanted her in his bed each and every evening she was willing to be there, and tonight was no exception.

Easy fix, he told himself. He'd simply take a cab to her condo complex and surprise her. He'd been curious about her living space; what better time to arrive with a magnum of champagne, another half dozen chocolate truffles, and a sincere apology for forgetting their date?

As a precautionary measure, he taped the keys for each of the Sky Tower suites to the underside of his desktop, just in case word got out that he'd been looking for entry to those apartments. Then he tucked the elevator key in his billfold and locked his office door.

He'd memorized Kyra's address and knew the exact location of her complex. After a quick visit to the kitchen for the truffles, and a stop in the hotel's wine cellar for the champagne, he'd hail a taxi and be on his way.

Kyra sat at her desk, drumming her fingernails on her blotter, unsure of what to do. At half past seven o'clock, the Wheel Deal had been over for an hour. The only call she'd received was from Buddy Blue, trying to convince her to take another look at his act—without the "big bossy guy" who had accompanied her last night.

She tried Jake's office for the third time and was connected to his voicemail, but she refused to leave a message. Had his meeting with Rob run over? Listening to the droning ring, she realized Rob was probably out with Lou. Which told her at least one couple was having a little fun tonight.

So much for Jake's dinner invitation, and their discussion of her imaginary cat. And so much for planning to share her last week on Earth with him. He'd been crystal clear when he said the only thing he was interested in was a no-strings relationship, and she now realized he'd meant every word, but she had hoped . . .

Miffed that he hadn't been considerate enough to slide a note under the door, she put on her coat, locked her office, and headed for the parking lot. On the ride home she recited a mental diatribe of the reasons why it was a bad idea to let herself care for him.

What had come over her, fantasizing that an affair with Jake could be anything more than a pleasant diversion? Had avoiding sex for as long as she had warped her brain and twisted her common sense?

What kind of fool was she to think a man like him, someone without roots who gave the impression of hopping from casino to casino, would ever contemplate spending even a week with one special woman?

And what right did she have to hope for anything, when she had her own specific goal: return to Mount Olympus in triumph and live a life of luxurious decadence until the end of time.

She climbed the steps to her condo, zeroed in on Rob's dark apartment, and felt marginally better. At least something was going right for Lou. Thanks to her intervention, whether or not Rob won the singing contest, Lou and Rob would have a happy life together.

In the kitchen, Kyra took out her stash of Orange Milanos, stood at the sink, and wolfed down a half dozen while she thought about the pesky things she *wouldn't* have to concern herself with after she returned to her mountaintop home.

Mortal women were expected to watch their weight, exercise, swallow vitamins, get a yearly mammogram, and visit the dentist regularly. No need for any of that on Mount Olympus, because no one ever got sick or had a cavity.

They had to read newspapers, pay attention to current events, compete with men for jobs and equal wages, while looking their best each and every day. On Olympus, there was no competition for anything because there was no need for money and, in accordance with Zeus's edict, everyone was beautiful.

Further worldly miseries included pantyhose, cellulite, armpit and leg hair, pointy-toed shoes, bad breath, bifocals, wrinkles, and sagging body parts—unnecessary worries for a goddess who needed no physical enhancements. Mortal women even got a monthly curse, and later in life went through menopause, none of which would ever happen to her.

The list of indignities mortals suffered and the chores they had to perform just to stay in step with the world around them seemed never-ending. The only things the females of Mount Olympus had to contend with were soft sunny days, warm breezy nights, and endless bouts of pleasure with whatever god they chose.

It was much wiser to think of Jake Lennox as a form of stress relief, a balm for whatever itch plagued her at the moment, just as Chloe and Zoë did with the men they took to bed. Her sisters had the right idea—love them until they dropped, kiss them good-bye, take off running, and never look back.

And speaking of her sisters, tonight was chat night. She retrieved her cell phone and speed-dialed Zoë's number, then waited while Zoë got Chloe on the line.

"So . . . how is everyone," asked Chloe, her voice oddly tentative. "Anything to report?"

"I'm fine," said Kyra.

"Nothing new here," Zoë added.

"Well, neither of you sound fine," Chloe asserted. "What have the two of you been doing?"

Kyra didn't even want to go there. "Same old, same old," she said, punctuating the sentence with a yawn of boredom.

"Just enjoying my job," said Zoë, though her tone was dour. "Not a thing to report."

Kyra sensed the uneasiness in both her sisters. Maybe, if she concentrated on them, they wouldn't mention Jake. "How's Miss Belle," she asked Chloe.

"Miss Belle is fine. It's her oh-so-perfect grandson who has me in a snit."

"I thought you said he wasn't due home until after your return to Olympus," said Zoë.

"Change in plans—just what I didn't need," Chloe snapped. "He's a selfish, boorish, bully who's always in the way. I can't wait to leave this cursed planet." Her sigh came over the line loud and clear. "But enough about me."

"Zoë, you're awfully quiet," said Kyra, when her sister muse didn't offer another comment.

"Hmm?"

"You're quiet. Don't you have anything to say?"

Zoë's sigh echoed over the line. "Sounds like Chloe is handling things at her end. I just wanted to check in and let you know everything in my life was on schedule."

Kyra remembered her conversation with Hermes and his report on Hera. Her sisters needed to know about the ever-present danger of the father god's vengeful wife. "I had a surprise visitor. Hermes, in his complete winged glory."

"No kidding? I thought he never left the computer room. What did he want?" asked Chloe.

"Zeus sent him. It seems I was too slow responding to his e-mails and it cheezed him off."

Zoë snorted. "You've never been on time, so why start now? Can't the old poop wait another week?"

"That's what I said, but I think Hermes used it as an excuse to warn me personally. Apparently Hera's returned to Earth. Our fellow gods are worried . . . about us."

"Us!?" her sisters chimed.

"Great," said Zoë.

"Well, crap," muttered Chloe.

"The hint was subtle, but I could tell he thought it was important we know. Since none of the others are fans of Hera, they want us to watch our backs."

The silence was deafening. Kyra managed a strangled chuckle. "Lucky for us we're playing by the rules, huh?"

"Of course," mumbled Chloe. "What else would we be doing?"

"Absolutely by the rules," agreed Zoë. "Not to belabor the point, but I have to make this an early night. I'm sort of involved in planning my big exit."

"Me, too," Chloe added. "And remember I love you both, more than I could ever say. You're wonderful sisters, and—well—good night."

"Same here," uttered Zoë.

Coupled with Zoë's strange attitude, Chloe's tender words sent a ripple of fear down Kyra's spine. It wasn't like the fashion maven to be so quiet, or the diva to be so caring. On the plus side, a short session meant she could fall asleep sooner, so she wouldn't have to think about Jake.

"Are we going to have time for a final chat?" she asked. "So we can discuss our glorious reunion and how much fun it will be to laugh in Hera's face together?"

"Um . . . don't count on me for a talk. I have a lot of loose ends to tie up," said Chloe. "Let's just say, 'See you on Olympus' and good night."

"I have to agree with Chloe," said Zoë. "See you on Olympus, and good night."

Puzzled by the direction the call had taken, Kyra signed off in the same manner, and pressed the disconnect button. Something wasn't quite right with either sister, but she hadn't a clue what that might be. Unfortunately, she was too beat to ponder it now. She had enough to handle dealing with her own problems.

Walking to the bedroom, she remembered the lovely nightgown she'd purchased for her special evening with Jake. Too bad it was still in the bag on his coffee table. Sighing, she changed into a diaphanous, thigh-high sleep chiton, brushed her teeth, removed her makeup, and vowed her dalliance with Jake Lennox was at an end.

Easing onto her mattress, she turned out the light, her one wish a peaceful and dreamless night's rest.

Kyra bolted upright in bed. The thumping in her head matched the drumbeat of distant pounding coming from somewhere in the vicinity of the front of her condo.

Was someone knocking on her door?

She glanced at the bedside clock. Who in the world would come calling at midnight?

It's Rob, jazzed about his date with Lou, and ready to fill you in, her brain answered.

Without a thought to her appearance, she jumped off the mattress, shot down the hall, and swung open the door. "Keep it up and someone will call the police," she said in a whispered hiss. "If they haven't al—"

Jake's dark brows rose as he inspected her from head to toe. "Were you expecting someone else?"

Kyra quickly closed her gaping mouth. "Excuse me?"

Bold as a Titan, he strode past her and into the kitchen. After setting a box and a huge bottle of champagne on the table, he slipped the jacket from his broad shoulders and hung it on the back of a chair.

Staring, he ran his gaze over her sleepwear a second time. "Nice outfit."

Kyra made a move to cover herself, then thought better of it. He'd already seen her nude. What was so unnerving about her chiton?

When his heated stare turned molten as lava from a newly erupted volcano, she peered down and noted the reason. The gown was thin as gossamer, and so short it barely covered her hips.

"It's what I sleep in when I'm home. I'm not in the habit of entertaining guests at midnight."

He raised his head and their gazes met. "I'm here to apologize."

"Apologize? For what?" she asked, hoping she sounded blasé and totally disinterested. He'd have to beg on his hands and knees before she'd consider forgiving him.

"I should have called when I realized I wasn't going to make our dinner date, but—"

"Oh, did we have a date?"

"Yes, damn it, we had a date. But something important came up, and I—"

"Something more important than me?"

He rolled his eyes. "Of course not."

"Then you must have forgotten where I was from four until oh, say, six-thirty."

"Um . . . no."

"You got a phone call from your uncle?"

"Themopolis? No."

"You fell from a ladder and broke your leg."

"Shit, Kyra." His lips thinned. "You've canceled on me before, and I always understood."

"And if you remember, I called whenever I did." Stepping back, she stretched out an arm to usher him from the room. "It's late, I'm tired, and you're delusional. Now if you'll just go quietly . . ."

Jake leaned down and pulled a champagne glass from each pocket of his jacket. Grabbing the bottle of bubbly, he went to the sink, set down the flutes, and found a towel. Turning in her direction, he began opening the bottle. "You're right. I know. I'm a jerk."

She gave a bored yawn, and plopped into a chair. "And I'm *so* not in the mood."

The cork popped to the ceiling and bounced off the light fixture before falling to the floor. He poured the foaming wine into the glasses and carried them to the table. "I'm sorry. Please forgive me."

Kyra tamped back a grin. Now they were getting somewhere. She arched a brow. "Not in this lifetime."

He dropped to one knee and offered her a drink. "It won't happen again. I swear."

Better, she thought. But not much. "How do I know that?"

"Because you have my word." He raised his glass and grinned, his blue eyes devouring her. "To us?"

She sighed. Damn, but he knew exactly when to use that sexy, *come here, baby* smile. The temperature in the room rose to blast-furnace level when his stare drifted to the front of her chiton and her peaked nipples jutted against the thin fabric. She sipped at the fizzy liquid, hoping to cool her burning libido, but the bubbles went straight to the apex of her thighs and ignited a slow simmer.

Gazes locked, they finished their wine. Jake rose, removed the glass from her fingers, and set it on the counter. In three steps, he stood before her and pulled her to her feet. His hot-as-Hades smile seared her skin, burning away what little was left of her resolve.

Reaching out, he palmed her breast. "You are amazing." He lifted her in his arms, carried her to the counter, and sat her next to the champagne bottle. Filling his glass, he dipped his finger in the bubbly wine and swirled it around the fabric covering her nipple.

The sizzle in her core spread outward, sending jolts of desire through her body. Jake read her reaction, inserted himself between her open legs, and captured her lips. His tongue teased hers and she tasted the sweet tang of champagne mixed with a potent dose of lust.

He trailed his mouth to her ear, her throat, her collarbone, and finally, the champagne-dampened nipple. Catching the aching tip between his lips, he suckled though the filmy fabric, drawing the throbbing peak into his mouth.

His hand grazed her thigh and inched upward into her damp curls. Inserting a finger between her folds, he circled her clitoris, massaging the pulse point.

Kyra lowered her eyes as bright lights again swirled behind her closed lids. After three long strokes, she cried out with the force of her orgasm.

Trembling in pleasure, Kyra wrapped her legs around his waist, and he lifted her off the counter. "The bedroom. Where is it?" he rasped.

She melted against him. "Down the hall. Hurry."

His chuckle was harsh, desperate. "Baby, you can't imagine how much I want to be inside of you."

Jake stumbled down the corridor, found the bed, and fell on top of her as they tumbled to the mattress. Lost in a battle of wills, he let Kyra roll him to his back. Buttons flew as she ripped his shirt apart and exposed his chest.

He pulled the gown from her shoulders and it pooled at her waist, baring her breasts.

She undid his belt, clawed at his zipper, dragged his pants and boxers to his knees. Then she took him in her hands, bent to lick his engorged shaft and cup his balls. Afraid the touch of her tongue would send him to the point of no return, he ground out, "Wait. I need a condom."

He struggled to reach the pocket of his slacks, found what he wanted and ripped the packet, but Kyra snatched it from his hands and slid the rubber onto his erection. Jake grasped her waist and guided

261

her over and down, impaling her on his penis. Arching up, he slammed against her until he felt himself locked inside her hot, wet core.

She leaned over him and he found her breast, scraped the nipple with his teeth, sucked her into his mouth. Her cries of pleasure spurred him on, faster, deeper, harder, until she shouted her completion in the curve of his neck.

She slumped to his chest and settled her still quivering body on him like a blanket. Jake enveloped her in his arms and held her, stroking her back until her frantic pants became slow, steady, even. Cocooned in her slick warmth, he ran his hands over her rounded bottom. Never happy with stick-skinny women and their store-bought breasts, he reveled in the lush curves and womanly softness he knew belonged to Kyra alone.

She squeezed her honeyed walls, and he moaned. "You're killing me."

"Funny, it feels like you're alive and doing very well."

"Not so funny," he muttered. "I'm barely breathing."

"I thought you worked out in the hotel health club."

"I do. Unfortunately, there's no specific piece of equipment that prepares a man for this type of exercise." He smiled. "The only thing that helps is practice."

She giggled. "Must mean you need dozens of hours of repetition to build up your stamina, huh?"

"After that kind of workout, I think it would be more like hundreds," he said, trying to keep his tone serious.

She gave a contented sigh and burrowed deeper. "Maybe we could start in the morning?"

Thank God she was exhausted, because he wasn't sure he could handle another round right now. She'd worn him out, wrung him dry, used him up in the best way possible. Next time, they'd take it slow, savor the moment, make it last, instead of burning the sheets.

Kyra's breathing turned to a soft humming of breath, and he realized she'd fallen asleep. Easing her off his chest, he tucked her tight against his side, snuggled her head on his shoulder, and pulled the comforter over the both of them. Then he gazed at the shadows playing on the ceiling.

He'd had sex with dozens of women, and most of it had been meaningless. Oh, he'd loved Corinne, or at least he thought he had, until he found out she'd cheated on him. He now realized what they'd had was more the other four-letter word, because lust and love were often confused. After his divorce, he never believed he would find that special woman who could fire both in his life.

Kyra muttered an unintelligible phrase and he grinned, but the smile was short-lived. How in the hell was he going to tell her he'd begun this *affaire* in the hope of wheedling his way into her good graces and trapping her in a lie?

What would she say when she learned he'd been sent here to catch a thief, and she'd been his first suspect?

Now that he was certain she was innocent, how could he put the brakes on this . . . whatever the heck they were doing, and get back on the straight and narrow?

Beautiful, competent, loyal, witty, kind. Kyra was all those things and more, yet there was an innocence about her, a wide-eyed way of looking at things, her computer for instance, that made him laugh. She cared about her job and her friends. Eddie, Rob, and Lou, even the people she graced with her good luck taps, were in her thoughts on a daily basis.

The reality of it all gave him pause. Now what the hell was he supposed to do?

Chapter 17

The next morning, Kyra woke with her bottom nestled firmly against a part of Jake that felt as if it had never gone to sleep. Though his breathing was slow and deep, his hard-as-steel erection prodded her backside, letting her know he wanted her even after their night of passion.

With his muscular arms wrapped securely under her breasts, she sighed with contentment. The protective, almost possessive embrace sent a hum of comfort thrumming through her veins. Lost in a morning daydream, she couldn't help but wonder what it would be like to know Jake was hers not just for the next few days, but forever.

Love 'em and leave 'em, like a smart goddess. Run as fast and as far as you can, and do not—repeat—do not look back.

The mantra played a taunting drumbeat in her brain, returning her quickly to reality. When in Hades would she learn to listen to logic? Even after all the warnings she'd given herself last night, it had taken only one of his seductive smiles and a bit of sweet talking, and she'd fallen straight into bed with the man.

Disgusting!

Why would she be so stupid as to throw away an eternity of decadence for the love of a single mortal? What kind of fool would give up endless days spent lounging on a snow-white cloud populated by immortals with just one thing on their minds: to live in the most pleasurable way possible.

No god with a brain in healthy working order would choose a shorter lifetime of toil over one of splendor, and she'd bet her last sip of ambrosia that if she posed the question to a thousand mortals, each would agree.

She was an idiot to be contemplating these ridiculous thoughts, especially since Jake hadn't once said the L word. Not in the throes of passion, nor in the cuddling afterward. Not even when he tried to coerce her into bed.

He expected her at his side for that moment alone. No promises, no demands. No happily-ever-afters.

Her mind stood still at the very words.

Goddess*

She was already committed to *happily ever after* on Mount Olympus, the only home she'd ever known. To lose it for one man would be more than foolish.

It would be total devastation.

The sensible decision so cheered Kyra, she felt ready to face the day. After carefully removing Jake's hands from around her middle, she inched off the mattress, let the chiton still circling her waist drop to the floor, and tiptoed into the bathroom. A brisk shower was exactly what she needed to put her brain to rights. Then she would offer Jake a mixture of pineapple and orange juice, tea, and toast, the same breakfast she made for herself every morning, and they would leave for the Acropolis.

No sweet words of seduction or tender sighs of longing to muddy the waters and keep them from their scheduled tasks.

She turned on the taps and let the water warm, then opened the curtain and entered the steaming spray. After squirting a froth of frangipani-scented shower gel onto a small towel, she drew the foaming cloth over her shoulders and . . .

"Good morning." The metal rings holding the shower curtain scraped as Jake pushed the plastic aside and stepped into the tub. "Glad to see you're awake and ready to go."

Kyra held the cloth to her breasts and spun in place. Treated to a view of his fully engorged penis throbbing in anticipation, she swallowed. "What are you doing?"

The swirling mist spiked his dark lashes, making his blue eyes sparkle. "Isn't it obvious? I'm taking a shower."

"But—"

"Or should I say *we're* taking a shower. Which, by the way, is the best of morning rituals—get clean and have a little fun at the same time."

"It is?" Could she sound any more stupid? "I mean—since when?"

"Since Adam and Eve and the garden of Eden, I'd imagine. You know, man—woman—water—important body parts slipping and sliding, skin to skin. Trust me, it beats slipping and sliding alone."

Warmth pooled in Kyra's belly, flowing into all the *important* body parts she assumed he was talking about. When faced with the river of water trickling over his well-formed chest, corded stomach, and straining erection, she could barely think straight.

She caught his sexy grin and frowned, turning her back. "It's getting late. The Voice of Vegas walkthrough is scheduled for 10 A.M. We don't have time to fool around."

"I promise it will be worth the time." He plucked the terrycloth from her fingers and began to rub. "Just go with me on this, sweetheart. I'll make it worth your while." With one hand on her belly, he used his other to massage her back in a slow, relaxing circle, moving in downward strokes until he captured her bottom.

"Your ass feels too good to be real." Jake nipped

at the nape of her neck and slid his hand to her breast. "And so do these." Catching a tightened nipple between his thumb and forefinger, he squeezed. "Everything about you is out of this world."

If not for the fact that her knees were buckling, Kyra would have pointed out that, of course, everything about her was *out of this world.* She was a goddess, after all. But when he pulled her rear tight against him and continued to fondle her nipples, a groan was the only sound she could manage.

Moving the cloth to her front, he laved her breasts with one hand while he positioned the other into the curls at the apex of her thighs. She spread her legs in automatic reaction, enabling him to find her sensitive core, and leaned back and into him as he moved his fingers in a slow seductive rhythm. Teasing her most sensitive spot, he brought her to the brink of arousal, just short of cascading over the edge.

Quivering, she grabbed his hand, turned, and gazed into his incredible eyes. "We can't—"

"I know you *think* we can't." He pulled her close and reinserted two fingers, sending shock waves through her system. "But Lord knows it's impossible for me to keep my hands off you." Bending forward, he continued to plague her, sipping at the water trailing down her cheeks, drinking at her lips, invading her mouth with his tongue.

"Just tell me you don't want this," he whispered, rotating his fingers against her most sensitive pulse point. "And I'll leave you alone."

When she whimpered in pleasure, Jake guided her to the tile wall, grasped her by the waist, and raised her up. Levering her onto his erection, he supported her with his arms and captured her lips in another commanding kiss. Then he thrust his hips upward again and again, slipping and sliding those important body parts together until she was wild with need.

His orgasm surged, threatening to burst like an overflowing dam. Kyra rolled her head from side to side, keening his name as her orgasm crested. He shouted hers at the same moment, and gave a final thrust, taking them over the waterfall where they drowned in each other's arms.

Kyra settled against his chest as reality turned to a steamy mist around them. Gently, he eased her to a stand. "If you ask me, that's a damn sight better than an alarm clock." When she didn't comment, he said, "You okay?"

She took a breath, her body trembling on a sigh.

He continued to soothe her with the washcloth, soaping her sensitized skin. Finally, he handed her the cloth and showed his back. "How about you do me while I wash my hair, then I'll get out of here and let you finish."

He braced his hands against the tile and let Kyra soap him, much the way he'd done to her. His muscles flexed under her ministering hands, and he moaned at the heady sensation. Overcome with emotion, he turned to tell her what was in his heart, but the words lodged in his throat. Instead, he kissed her long and deep, then touched his fingers to her cheek, and left the shower.

Kyra's very presence in his life made him feel like a giant among men. Only he knew he wasn't. In fact, there was only one thing he knew for certain.

He was well and truly fucked.

Jake sat at the kitchen table, admiring Kyra's curvaceous figure while she made a fuss over their breakfast. Dressed in a tasteful navy skirt, white blouse, sexy black hose, and red sling-back pumps, she put him to shame. But there wasn't a thing he could do about his buttonless shirt and rumpled slacks until he returned to his hotel room.

It was a kick seeing her in the role of a domestic goddess, though it was obvious her skills were limited. When he'd offered to take her out to breakfast, she'd insisted on fixing a meal for both of them, and he'd decided to let her do whatever made her comfortable.

"I know it's not very hearty," she said, setting a plate of toast in front of him. "But it's all I have in the pantry."

"I'll need more food than this if we keep burning calories the way we did this morning," he teased.

"Unfortunately, we're running late, so you're not going to get your wish." She brought glasses of juice to the table and took the chair across from him, her expression noncommittal. "I guess you're used to the fancy meals provided by the hotel kitchen."

271

"Yeah, but that gets old fast." She passed him a jar of orange marmalade, and he cleared his throat. He'd thought about it, and decided this might be the time to share his earlier thoughts, but the words "Got any peanut butter?" slipped from his mouth before he had a chance to stop them.

Kyra took a dainty bite, then chewed and swallowed. "No. Is peanut butter good?"

"Don't tell me you've never tasted peanut butter."

"I . . . uh . . . of course, I have," she said, worrying her lower lip. "Just not on toast. I guess I should try it."

"Definitely. My mom used to make peanut butter on toast for me almost every morning while I lived at home. She's a great cook, but she always tried to make what I enjoyed." Relieved his subconscious had deemed it too soon to divulge his feelings, he reached across the table and entwined their free fingers. "I'll bring a jar the next time I plan to stay the night."

"You're going to make a habit of these . . . surprise visits?"

"Does the thought of my coming here unannounced bother you?" he asked, trying to keep his tone casual.

She unlaced their fingers and wrapped both hands around her juice glass. "No, but there might come a day when . . . I'm not here. Then what would you do?"

"Find you, of course. Unless you left town without telling me." He frowned at the thought. "I thought you were happy at the Acropolis?"

"I am. I was joking."

You could move in with me, he almost blurted, but swallowed those words, as well. "If you don't approve of my coming here without calling, just say the word. I don't want to be a pain, Kyra, but I do want us to . . . take the time to see where this attraction leads."

"You're not a pain," she quickly said. "At least, not when you're being sweet. Like now."

There was that sappy word again. But if being sweet bought him points with Kyra, he'd get used to the girlie expression. "I'll try to be *sweet* more often," he promised. "Especially after a night like the last one. A couple more and I'll need vitamins."

"I . . . it was . . ." She inhaled a breath. "I'm glad you came over, even though it was late."

"Sorry, it won't happen again."

Kyra simply smiled as she finished her toast. Then she stood and cleared the table, depositing the dishes in the sink. After that, she slipped into a red wool blazer and hoisted her tote bag over her shoulder. "What else did your mother do special for you?"

"Anything and everything." He raised a brow as hope blossomed in his chest. "Why, are you planning to serve me dinner?"

"Only if you want to starve. This breakfast was the top of my meal list." She trotted into the foyer, then poked her head around the corner. "You coming or am I leaving without you?"

Jake wasn't sure why, but somehow their conversation had gotten off track. Kyra's suddenly dismissive attitude was not what he expected, and he wasn't sure how to proceed. He'd been prepared to tease her about her lack of culinary skill, then offer to have her meet his mother and take a few lessons, as a sort of lead in to the possibility of their living together. He now realized that might be the furthest thing from her mind.

He followed her into the hall and waited while she locked her door, then strode beside her as she headed outside jingling her keys. After hitting the automatic door lock, she said, "And before you ask, no, you cannot drive my car."

"Why can't I drive? I'm good behind the wheel."

"Seems to me a *good* driver would have his own automobile." She batted her eyelashes. "Don't you agree?"

Grinning, he opened her door, then hurried around and slid in the passenger side. "I never lived long enough in one place to bother with a car." And when he was home, he drove the SUV he'd bought his mother. "I planned to shop for something this spring." *After I sew up this job.*

He took in the sedan's luxurious leather interior, walnut paneled dash, and top-of-the line stereo system. Still curious how she could afford the BMW on her salary, he said, "This is some set of wheels. Must have cost a bundle."

"My father gave it to me." She fired the ignition. "Though I didn't ask for it."

"Nice gesture," Jake commented. "Sounds like he's an okay guy. Maybe I should meet him."

Kyra tromped on the gas pedal and the car shot from the parking space. "You can't—I mean you wouldn't like him if you met him. He's controlling and nosy and pushy and . . . and . . . oh, never mind. Forget I said anything."

"You and your dad don't get along?"

"Not as well as it sounds like you and your mother do. I think that's sweet, by the way."

Jake stifled a snort as she pulled into traffic and picked up the pace. He drove at a good clip himself, but when Kyra breezed through a yellow light, he cringed. "You do know yellow means it's time to stop?"

"Yellow means it's time to step on the gas," she countered, peering past the steering wheel with a look of determination on her face.

They careened around the next corner, and Jake clutched the strap hanging over his window and held onto his seat belt with his other hand. "Are you aware there's a speed limit, and it's about fifteen miles per hour *less* than what you're going?"

"There aren't ever any police on the road at this time of the morning," she lectured. "Where's your sense of adventure?"

"I guess I left it in your bedroom," he quipped, but her laughter didn't induce him to release his death grip.

When the next light turned from red to green just before Kyra coasted through the intersection, he swallowed a curse. By the time they arrived at the hotel he was worn out from jamming his foot against the floor and holding his tongue for fear of making Kyra angry. He wasn't sure whether she had the timing down perfectly, or she was the luckiest driver on the planet, but she'd managed to hit every light at the exact moment it turned color.

Finally at the Acropolis, they walked in side by side, giving Jake a chance to calm his nerves. He thought of Herb watching them from the surveillance screens, and pulled his sports coat closed to cover his gaping shirt. After this morning, there was no way he could lie about his and Kyra's friendship, and he had a sinking feeling Herb was going to rub it in whenever he could.

Intent on skulking to his suite to change, he skidded to a stop when Kyra halted abruptly in front of the huge statue of Zeus in the entryway. As usual, she flipped the sculpture the bird, which brought a full-blown smile to his lips.

"I just have to know, why do you do that every morning when you come in?"

She wrinkled her nose. "At first, I did it because I was angry for something that happened—something over which I had no control. Now it's just a habit . . . most of the time." She gazed at the statue with a stony smile. "Do you think he's real?"

"Zeus?" Jake asked. "Not a chance. I mean, he's a

myth, one of many gods some of the ancient civilizations once believed in. Sort of the way the early pioneers thought of Paul Bunyan and his pal Babe, or how we think of Bigfoot now."

"Big ego, is more like it," she muttered. Then she sauntered past him, turned and said, "I'll see you later today, but I've got a ton of work, so I'm not sure when."

Jake went to his room and changed clothes. No doubt about it, being with Kyra beat gambling in Monte Carlo and every other glamorous place on the map he'd visited, and not just because of the way she handled a car. She was a trip . . . an entertaining and exciting journey he wouldn't mind taking for the rest of his life. And soon, he would tell her so.

He shook his head at the thought. Man oh man, he had it bad. He had to concentrate on his current objective or he was going to screw himself big time and not in a good way. He'd been so absorbed in the idea of surprising Kyra in the shower, he hadn't even used a condom. Something he never forgot to do.

When he reached his office, he picked up his voicemail and noted there was only one message from Rob, saying he could meet for lunch to discuss his findings. The time line was all right with Jake. He just hoped he could keep his mind on business, instead of Kyra.

Because nothing he did could rid his mind of the way she'd looked in the shower. Her russet hair had framed her face in a cap of ringlets, and her damp silky skin had glistened like a living work of art. She'd reminded him of a painting he'd once seen in a museum. The female subject of *Venus Rising From the Sea* gazed at the viewer as if begging for the touch of a man's hand, just the way Kyra had stared at him this morning.

He flexed his fingers and swore he could still feel her trembling under his palms while he stroked her to a climax. Closing his eyes, he envisioned her expression of wonder when she saw his aching hard-on. Thanks to his regular workouts, he had nothing to be ashamed of in the male equipment department, but he couldn't remember any of his past lovers ever looking at him as if they were a cat who wanted to lap him like a bowl of cream, the way Kyra had.

He glanced down at the spreadsheet on his blotter and forced his mind to focus. The form clearly stated that Fast Track Design and Restoration had been receiving a hefty amount of cash, over a million bucks a month, for the past year.

When Themopolis had asked him to take on this task, he'd never brought the remodeling project to the table, but that wasn't unusual. Unless brand new, the big casinos were always going through some sort of updating: replacing wallpaper in the suites, new carpeting and paint in the hallways, a change of art throughout the building. Sometimes hotels remodeled entire floors, one or two at a time, just as it appeared they were doing here.

There were several explanations Jake considered reasonable for the current irregularity. Maybe Fast Track Design and Restoration required a big down payment, and the job had been suspended until the entire amount was paid. Or Ardmore had decided on the renovations himself in hopes of impressing Mr. T, but he'd gotten sidetracked because, as Herb had said, there were material shortages.

He'd even go so far as to believe the problem was due to some type of labor dispute that had halted the job before it began. Nothing else made sense, which led to a glaring problem. Something was rotten in Vegas.

Right now, Herb was investigating the security clearance for the design firm and its workers, while Rob was scoping out the contracts and snooping around accounting. In the interim, he'd assigned himself another chore, and it was about time he got to it.

He dialed the number imprinted at the top of the spreadsheet. After several rings, he heard a standard taped message. Well, hell. He could try calling information for another number, but he had no address. He knew it was useless to take a look at the disk, because he'd already checked, and there was no contact name or other data on file.

Jake scratched his jaw. Then he punched in a number he'd used so often in the past week he knew it by heart. The phone was answered on the third ring. "Mr. Themopolis's office. How may I help you?"

279

Taken aback by the live but oddly accented voice, Jake wasn't sure what to say. "Ah . . . Jake Lennox for Mr. T."

"He's not in at the moment. Can I help you?"

The unfamiliar speaker confused him. "Maybe, I mean, who are you?"

"His administrative assistant," the woman answered, as if Jake were phoning from the planet Jupiter. "Would you like to leave a message?"

Hell yes, he almost shouted. "Ask him to call me at his Vegas hotel, please. He'll know what it's about."

"Will do," she said in a too-chirpy tone.

Jake set the receiver in the cradle and leaned back in his chair. At least he'd spoken to a human being instead of a machine, which meant he was one step closer to getting Themopolis's attention.

He checked the time and noted it was noon. He had to get cracking on this case, before he could settle things with Kyra. He wasn't going to ask her to take a chance on him unless he had a regular paycheck and a future. He wouldn't do to her what his dad had done to his mom.

His next call was to Rob. They had plenty to discuss, and it was time they got down to it.

Chapter 18

Kyra sighed as she viewed her piled-high, paper-strewn desk. She was getting nowhere fast with the work she had for the Voice of Vegas. The walk-through rehearsal had gone well, but unless she concentrated the event would be a grand fizzle instead of the grand finale with which she was hoping to end her time on Earth.

Unfortunately, her libido refused to listen to her brain.

Whenever she closed her eyes she envisioned Jake, water cascading down his hard-muscled chest, his ripped abs, and his thick shaft waiting for her to welcome him into her arms. Then she remembered how the touch of his demanding mouth, gentle hands, and invading fingers had made her feel. Before she knew it, she became so itchy in *those* places she had to squirm in her seat just to get a little relief.

If this kept up, she'd have to do something drastic like . . . like . . .

She raised her head at the knock. Anything to get her mind off Jake. "It's open."

Lou poked her head around the door. "You got a minute?"

"I've got hours for you," Kyra said, grinning. "I was going to drop by the floor later to ask how it went last night."

The waitress sat in the chair across from her and gave an innocent smile. "How what went?"

Kyra quirked her lips. "Don't be so smug. Your date with Rob? How did it go?"

"What makes you think we went on a date?"

"For one thing, you didn't have your car, and he's too much a gentleman to let a girl take the bus, so of course he asked to drive you home. I also assume that you, being the intelligent woman you are, said yes."

"Okay." Lou heaved a sigh. "I said yes."

"Then it stands to reason he also asked you out."

Her expression turned solemn. "Okay, he did. After he drove to my apartment, he insisted on meeting my mother and Katie, then he took us all out to dinner. When we returned, I invited him in, and Mom was smart enough to put Katie and herself to bed without a comment. We talked for hours, and it was . . . nice."

Kyra remembered where her *dates* with Jake always landed, and decided to be blunt. "Did you have sex?"

"Kyra!" Lou's shriek echoed in the room. She held her hands to her face. "No, but I wanted to." When she raised her gaze, tears glimmered in her eyes. "I really really wanted to."

"Oh, honey," said Kyra, connecting with her friend's misery. "It's okay to admit you're crazy for the man."

The waitress sniffled, then dabbed at her cheeks. "It's not only that . . . I mean it is . . . he is. It's just, well, I never thought I'd feel this way again."

"What way?"

"As if I'm heading over Niagara Falls without a barrel. After Mom put Katie to bed, I completely forgot about both of them and went to sleep thinking of Rob. I woke up with a vision of him burned into my eyelids. I even saw his face in the jam I spread on my toast. I—it's—"

"Yessss?" said Kyra, worried because she had the identical reaction to Jake.

"My stomach turns inside out whenever I think of him, and it's only been forty-eight hours since we met in person. If this continues, I'll go nuts."

"So do something about it," Kyra advised. *Like I've done*, she wanted to add, but couldn't voice it out loud. It wouldn't do to let Lou know how she felt about Jake.

"Not so easy. I think I'm falling in love with him. And that's impossible!"

Kyra gave herself a mental pat on the back for not using the L word where Jake was concerned, and focused on one of the more positive things she'd accomplished in her time here: seeing to it Rob and Lou got together. "No, it's wonderful."

Lou reached for a tissue from the box sitting on the corner of Kyra's desk. After blowing her nose, she shrugged. "I just wish he returned the feelings."

"Didn't he say so?"

"Not in so many words, but . . ."

"Did he kiss you?"

"Oh, man, did he ever."

"And you kissed him back?"

"As if I was sucking on a ripe peach. It was . . . embarrassing."

Kyra giggled. "Then what's the problem?"

"Fear of rejection. Fear of making a fool of myself . . . again. Fear of heartache so cutting it hurts just to think about it." Lou exhaled a weary-sounding breath. "I'll only have myself to blame if I fall for the guy, even though I already decided I'll survive if it doesn't work out. I can live with being rejected. I'll even accept being called a fool. But what can I do to protect my heart?"

The words resounded in Kyra's head, bringing her own biggest concern to the fore. No matter how strongly she wanted to be recalled to Mount Olympus, she cared for Jake. Would she be able to leave him, knowing her heart would probably break into a thousand pieces once she did?

"Sorry to sound so depressing," muttered Lou. "Let's change the subject. How are things going with the competition?"

"Fairly well," Kyra answered. "Rob did a great job at the walk-through. I'm supervising a full rehearsal this afternoon, and tomorrow, I have a lunch meeting with the judges."

"Sounds as if you're up to your fanny in work. Funny, Rob didn't mention a thing about a walk-through, or the rehearsal," said Lou, frowning.

"It'll be a practice with the director and cameramen, to get the singers used to their spots on stage and warm up with the orchestra. Then we'll go over costumes with wardrobe. We have one more dress rehearsal before the big night, and a short pre-show practice."

"Doesn't sound like enough to me."

"It has to be. The event's a sellout, the schedule's been promoted in the papers, radio, and television. It's too late to postpone now. I can't wait to see Rob win. How about you?"

Lou's face crumpled as her crying jag took an encore. Kyra grabbed a tissue, and began to blot. "Now what did I say?"

"It's no-not you," Lou muttered between sobs. "I'm being stu-u-pid. Just ig-ig-nore me."

Kyra gazed at the ceiling. "That's kind of tough to do. Here." She passed her friend another tissue, then sat on the edge of the desk while Lou gathered her composure. "Mind telling me what's so terrible?"

"Rob's going to win and become famous—a huge star with a real career. He'll have so many beautiful woman chasing after him he won't give me a second look."

"There's a good chance his career will take off, but the rest wouldn't happen in a million years," Kyra stated.

Lou gazed at her through red-rimmed eyes. "I wish Rob looked at me the way Jake looks at you."

"Jake—at me?" Kyra blinked in shock. "What way is that?"

The waitress blew into her tissue. "Obviously, you've never paid attention to the man. Whenever you talk, he stares as if you were a glass of ice-cold beer, and he's just crawled in from the desert." She gave a watery smile. "Jeesh, for all your talk about past experience, I would have thought you'd recognize the signs by now."

"Jake and I have an arrangement. We've promised to keep things impersonal. Instead of getting involved, we're going to have fun together for as long as it lasts, then move on."

"Hah! That's just an excuse, because you're afraid of letting go, like I am, I guess." Lou rubbed her nose. "We're a pair, aren't we?"

"You and Rob were made for each other. The jury's still out on me and Jake." She hefted her tote bag. "Let's grab a bite, then go to the seamstress for your fitting."

* * *

Rob had arrived in Jake's office with sandwiches for lunch, his jaw rigid, his fingers clenched. For the past thirty minutes, they'd gone over the details Jake had amassed on the spreadsheet. Impressed by the soon-to-be-crowned king of crooners' show of temper, Jake raised a brow. Since they'd met, he'd never seen the guy show any specific emotion other than dogged cheerfulness. The moment Garrett had a good look at the spreadsheet, he was a changed man. If he learned to channel his anger into determination, he had an excellent shot at winning that competition.

"I want the whole story, everything you know from top to bottom," Rob ground out. "I don't condone crooks, especially if they're in a position of trust."

Damn right, Jake silently agreed. "I'm still putting the pieces together. It's going to take some thinking, and Herb's findings, to get it straight."

Rob speared him with a glare and began to pace. "I think it's time you told me what is going on, don't you?"

Well, hell. Wouldn't that sit well with Mr. T?

"I suppose you want the entire story, beginning with the real reason I'm here."

Nodding, Rob sat down across from Jake and folded his arms.

Jake glossed over his past, and began a sketchy story of his last meeting with Themopolis, telling Rob no more than what was needed to appease the

287

singer's temper. Then he got to his inspection of the towers and the little he'd found in the way of a remodeling job.

Rob went ballistic as soon as he heard that, aside from some paint cans and drop cloths, there hadn't been so much as a change of wallpaper in the penthouse suites. Though he was wasting his ire on something he could do little about, it appeared the guy planned to involve himself come hell or high water.

"So tell me," Jake began, hoping to settle Rob down. "How did you convince the geeks in accounting to let you into their precious files?"

Rob stopped wearing a path in the carpet and turned, his expression a couple of notches lower than red alert. "I just told them I ran a monthly recovery program and discovered a glitch in the system. Said it wouldn't affect them now, but come end of the quarter, it would be a real headache." He shrugged. "You know bean counters. The second they hear 'trouble' and 'end of quarter' in the same sentence, they start tearing their hair out. After that, I had a quiet corner to myself and open access to the books."

"Not bad," Jake stated. "In fact, I'd say there's hope for you yet."

"What's that supposed to mean?" snapped Rob.

"Nothing, and take it easy. I'm not the enemy here."

Rob grabbed a chair from a corner of the office, set it in front of the desk, and sat in a straddle. "Then who is?"

"Isn't it obvious? Rupert Ardmore."

"Considering whose computer you got that file from, I guessed as much, but I had to hear it from you. What I want to know is *how*."

"It's conjecture on my part, but from the specs on the spreadsheet, I'd say Fast Track Design and Restoration is a dummy company Ardmore's been funneling hotel money through for the past year, maybe longer. It all depends on how he's rigged the remodeling budget."

"A whole year? And no one suspected?" Rob shook his head. "I find it hard to believe."

"Because . . ."

"Because everything in this business, down to the bolts holding the slots in place, is under scrutiny. The auditors and accountants stick their fingers in the casino records, on and off, all year long."

"That's one of the reasons he's been able to get away with it. It's not the casino he's skimming from—it's the hotel."

"How?"

"The hotel reports combined monthly incomes of lodging, food, and spa services, but the gambling numbers are kept separately. The hotel records undergo a basic monthly report until the end of the fiscal year. That's when its books will be turned inside out, and even then, what accountant would wander to the Sky Tower to verify work was being done? Ardmore is in charge. If he says pay the bill, it gets paid."

Judi McCoy

"He won't be able to continue the scam much longer."

"Yep."

"What do you think he'll do then?"

Jake tapped the end of a pencil on the blotter. "He's socked away a tidy sum, and he's clever. Since it's getting close to crunch time, he'll probably fly the coop and land in the Grand Caymans. The island's been the Switzerland of shady deals since the eighties; you can deposit any amount of money into one or a dozen of their many banks, no questions asked, and there's no reporting to Uncle Sam. It's a perfect place for a crook to spend the winter and celebrate his success."

"You sound pretty sure of the guy."

"Just a healthy guess."

"So how does Kyra figure into it?"

"That's personal," Jake said, his voice low.

"I assume you finally told her what we're doing?"

"I'll get to it."

Shaking his head, Rob said, "Besides the fact that the two of you are dating and you're working on a project together, you found the spreadsheet on her computer. I think you owe her some kind of explanation . . . before she asks."

Staring at the pencil, Jake kept mum. He wasn't about to let anyone tell him how to handle his relationship with Kyra, even if he had no idea what to do about it himself. Sooner or later, something would—

290

Rob stood. "You have to tell her. She's a smart woman, and she might come up with an angle we haven't thought of."

"I don't want her involved in this." *Or have her find out she was a prime suspect.* "If Ardmore thinks I'm on to him before we have all the evidence, he could get desperate, and desperation often leads to violence. My aim is to keep her, and anybody else working with me, safe."

"What's in this for you? Did Mr. T offer you a big reward or something?"

"Let's just say if things go as planned, I'll be your new boss. Unless, of course, you ace that singing contest."

Rob started to smile. Then he glanced at his watch and his eyes bugged. "Oh, hell, I'm late for my second rehearsal."

Herb took that moment to stroll into the room, his bulldog-like face set in frustration. Rob ran past him without a word. "What was that all about?"

"He's got a lot on his plate, but he'll handle it," Jake said with a laugh, then he eyed the overhead camera. "I assume you remembered to turn off the surveillance room Cyclops?"

"Damn straight," said Herb, commandeering Rob's chair. "It's been a tough row to hoe. I had to make a dozen phone calls, wait for people to call me back, even listen to remodeling professionals complain about the state of the industry. As of my last phone conversation, I'm ninety-nine percent positive there is no physical company by the name of Fast Track Design and Restoration."

"Just the dummy number I called."

"Yep." Herb tossed a manila folder on the blotter. "The phone bill goes to a PO box in town. There's no business by that name registered with the building authority. Permits only go back two years, but there hasn't been one issued to the company during that time, and none of the trade unions, electricians, plumbers and such, have ever had anyone on their roster working for them. The video cams in the Sky Tower have been shut down for close to fourteen months, and far as I can tell, there's never been any investigation run on an outside contractor."

"Rob is supposed to go back to accounting and get copies of the canceled checks or find out where the payments are going."

Herb leaned forward in the chair. "I'm still not sure how Ardmore managed it."

Jake gave him a quick run-down of his theory.

"Makes sense to me," said Herb when he finished.

"So we're in agreement," said Jake. "Everything stays between the three of us until I clue in Mr. T. Understood?"

The day passed in a blur. Kyra hadn't seen Jake since they'd driven to the Acropolis together, and she wasn't about to go looking for him. The walk-through had gone well, and the first full rehearsal was scheduled to begin in a few minutes. Willing her feet to take wing, she made it to the pavilion with seconds to spare, and found the director and camera crew already working with the contestants for the show.

The orchestra tuned up, while one of the female singers stood by a grand piano and practiced her number. Other entrants milled about the stage, getting their orders from a production assistant. Kyra recognized the competitors, who'd been introduced to her yesterday morning. The entire group consisted of three women and three men, all about the same age, who seemed eager, willing, and hungry for fame.

Taking further stock of the singers, she realized one of them was missing. Where the heck was Rob?

In a panic, she used a house phone and left a message on both his voicemail and Jake's. Then she called the front desk and asked them to keep an eye out. There was little else she could do but cross her fingers and hope he hadn't forgotten or been called to a meeting and couldn't break free.

Kyra chatted with the group in general as she accompanied them to the dressing rooms. After the walk-through, the contestants had discussed clothes with the head stylist and gone over what they might wear for the performance. The stylist had taken everyone's opinion into consideration, including Kyra's, and reported she had a trailer full of clothing available for their use. Now, the wardrobe assistants were on hand with a variety of gowns for the women and a choice of tuxedos for the men that Kyra hoped would be to each singer's liking.

A few minutes later, consultants arrived to speak with the contestants about their hair and makeup, which would be done by individual stylists immediately before the show. Listening to the chatter of professionals who took pride in their work, Kyra had to admit the Voice of Vegas was turning into a class act, instead of the pop idol-blue jeans-and-T-shirt free-for-all it could have been.

She surveyed the singers as they filed back to the stage. One by one, each vocalist ran through his or her number with the orchestra, while the others stood in a corner or disappeared behind the huge viewing screens to study alone. The girl Rob had compared to Alicia Keyes was quiet, almost shy, but her voice was lovely. Kyra decided the other female entrants were a bit too brassy to do justice to the title Voice of Vegas and put them out of the running in her mind. And neither of the men had Rob's hunky good looks or the deep rich baritone that set his voice apart.

With each passing moment, Kyra felt more confident of the computer guru's chances at winning, and threw herself into the rehearsal with gusto. She'd already coerced the director into believing Rob would be there shortly, but she couldn't continue to make excuses. If word got out he wasn't prompt, and the negative trait leaked to the judges, it might go against him in the voting.

The production assistant called everyone in a huddle and Kyra hurried to join them. "Ms. Degodessa," said the director when they arrived on their marks. "We're still missing two important pieces of the show."

Two? She knew about Rob, but who else was missing? As she did a quick recap of the names, Buddy Blue bounded onto the stage.

"Never fear. Blue is here." He snapped his chewing gum for emphasis. "Better late than never." He put an arm around Kyra. "Hi'ya, doll. How ya doin'?"

The director narrowed his eyes, then raised them to the ceiling as if praying for patience. "Okay, we'll start the run-through from beginning to end. Mr. Blue, I assume you know what's expected?"

"Hey, D-man, I could do this gig with my eyes closed, and still get a standing ovation from the fans. Ain't that right, doll?" Buddy commented to Kyra.

"I certainly hope so," she replied, squirming from under his possessive hold. A noise at the front of the auditorium made her turn. The massive double doors swung open and she breathed a sigh of relief when Rob trotted down the aisle. After apologizing profusely to the director and the other contestants, he stood tall, paid attention, and quickly got into the swing of things.

Kyra calmed as the show took shape. Rob had gotten her so worried, she didn't know whether to kiss him or kill him. When he sang his number with the full orchestra, her confidence grew. Between fussing over him and thinking about Jake, she was worn out, but her hopes were high.

Unfortunately, she still had to take care of the afternoon drawing. If Jake wasn't around when the Wheel Deal finished, she'd weather it in stride and think about the wonderful things in store for her on Mount Olympus.

She didn't need anything from a mortal man to make her life complete. She was a goddess, in charge of her destiny.

Chapter 19

Kyra ran the Wheel Deal and made sure there was a winner. Then she waited in the lobby, bombarded by jovial tourists and the clanging of slot machines, until she assumed Jake was a no-show. Torn between phoning his office and hotel suite to locate him, or simply going home, she opted for the latter. The less time she spent with the man, the easier it would be to leave when Zeus called her home.

On her way to the employee parking lot, she ran into Lou. "Have you heard from Rob?" Kyra asked as they fell into step together.

"Nope. And he didn't turn up on the casino floor this afternoon, either."

"He was late for the dress rehearsal, too. I wanted to clobber him."

Lou stopped when they reached her ancient gray sedan. "I'm so confused. I thought Rob would ask to see me again, tonight—at least he hinted that he would. I can't help thinking I'm being dumped before we even have a second date."

"Rehearsal went overtime," said Kyra, not telling her that Rob had barely made it for one run-through. "Besides, it's *so* not Rob's style. He'd be man enough to tell you if he didn't want to see you anymore."

"I don't understand how you can be such a cheerleader for the guy. How well do you know him, really?" asked Lou, the suspicion in her voice clear.

"Very well, and not in the way you're implying. He's a nice man with a crush on you I'm certain will develop into something more, if it hasn't already. I'd lay odds on it."

Lou rested her backside against the driver's door. "Okay, okay. I'm sorry. And I apologize for talking about my love life like it's a broken record, when you look more dejected than I feel. Since you're heading to your car, I assume you don't have a date with Mister Tall, Dark, and Dangerous. Or do you?"

"I haven't seen or heard from Jake since this morning, when we—" Kyra almost said "drove in together," but realized that would be a mistake. Lou didn't need to know every detail of the arrangement she had with the man. "When we parted in the lobby, he mentioned that he and Rob had more to discuss. Maybe they went someplace to talk and they're still going over things."

"Maybe." Lou chewed on her lower lip. "Do you have an inkling as to what they're working on? Rob's a computer person, and Jake doesn't fit the mold, so I can't imagine what they have in common."

"I'm not sure, either, but I have a suspicion it's the reason Rob is distracted. I don't really know what Jake does here." She figured the project had something to do with the document that had popped up on her PC, but she'd given her promise not to mention it to anyone.

"There's plenty of speculation around the hotel. Eddie says he got word from a reliable source that Jake really isn't Mr. T's nephew. Says a couple of people know it for a fact, and it's raised some eyebrows."

Kyra made a mental note to question Jake on his job and the spreadsheet. If she ever saw him alone again. "Guess I should ask him about it."

Lou opened and closed her mouth. "You really don't know?"

"We've discussed his job, in a roundabout way, but he's never given me a definite answer," said Kyra, confused by the anger inching through her system. Even though their relationship was supposed to be casual, she thought Jake trusted her enough to be truthful. Unless he was involved in something illegal or dishonest . . .

"Then you should ask. Gosh, I'd be so curious I'd pester him like crazy or worry he was . . . ."

"He was what?"

"Nothing."

"You're not getting off that easily," said Kyra, crossing her arms. "What should I be worried about?"

Lou studied her fingernails. "I'm sorry I said anything."

"Come on, tell me what you think you know."

"Okay, but don't say I'm nutty until you hear me out." She straightened, then scanned the parking lot as if preparing to spout military intelligence. "What if they're planning something that's not quite . . . legal?"

Shocked Lou had read her mind, Kyra snorted a laugh. "Why in the world would Rob do that, when he's about to take the city by storm? He's going to be a national singing sensation."

"Maybe, but there's no guarantee."

"Even if that were a possibility, and I'm not saying it is, Jake seems fairly well off to me. Why would he need more money?"

"Maybe it's not the money, but the power. His man-of-the-world attitude reminds me of a risk-taker, someone who enjoys being in the hot seat. The idea of scamming a major casino might appeal to his sense of adventure. Remember *Ocean's Eleven*—and *Twelve*." Lou snapped her fingers. "It's so clear—don't you see the resemblance? Jake is like

300

George Clooney, Brad Pitt, and Matt Damon, all rolled into one. I wouldn't be surprised if—"

"Will you listen to yourself?" Kyra practically hooted. "You're talking about a movie scenario, not real life. Men who are that over-the-top don't exist." Okay, so Jake was a professional gambler, or at least it's what he'd told her. And he did impress her as someone who enjoyed *living large*, as people often described high rollers. He'd even introduced her and Terpsichore to a whale, so he had friends with money. He might not be Mr. T's nephew, but they had to have some connection or he wouldn't have been able to waltz in and take over the way he had.

"It's common knowledge that, in this town, money greases the wheels," Lou continued. "Maybe Jake's tired of being a working stiff, and he plans to make a killing at Mr. T's expense. He's befriended Rob, because Rob's a computer nerd who knows how to get into the system and—"

"Stop it right there," said Kyra, raising a hand. Even if she couldn't reassure Lou by explaining the spreadsheet or mentioning Rupert Ardmore, she could talk sense. "You're starting to sound like an amateur sleuth from one of those old detective movies. I'll simply ask Jake, flat out, what he and Rob are doing, and I'm sure he'll tell me."

A gust of wind blew across the lot, and both women shivered. Lou sighed, then her face brightened. "Say, how about you follow me home? It's Mom's night to play bingo, which means delivery pizza for dinner and a video from the rental palace for Katie. We can get a cartoon for her and watch one of those detective movies after I put her to bed. Maybe Bogie can shed a little light on what Rob and Jake are up to."

"Sounds good to me," agreed Kyra. It would serve Jake right if he came to her condo, and she was gone. "Lead the way."

Sitting at his desk, Jake weighed the possibilities. He had two choices: go to the Sky Tower penthouses now and take photos of the untouched suites or wait until early morning, when the hotel was quiet and there was less activity.

Going now was good, because there was so much happening in the casino during the evening that every able body was occupied. But it was bad because more people and guards meant more prying eyes to monitor his actions.

If he waited, there would be less security, but his taking the penthouse elevator would make it easier for the few who were around to see him and report the trip to Ardmore. Who knew which of the guards had orders to follow anyone going to those floors, and what they were supposed to do if it happened?

Neither was a comforting scenario, but he had to choose one or the other in order to continue his investigation.

Checking his watch, he frowned, then checked his

voicemail. Kyra had called, but she was looking for Rob, not him. And he didn't blame her for the snub. He'd been so involved with Herb that he'd forgotten to contact her, which probably had her spitting mad. Sure, he could cab to her apartment, as he'd done last night, but he was fairly certain she'd be ticked as a wet cat if he awakened her from a sound sleep for the second evening in a row—even if it was for fantastic sex.

He'd groveled so often in the last couple of days his knees ached, so he decided to postpone the next round until tomorrow. He'd go upstairs now, and take those photos. Then he'd have proof positive the money allocated to Fast Track Design and Restoration wasn't being used as it was intended.

Rob's mission, to talk his way into accounting and find out about the checks, was the key. If the casino's returned checks were handled the same way as most were these days, the accountants never saw an actual canceled check unless they requested it from the bank. And no one in the department would do so, because they figured the expense was legit.

Jake tucked the camera he'd been given by Herb into his jacket pocket and untaped the keys hidden on the underside of his desk drawer. Then he took the stairs to the main level. The senior guard had promised the date and time would be recorded at the bottom of the photos so there would be no mistaking the evidence. When the pictures were developed, he'd add them to the file he'd amassed and send another message to Mr. T telling the hotel magnate to get to town ASAP, because he was ready to reveal his findings.

As he climbed the staircase, a vision of Kyra slipped into his mind. He imagined her sassy attitude and stormy scowl when he hadn't appeared after the Wheel Deal this afternoon. The way he kept dropping off the radar screen like a phantom fighter jet gave her every reason to be angry. He had a lot to make up for in their relationship, and he intended to spend the rest of his life doing so.

Aside from this mess with Ardmore, all he'd been able to think about was being with Kyra—in his bed, at her condo, even sharing a ride to the office, though he'd put his life in jeopardy by doing so. It didn't matter where, as long as he could breathe her air, bask in her smile, and listen to her laugh. It might take a while, but he'd make her understand why he couldn't tell her the real reason for working at the Acropolis. He only hoped to heaven she never found out he'd begun their relationship with a lie.

He realized that what had started out, for him, as an act of redemption, was now a step toward their future.

He was almost ready to confess that he loved her, and he wanted to spend the rest of his life with her. But besides offering himself, he wanted to give her something his father had never given his mother: the gift of security.

He'd begun his marriage to Corinne on the road, expecting his wife to wait patiently at home while he made a killing, the same as his dad had done. By the time he recognized his error, he was repeating the emotionally damaging pattern, and it was too late. His ex had found someone else to love her and make her feel secure.

And that was what he wanted to do for Kyra.

Winning the position of manager would give him a place to put down roots, make a home, and raise a family, a challenge he'd always thought about attempting some day. Now that he'd met Kyra, he was ready to try again—with her.

He longed for the two of them to build a marriage based on equality, with a healthy dose of lust and an infinite amount of love to balance the mix. If only she would let him.

Now in the lobby, he glanced around in his best casual manner. A guard nodded as he passed, and Jake tipped his head in return. Then he sauntered to the front desk and chatted with the clerk about the upcoming competition. After removing the key to the private Sky Towers elevator from his pocket, he wandered to the correct set of doors, slid the card home, and slipped inside without a look at the guests.

The car flew to the twenty-fourth floor, where he

got out, went to each suite, and took pictures. Then he rode to the next floor and did the same.

Feeling marginally better, he returned to the lobby and caught a regular elevator to his room. Instead of using the hotel's development service, he'd pass Herb the camera so he could take the film to a local one-hour photo shop. The rest of the plan depended on what Rob was able to dig up.

Chapter 20

The next afternoon, Kyra bent over her clipboard and jotted a note. She had stayed too long at Lou's last night, gotten little sleep, and arrived late to work to find no message from Jake on her voicemail—the typical male way, she'd heard, mortal men dumped the women they'd been dating. Instead of brooding or throwing a fit, she faced the fact that, except for coordinating the Voice of Vegas, she'd seen the end of him on a personal level.

After going over paperwork on the contest and trying not to dwell on Jake, she was now with the celebrity judges and their assistants in one of the hotel's six smaller yet formally appointed dining rooms for their lunch meeting.

"Miss Malone and I will have a salad of mixed field greens with lemon juice on the side, and a glass of iced herbal tea with two slices of fresh lime to go with lunch."

The speaker, a ruler-thin woman with a short gelled hairdo that reminded Kyra of an eraser stuck on the end of a pencil, had been lecturing from the moment she and the pop star entered the dining room. The singer's only reaction had been a toss of golden curls, much as Chloe did when she was in diva mode.

Missy Malone's assistant arched a thinly penciled eyebrow. "We assume your chef prepared a macrobiotic meal, as requested."

Pretending to study her notes, Kyra rolled her eyes, then gazed politely at the assistant. "Of course."

As the woman continued prattling, she held her tongue and kept her smile in place. She found paying attention to the demanding duo difficult, even when only one spoke while the other stared vacantly into space. She'd inspired a tempting menu for this meeting. Unfortunately, each of her carefully chosen items, filet mignon, braised asparagus tips, and warm endive salad, or sautéed scallops on a bed of wild rice with a side of fresh bread and citrus butter, had been dismissed.

"Would you gentlemen prefer something else, as well?"

Simon Cloud, who reminded Kyra of one of Zeus's too-big-for-his-toga sons by a minor goddess, gave his order, then Dr. Slick. Of the three judges, the popular rap artist seemed the most friendly. In fact, when compared to Missy Malone and Simon Cloud, he was a pussycat.

Buddy Blue, who had arrived late for this and every other appointment, said, "I'll have a double serving of the filet mignon, sweet cheeks. More for me if some folks don't know what's good."

"Thank you, Buddy," said Kyra, pleased with the comedian's brash comment. At least someone appreciated her efforts. She handed a hovering waiter the orders, and he immediately scurried off toward the kitchen. "Your meals will be out shortly, as will yours Miss . . . uh . . ." she groped for the pencil's name.

"Ms. Ennis. Penelope Ennis," the woman said curtly.

"Penny Ennis, eh? No pun intended, but your mom and dad must have thought long and hard about that one," said Buddy with a naughty glint in his eyes.

Ms. Ennis acted as if Buddy didn't exist, but she did wave her hand as if shooing away a bee as she glared at Kyra. "Thank you. And while you're seeing to requests, can something be done to clear the room of this noxious cloud? It could harm Miss Malone's voice for the number she's scheduled to sing at the competition."

The meeting with the judges reminded Kyra of the last round table discussion she'd shared with her fellow Olympians, which turned into a contest to see who could be the most officious and the biggest suck up to Zeus at the same time. But the citizens of Mount Olympus were immortals who had come by their overbearing attitudes legitimately, inheriting either Hera's haughty demeanor or the father god's might-is-right personality. What excuse did these self-important mortals have to be rude?

She locked gazes with the record executive. "Mr. Cloud, please extinguish your cigarette until we find a better way to dispose of the smoke."

Simon frowned, inhaled a lungful of the offending weed, and dropped what was left of the cigarette into his glass of mineral water. "I thought this was a casino," he groused, a gray cloud drifting from his nose. "Why can't I light up?"

"The Acropolis is a casino, but smoking isn't permitted in any of the eating areas, only on the gambling floor, some of the private salons, and certain guest suites."

"Then see to it we have one of those suites," he said, curling his upper lip. "Or Jeffy will be inconsolable."

The well-built, almost pretty man who sat to the right of Simon sniffed in agreement. Sporting eyeliner, mascara, and too much cologne, Jeffy was dressed in a tight black T-shirt and even tighter white jeans. Introduced by a single name, he'd been touted as Cloud's personal trainer, with emphasis on the word *personal*.

"Come on over to my club tonight, Simon. There's so much smoke in the air you and your friend can get a nicotine fix just by breathing," added Buddy in a convivial manner. "We even got a drag queen on tap for tonight. Ruby Slippers should be right up your alley."

Kyra resisted the urge to giggle, made another notation on her clipboard, and turned to Dr. Slick. "Is there anything special we can do for you?"

The rapper removed his purple fedora and revealed his shiny bald head. Aside from his matching designer suit and the two-carat diamond studs in each ear, he seemed congenial and, dare she hope it, devoid of a bossy nature.

"No, ma'am." His smile gleamed white in his coffee-colored face. "My people have checked the accommodations and given their approval."

She recalled the two six-foot muscle-bound men who had accompanied the rap artist and were currently waiting in the hall, and realized they were bodyguards. "Good. Now, if you don't mind, I'd like to begin."

Three hours later, Kyra sat back and breathed a sigh of relief. Closing her file, she was ready to adjourn the meeting, which had centered more on the judges' personal requests and Missy's and Dr. Slick's vocal numbers than the rules of the competition. Amazingly, Buddy Blue had been the most sensible participant, even though his outrageous comments had grated on everyone's nerves.

In the end, it was decided the judges would consider just two things when choosing the first Voice of Vegas: the quality of each contestant's talent and their audience appeal.

Ms. Ennis stood. "If you would be so good as to call hotel security, Miss Malone and I need an escort to our rooms."

"You didn't bring your own entourage?" Kyra asked in an even tone.

"We already informed Rupert Ardmore that we'd only be bringing Miss Malone's hairdresser and wardrobe stylist, and requested a security team. He said you would take care of it."

Kyra gritted her teeth and tallied the extra cost of paying several guards overtime and the result it would have on her carefully balanced budget. It figured Rupert Ardmore would *forget* to let her know. But did it matter, when she'd be gone before the manager called her on the added expense?

"If you'll give me a second, I'll see what can be done." Though Jake was in charge of security for the event, the request was a hotel matter, which meant it would be more professional to go through Herb or whoever was in charge in the surveillance room. If Jake complained that she didn't ask for his help, it would be a logical explanation.

Jake observed Kyra's meeting from a monitor in the surveillance room. He'd tried her office earlier, intent on apologizing for not contacting her last night, but she wasn't there, so he'd gone to his cubbyhole to read over his records on the Sky Tower suites.

Now that he'd found her in one of the smaller dining rooms, he remembered she had an appointment with the celebrity judges.

He didn't want to step on Kyra's toes by interfering in a task that was hers, but he was curious. He'd met a few Hollywood notables and their traveling companions in his rounds of the European casinos and always got a kick out of their smug expressions and "look at me" attitude. From what he'd seen of the judges so far, this group was cut from the same cloth.

Simon Cloud was a regular on a popular television reality program that searched for the next great recording star, and Jake had heard Dr. Slick's chart-topping rap hit on the radio. As for Missy Malone, well, she was better to look at than listen to, but her kittenish appearance couldn't hold a candle to Kyra's classic beauty and regal bearing.

"Yes, Ms. Degodessa." The shift supervisor answered the phone within earshot of Jake. "I'll get right on it."

After a short conversation with the man, Jake realized Kyra could use a little help. Since neither Herb nor Rob had arrived for another meeting, he had time to introduce himself to the VIPs, and take some of the burden off Kyra's shoulders.

He rode the elevator to the proper floor, and, after waving his badge, shouldered past two beefy guys wearing what could only be guns under their jackets. Then he knocked and pushed open the door.

"Thought I'd drop by and introduce myself," he said to the room in general. "Name's Jake Lennox. I'm partnering with Ms. Degodessa on this project." He shook the rapper's hand, then Simon Cloud's, and nodded to Missy Malone and the reed-thin woman beside her. "If there's anything you need and you can't reach Kyra, just give me a ring and I'll see that it's taken care of." He met Kyra's unenthusiastic smile. "I was downstairs when you called for a security team."

She straightened, as if composing herself. "The guards will be needed whenever Miss Malone walks the hotel."

"Just give me a minute to make the arrangements," said Jake, continuing to flash a grin. He sidled to Kyra, clasped her elbow, and led her into the hall. Using the house phone, he contacted the senior official, verified the request, and gave Kyra the report. "The men will be here soon."

Kyra tugged, but he wouldn't release her. "I know. You're ticked off."

Her eyes opened wide. "Ticked off? Why would you think such a thing?"

"I should have called you last night or this morning, and I didn't." He backed her against the wall. "I don't have anything to say, except that I'm working on something important and it's cutting into my time. The best I can do for now is apologize . . . again. As soon as the project is over I'll—"

"I don't want to talk about it," said Kyra as she gazed toward the dining salon and Dr. Slick's men.

"Who cares if they hear? We have things to discuss. When can we get together?"

"Not right now," she said in a hushed voice. "I'm due in the pavilion to make sure things are on track, then I'm scheduled to be in the lobby for the new drawing. After that, I have to meet Lou for the final fitting of her gown."

"New drawing?"

"We're giving away a car, in place of the Wheel Deal."

"Right, the Mercedes," he answered. He'd passed the white luxury sedan sitting smack in the middle of the hotel lobby several times today. "So, are we going to have a winner on the first try?"

"I imagine so," said Kyra, raising her nose in the air. "The winner doesn't need to be present, just a currently registered guest. Now if you don't mind—"

Jake turned his back to Dr. Slick's companions, effectively blocking Kyra from their sight. Stepping closer, he whispered, "I do mind. I was hoping to spend the night with you. I have something I need to tell you."

He'd paced all morning, waiting for Herb and Rob. While wearing out the carpet, his mind had ping-ponged between Ardmore's sneaky scheme and Kyra. Now that he was in her presence, he realized how dull his day had been without her.

"It will have to wait."

"How am I going to fall asleep without you curled into my chest making those cute little gurgling noises?" he asked, egging her on. Since they'd begun sparring, he had to admit he'd rather be on the receiving end of her sassy attitude than the subject of her indifference.

"I do not gurgle," she sputtered. "And your sleeping arrangements are *so* not my problem." She slid from his embrace, then smiled at two security guards who strolled around the corner. "Gentlemen, I'll be right back with your charges."

Jake nodded to the men. "It's simple escort duty, so I assume you know the drill."

Missy and her assistant appeared in the doorway, followed by Kyra. Introductions were made, and the quartet left. When Kyra trotted after them Jake blocked her way.

"Dinner?"

"No."

"Late-night supper?"

She bit her bottom lip. "I don't think so."

"How about I ride home with you?" *And we have wild monkey sex. Then I'll tell you I love you, and we can do it all over again.* He cocked a brow to let her know he was serious.

"You've got to be kidding."

"Come on, you'll need a break and so will I. We might as well take it together."

Her indignant stare told him his suggestion was out of the question. "I plan to go home and catch up on my sleep. Tomorrow's the big day, and I have to be on my toes. I have no idea when I'll be free."

"Not a problem. I'll find you."

An expression of profound sadness crossed her face, and Jake gave himself a healthy mental kick. He'd been an idiot this past week, but he would convince her to forgive him, even if it took the rest of his life.

"I don't think we have anything more to say to each other."

Before he could argue the point, Kyra turned and disappeared down the hall.

"Those photos are proof positive Ardmore's been siphoning money," said Herb, leaning into the desk as Jake studied the pictures the security chief had retrieved from the drugstore.

"The only thing they're proof of is not getting the job done," Jake said in a dour tone. "We have no paper trail to Ardmore."

"Too bad Ms. Degodessa's computer didn't have any other info on it, though I still don't understand why you need more."

"Since there's nothing to connect the sheet to Ardmore, it'll be our word against his. He can always say I planted the data to get him in trouble or deny the computer was ever in his possession." Jake slid the photos into the file. "He probably knows I'm after his job, too. That's why it's important we have something in writing."

Herb eyed his watch. "So, where is the singing detective?"

"He was scheduled to rehearse with a pianist a while ago, so I hope he's in accounting right now, searching for what we need. Come tomorrow, preparations for the show will be in full swing; who knows when he'll get the chance again."

"I have a set of master keys. We could always let ourselves into Ardmore's office after he leaves, and snoop."

Jake admired the guy's fighting spirit. "If we got caught, we'd have a hard time explaining things. Let's see what Rob finds before we make the decision to do something not quite legal."

"Jeez, talk about taking the fun out of life. I never figured you for a stick in the—"

Jake raised a hand and answered his ringing phone. "Lennox here. Yeah . . . yeah? You're sure? Okay, then, that's good enough for me. You've got a lot going on, so just hang in there. Uh-huh. Later."

"Well . . . ?" Herb asked.

"Looks like we won't have to resort to anything dicey. Rob was able to dig further into the accounting records and found a memo signed by Ardmore, instructing the department to pay Fast Track from the remodeling account. The memo says the monthly fee should be mailed to the same address as the one we have for the telephone bills. With that document, I doubt we'll even need a canceled check."

"Then it's a slam-dunk," said Herb, a huge smile on his face. "Have you heard from Mr. T?"

"No, but I'm going to try him again."

The chief guard backed toward the door. "Let me know if I can do anything else. I'll be here the rest of the afternoon."

Jake waited until Herb left before picking up the phone. He was fairly confident that, with this latest development, he could safely show the evidence to Mr. T, and wrap up the investigation, but there was always a chance Ardmore had an airtight alibi. If so, the guy would be gone a nanosecond after giving his explanation, leaving the rest of them with nothing.

It was late evening in Europe, but Jake wasn't sure of the exact time, because he didn't know where Themopolis actually was located. The mogul had an office in every casino he owned, but he'd given Jake a number he said was private, which meant it was probably a mobile phone. Inhaling a breath, he punched out the numbers and listened to the ring.

"Mr. Themopolis," a woman answered.

Jake recognized the voice as belonging to Mr. T's new assistant. "It's Jake Lennox. Is he available?"

"Not at the moment, but he did leave a message in case you tried to reach him again."

So maybe it wasn't a cell phone, Jake thought, but it did bring him one step closer to his boss. "Let me have it," said Jake, encouraging the woman to talk.

"He says he won't be able to make the contest."

Not make the contest?

"That's it? No explanation as to why?"

"Sorry, but no."

After a second, he heard a click and the buzzing of the phone line. Well, damn. The woman had to be a couple of chips short of an ante if she thought she could just hang up on a caller. Speaking with her had been little better than holding a conversation with a message machine, but at least she'd relayed information. Mr. T had to be distracted by one hell of a business deal if couldn't make the biggest promo the Acropolis had seen in a decade.

It just didn't seem possible.

He ran his fingers through his hair, read his watch, and pushed from the desk. Handle things, his brain instructed. Lie low and watch Ardmore; if Mr. T doesn't call with instructions, you contact the authorities when you're sure you have enough to nab him, and get the job done.

According to Rob, the song rehearsal had just started. This was the perfect time to go to the pavilion and listen to the contestants practice their vocals. Kyra was sure to be there, so he could kill two birds at once. He and Garrett could play "pass the memo," then he'd hang around and work his charms, maybe escort Kyra to the drawing for the Mercedes. When it was over, he'd find a way to get her alone and show her how much she meant to him.

On the main level, he took the path that led to the outdoor market. He stopped in the florist shop and ordered a dozen roses delivered to her office. It was the least he could do by way of apology.

Then, walking past a booth that specialized in items from Greece, he did a double take. Flowers were nice, but gold and diamonds lasted forever. Inspecting the U-shaped counter, he spotted something unique, just like Kyra.

"May I see that necklace?" he asked the clerk.

"You have a good eye," the woman answered, removing the golden strand. "This is eighteen carat, and the sapphires are from Burma. It's an exact copy of a piece found in an archeological dig in Athens. All of the jewelry sold here is guaranteed to be an authentic reproduction."

She laid the thick strand across a tray of black velvet, giving Jake a better view of the unusual design. Two gold dolphins, each about an inch long with a single sapphire for an eye, faced each other, their smiling mouths joined from behind by a security clasp.

"The clasp can be worn with the dolphins in the back or front, though I like them in view so everyone can see the intricate craftsmanship, and the sapphires, of course," the clerk stated.

Jake had to smile. Kyra was a beautiful woman; she deserved beautiful things. He had no cash flow problem, so why not buy her a token to show how much he cared? He'd give her the necklace tonight and tell her he loved her. When she got used to the idea, he'd propose, maybe after the Voice of Vegas. If Garrett won, it would be a dual celebration. If not, it would soothe the pain of his defeat.

He paid for the necklace, had the clerk wrap it in their best paper and ribbon, and tucked the long, slender package in the front pocket of his jacket. Striding through the market, he stopped at the Dionysos pavilion, flashed his ID at the guard, and opened a pair of entry doors.

Once inside, he scoured the performance area. Even from this distance, he could pick Kyra out of the crowd cluttering the competition area. She was standing in a spotlight, but it wasn't necessary. Her presence lighted the stage, her fiery hair a flame that drew him like a moth.

He shook his head at the cliché. No doubt about it, he was in hip deep. And the strange thing was the unfamiliar emotions swirling in his gut made him want to shout his feelings to the world.

Halfway to the stage, an announcement sounded over the paging system. "Mr. Lennox. Jake Lennox. You're wanted at the front desk. Paging Jake Lennox. Please report to the lobby immediately."

Well, damn.

He gave Kyra a final glance, then pivoted and re-traced his steps. Maybe the assistant had been wrong, and Mr. T had flown in anyway.

Chapter 21

Finished with the details she had to take care of in the pavilion, Kyra headed to the Mercedes giveaway. When the drawing ended, she planned to meet with Lou, then return to her office and answer the e-mail she'd received that morning from Zeus, something titled "final instructions." Afterward, she had every intention of going to her condo and settling in for the night.

She'd spotted Jake at the top of the central staircase a short while ago, but he'd left to answer a page without speaking to her. He had some nerve appearing at the vocal run-through, even if he hadn't made it onto the stage. Good thing he'd been interrupted before he was able to do whatever it was he'd come there for, because she was growing weary of his apologies. Considering the upheaval he'd caused in her life, it was best she continue to ignore him. Then he'd leave her alone, and she could forget he ever existed.

She groaned. Fat chance she could ever forget Jake Lennox. Even when he was out of her life for good, she would remember him. The man's seductive smile and sexy body, his every kiss and touch, the way it felt when he moved inside of her, were burned in her brain.

Jake was the last thing she thought of when she closed her eyes at night, and the first thing she thought of each morning. He even filled her dreams. She looked forward to their shared laughter, enjoyed his confident, take-charge attitude. She couldn't imagine her day without him.

Lou's description of love beat a heady tattoo, warning her she was dangerously close to a catastrophe. Stomping out of the pavilion doors, she refused to admit her feelings for Jake were any more than potent desire. Her involvement with him was merely an overblown case of infatuation.

She weaved through the customers walking the bazaar, followed the hall, and made it to the lobby with minutes to spare. Most of the people present were clustered around the sleek white sedan, admiring its high-end features and even higher price tag. It only took a short explanation from the promotions manager and she was ready to begin the contest.

My final customer giveaway, Kyra thought, refusing to give in to tears. She enjoyed the elation that churned inside of her whenever she inspired a mortal, but tonight was different. With so many people hoping to win, it wasn't possible to personally introduce herself to each member of the crowd. Fate would be the one to choose today's winner. If she hadn't brought her gift of good fortune to enough mortals by now, it was too late to meet any of Zeus's secret quotas.

She strode to the barrel holding slips of paper signed by the customers who had registered that day. Amidst the clatter and clang of the casino's background noise, a three-piece jazz band played a popular tune to accompany the drawing. Kyra cranked the handle, spinning the barrel to mix the names. Then she reached inside, pulled out a ticket, and announced the lucky contestant.

Screeches of delight vied with the musical trio's rousing melody, almost obliterating the never-ending racket of the slot machines. She led the jubilant winner to the head of promotions, where he verified the woman's driver's license and handed her the keys to the car in a flurry of camera flashes and hearty congratulations.

As the crowd dispersed, Kyra scanned the lobby and spotted Jake at the farthest end of the registration desk. Since he'd been paged a while ago, she couldn't imagine his reason for still talking with the afternoon reservation manager . . . unless he'd decided to lie in wait for her. Surely he had better things to do than waste his time spying?

He bent to speak to the diminutive woman standing next to him, and Kyra couldn't hide her curiosity. Especially when she noticed the suitcase at the woman's side.

"I don't mean to be nosy," she said to the nearest desk clerk. "But who's that with Jake Lennox?"

"Mr. Lennox's surprise visitor," the clerk responded. "When she tried to check in as Mrs. Edward Lennox, and asked for Jake, I assumed she was a relative. As soon as I found out she was his mother, I had him paged."

Jake's mother!

"What do you mean, *tried* to check in?" asked Kyra.

"She didn't have a reservation, and we're booked solid for the contest. Between the Hollywood types, recording bigwigs, and fans, every room is spoken for. We decided to let Mr. Lennox handle it. She's his problem now."

Hoping to catch Jake's eye, Kyra sidled to her old desk and picked up a file. When Jake raised his gaze and glanced in her direction, he didn't smile or act as if he saw her. His mother tugged at his sleeve and he redirected his attention to whatever she was pointing to on the desk.

Not wanting to admit his snub upset her, she headed for the elevators to think.

* * *

Jake took stock of the lobby and noted Kyra was busy at the bell stand. When his mom touched his sleeve, he looked down and pointed to the space she needed to initial on the reservation card. Drumming his fingers, he told himself he was in one hell of a mess. He should have known by the tenor of Laura's last phone call something like this would happen. His mother was at loose ends, and they hadn't seen each other in over a month. She thought he'd be in one place for a while, so she'd opted to fly out and surprise him. It was his fault this had happened, not hers, so he had to handle her with kid gloves.

Laura smiled sweetly, and his irritation melted. "I'm sorry to be such trouble," she said with a trace of apology. "Maybe I should go to another hotel."

Jake shuddered at the thought of his mom, on her own in a town she hated, taking off for a different hotel when she'd come all this way to spend time with him. "Over my dead body," he said jokingly.

"No, it's exactly what I deserve for not thinking. I should have called ahead or—"

"It's okay. I have a suite, and the living room sofa pulls out into a bed. You can have the bedroom, and I'll take the couch, no problem."

"Nonsense. I'm perfectly capable of sleeping on the hide-a-bed. You need your rest for the big event."

"What big event?" Jake asked, keeping his smile in check. He had an inkling they were finally getting to the *real* motive behind her visit.

"Tomorrow's contest. It's all the entertainment channels can talk about. I thought you might have something to do with it as soon as I heard the competition was being held here." She glanced around the lobby like a star-struck teenager. "Have you met any celebrities? I'm hooked on the television program Simon Cloud hosts. Maybe I could get his autograph."

Jake didn't have the heart to tell her the real Simon Cloud was far from the gentleman he portrayed on the show. He slipped the extra room key into his pocket and picked up her bag. "If you're up for it, I could probably arrange for you to see the Voice of Vegas in person."

Her eyes sparkled. "You'd really do that for me?"

To Jake, seeing his mother this thrilled was tantamount to someone pinning a badge on his lapel with the words "World's Best Son" spelled out for all to see. "I'm sure there are a couple of spare tickets lying around. I'll get to work on it right away."

As they walked toward the elevators, he searched for Kyra, hoping to at least nod a hello. The Mercedes giveaway had attracted a huge crowd and she had, as usual, handled it professionally. The car raffle, coupled with the singing competition, had gotten the Acropolis its fair share of positive publicity. He only hoped when the story broke about Ardmore, it would weather the negative buzz and stay on track as one of the premiere Vegas hotels.

He took stock of the dispersing throng, but didn't see his soon-to-be-fiancée, and figured she probably had another contest detail to take care of. Which was fine by him. He had to keep his mother and Kyra apart until after he explained a few things to both women. Kyra needed to know why he was here, as well as a few tidbits about his past, including the fact that he'd been divorced, while his mom deserved the truth about the last ten years of his life.

After the confessions, he'd probably have to juggle wounded feelings, though he was counting on his mom to understand. But Kyra would be furious if she learned about his ex from anyone but him. And if she ever discovered he'd come on to her because he suspected she was somehow involved in the casino's money troubles, he was toast.

He had every intention of introducing the two most important women in his life, but right now he needed to focus on nabbing Ardmore and the success of the Voice of Vegas, in that order. There was plenty of time for Kyra and his mother to get acquainted. Once he exposed Ardmore and the contest was over, the rest of his agenda was a piece of cake.

Kyra walked into the Dionysos Pavilion sporting one of the many horrific things that often plagued mortals: a skull-splitting headache.

She'd spotted Jake watching the Mercedes drawing from afar. His mother seemed pleasant enough, and she and Jake were co-workers, so why hadn't he called her over for an introduction?

Judi McCoy

When the ugly truth grabbed hold of her heart and gave a nasty twist, Kyra almost burst into tears. There were only two reasons a man wouldn't introduce the woman he was sleeping with to his mother. Either she was so unimportant he didn't think it necessary they meet, or he was ashamed of her. And both thoughts were too painful to bear.

Thoroughly disheartened, she followed the corridor that led behind the stage to the fitting rooms. Drawn by the sound of girlish laughter, she opened the door marked "wardrobe" and peered inside, where she found several dozen women in various stages of undress chattering about everything from undergarments to the proper color eye shadow to wear with their gowns.

Scanning the crowd, she spied Lou in a back corner. The waitress waved and Kyra forced a grin. Rob and Lou still had a chance at real happiness. Telling Lou what she suspected about Jake would only give the girl another excuse to doubt men, which might make her give up on Rob. She had to continue the façade, let Lou *think* things were going great with her and Jake, and play the game out until her retrieval.

"You look fantastic," Kyra shouted, threading her way through the milling throng.

Lou beamed, her smile almost as broad as Consuelo's, then twirled in place. The gold sequins scattered over her form-fitting, mahogany-colored gown glittered under the room's brilliant lights. "It's all due to this lady," she said, giving the seamstress a hug. "She did a phenomenal job with the alterations."

"Bah!" Consuelo's brown eyes shined with pride. "I did nothing but enhance what nature so graciously gave you. Now, take off the dress and hang it at station two. You have to get ready for your date."

"Date?" Kyra tried to hide her surprise. "With who?"

"Rob, of course," said Lou, stepping out of her dress. She hung the gown on a padded hanger and brought it to the makeup station she'd been assigned as Kyra followed. "I tried to find you today to tell you, but you were unavailable. He came to the apartment last night, and we had a long talk about . . . stuff. As soon as he finishes work, we're going to dinner. Mom even agreed to baby-sit without complaining."

Kyra pasted on a happy face, the thought of Lou's life taking a positive turn somewhat dulling the pain in her head. "I told you he was serious, didn't I?"

Lou slipped into her jeans and a navy blue sweater, then sat and put on her sneakers. Standing, she clasped her hands around Kyra's. "Yes, you did. And if Rob and I do nothing more than become good friends, we'll owe you a huge thanks." Her hazel eyes took on a dreamlike quality. "I don't know how I'll be able to repay you for making me see the light."

"See the light?"

"Even if things don't work out romantically with Rob, there's no reason why I can't take a chance on a nice guy. Who knows, I might even get married someday, and I already know who I want for my maid of honor."

Maid of honor? As in a wedding?

"Gee, Lou, I don't know." *Unless you plan to get married in the next twenty-four hours.* "Are you sure?"

"Of course I'm sure. If it ever happens, I'll need my best friend to help with the details. That's you."

Best friend? The two words softened the earlier blow Jake had given her heart. The few weddings she'd attended on Mount Olympus had been little more than an excuse for a night of debauchery, not the grand celebrations of a lifetime of love between two people, as they were here on Earth.

She'd never discussed men or cosmetics, or clothes, or anything of importance with a mortal woman. And never had she been asked to perform the joyful task of wedding attendant, because she'd never been anyone's *best friend.*

But she felt no better than a traitor, making a promise she knew she couldn't keep, so she skimmed over the idea with a laugh and a "thank you for asking." Together, they walked from behind the stage and into the pavilion.

"Where are you supposed to meet Rob?"

"Right here. Can you wait with me?"

"I wish, but I still have paperwork to do, and a million details to take care of before tomorrow. You and Rob have a good time without me."

"We'll try," said Lou, waggling her fingers as Kyra walked away.

Kyra waved in return, then headed for her office. She was *so* going to miss Lou and all the friends she'd made here. What would her life on Olympus be like without them?

Chapter 22

FROM: Topgod@mounto.org
TO: Kdegodessa@Acropolis.com
SUBJECT: Final instructions

In preparation for your journey home, it is imperative I remind you of the rules. Plan for retrieval anywhere from nine until midnight, Earth time, tomorrow evening. Attire: Chiton and sandals only. No property acquired on Earth will be allowed on Olympus, including clothing, jewelry, and documentation of your successes or failures.

Avoid transporting the following contaminants: Chewing gum, breath mints, cosmetics, and Orange Milano cookies.

I look forward to your arrival,

Zeus
CEO (and still Top God of the immortal world)

Kyra leaned back in her chair, dejected by the note's somber tone. When she'd logged on, the system asked for her password. Just a few days ago, Jake had insisted she tighten the security on her PC. Stupidly, she'd used the first word that popped into her head.

Home.

At the time, the four letters represented a place to live in royal splendor. Since she'd become involved with Jake, they signified a refuge, a place to heal her saddened heart, where, if she were clever, she would start her life anew.

But could she? After her last conversation with Lou, she wasn't even sure she wanted to *go* to Olympus. Aside from Zoë and Chloe, Lou was her one true friend, and she'd never see her again. No one would ever ask her to be a bridesmaid if she returned to the mountain.

She read her father's e-mail a second time. His reminder about Orange Milano cookies made her shudder. Either Zeus, or someone sent by him, had snooped into every aspect of her life here, right down to the food she ate.

It also meant he knew about Rob, Lou, and Eddie, and how much she cared for them . . . and Jake.

Her shoulders slumped in defeat. Could the top god really see inside her head and read her thoughts, or peek into her heart and take stock of her secrets? Was he aware of all the waffling she'd done of late regarding her feelings for Jake?

Throughout the ages, she'd suspected Zeus's mental manipulation was merely a ploy used to bring his subjects to heel. Because of his cookie comment, she was certain he spied, made assumptions, and formed opinions without giving the gods or goddesses a chance to defend themselves against his suspicions.

Worse, she knew she'd been deluding herself when she said it didn't matter that she'd be leaving, or that she dreamed of living in magnificence for eternity. She could no longer lie about the emotions in her heart.

She was in love with Jake Lennox.

Before she could absorb the statement, there was a knock on the door, then a voice announced, "Gift for you, Ms. Degodessa."

"Come in," she answered.

A bellman strolled into the room carrying a huge vase brimming with red roses, at least two dozen, set the flowers in the center of her desk, and left.

The intoxicating scent of the bouquet surrounded her as she opened the card.

There's something important I have to tell you.
Jake

Kyra's headache intensified. What did he want to tell her, besides good-bye?

She held her head in her hands, willing the pain to the farthest corner of Hades. Then, like a bulb in the midst of a power surge, her dim spirits brightened. There was still reason to hope. She had yet to announce her feelings for Jake aloud, which meant she might be able to hide them from her father. An eternity of frivolity and decadence on Mount Olympus had to be better than a life on Earth without the man she loved.

If she hardened her heart, she could protect it from Zeus's prying eyes. She was a demi-goddess, after all, with powers of her own and the will to wield them.

She could still salvage her pride and her future.

Focusing on her computer screen, she responded to Zeus's e-mail, then set out for her condo. She needed every bit of strength she possessed to prepare for the job ahead.

Jake pushed the remains of a slice of prime rib across his plate with his fork, his appetite as nonexistent as his will to concentrate. His stupidity at holding an important part of his life from his mother kept getting tangled with the many things he'd avoided saying to Kyra. Maybe, if he'd been truthful with Laura from the start, he wouldn't be feeling like such a jerk right now.

"Jacob, you're not eating. Is something wrong with your dinner?"

"Hmm?" He stared at his plate. "No, it's fine. I guess I'm not hungry."

"Well, my dinner was delicious," she said, forking up a last bite of shrimp scampi. "What's good for dessert?"

It had always amazed Jake how a woman who

Judi McCoy

tipped the scales at no more than a hundred pounds could eat her weight in food in a single meal and still stay slender. "The chocolate truffles are a specialty of the house. They also have a killer carrot cake, which is probably what you should order seeing as they only serve it if you sign a pledge promising to eat the whole thing."

She *tsked* at him and smiled at their waiter. "I'll have the truffles, and a cup of decaf coffee."

Jake drew back from the table and the waiter removed his nearly full plate. "Can I get you anything, Mr. Lennox?"

"No, thanks." He gave his mother a teasing smile. "I'll just have some of the lady's."

"I'll let you know if I'm willing to share, after I taste it," said his mother, her lips still curled in a grin.

He raised their bottle of wine, and she shook her head. "Not for me. If I drink any more, I won't be able to sleep."

Jake didn't think he'd be catching any shut-eye, either, considering the guilt that washed over him every time he met his mother's piercing blue gaze. He felt little better than a cheat in her presence. Aside from the whopper he'd told her about his career, he'd never lied to her about anything. She trusted him to be truthful, unlike his father, who had spouted so many sob stories it was tough telling fact from fiction.

"So, Mom, what type of entertainment do you

338

want while you're here? Besides a ticket to the Voice of Vegas, I might be able to scare up seats for one of Celine's shows. Or would you rather take a helicopter ride to the Grand Canyon, or a tour of the dam and a few other local sights."

"What I want," said Laura, "is to see you lose your pensive expression. If I'd known this visit was going to depress you, I would have stayed home."

Jake reached out and linked their fingers. "I'm happy you're here, honest. What with the show and a project I'm handling for Mr. T, I have a lot on my mind."

Laura rested her forearms on the table. "And does whatever or whoever's weighing on your mind have a name?"

He blinked at the comment. His mother was messing with his head, something she'd been fairly successful at when he was younger. More often than not, he was so surprised by her intuitive question he let the cat out of the bag without thinking. "You aren't going to trap me into spilling my guts, Mom. I'm not a kid anymore."

"I see." She waited while the waiter arranged the plate of truffles and two forks in the center of the table, then poured her coffee. "How about if I phrase it another way. What's the young lady's name?"

Well, hell. He kept silent and she *tsked* again.

"I wasn't born yesterday, Jacob. I can see it in your eyes. You haven't looked this way since you thought you were in love with Corinne. Now that you're older, and I hope wiser, I'm going to assume it's the real thing this time."

Jake swallowed hard. If he told his mother about Kyra, maybe she'd be so occupied fussing about the new woman in his life she wouldn't take it too badly when he told her what he'd been doing these past ten years. But would Kyra be angry if she found out he'd informed his mother about her before he introduced them?

Ignoring the sinking feeling in the pit of his stomach, he shrugged his agreement. "If I tell you about Kyra, you have to swear to me you'll play dumb when you meet her."

"Kyra. What a lovely name." Laura licked the rich chocolaty filling off the tines of her fork and gave a satisfied sigh. "You have my word, now here." She scooped half a truffle onto her fork and held it out to him. "Try a bite of this. It'll help soothe the pain of your confession."

He refused the bite of truffle with a shake of his head. "There's more, Mom. I have a lot to explain."

The next morning, Jake rode the elevator to the basement, deep in thought. Last night, besides coming clean about his career, he'd shared his feelings about the woman he loved with his mother, and told her he wanted a life with Kyra.

The moment Laura learned about Kyra, she put

aside his personal confession to her, and zeroed in on his stupidity. If Kyra was as wonderful as he said, she'd warned, then Jake had better "stake his claim" before someone else did.

This morning, he and his mom had eaten breakfast in their suite, and Laura was now taking advantage of the hotel's spa services. The spa's appointment schedule was tight, but the facility agreed to work her in for a pedicure and a hot stone massage provided she didn't mind killing time in one of the hotel's signature luxuries, the Acropolis's opulent Grecian-themed baths. After commenting on the "terrible inconvenience" with a laugh, she'd proceeded to ready herself for a morning of leisure, and left the suite.

His mother's advice only reinforced what Jake had already decided on, though it did change the time frame. Instead of waiting until after the Voice of Vegas and Ardmore's downfall, he was going to find Kyra right now, confess everything, and give her the necklace. Then he'd convince her to move in with him. Once that was accomplished there would be nothing to plan but the wedding.

He'd left Kyra a message on her voicemail from the phone in his suite. Once in his office, he'd make a few more calls, pin down her location, and meet her. Buoyed by his decision, he tucked the Sky Tower file under his arm and bent to unlock his office door. Surprised it was already open, he squared his shoulders and charged into the room, prepared to meet the interloper.

"I figured you'd get here eventually." Socrates Themopolis lounged in Jake's padded chair, his feet propped on the desktop.

"Mr. Themopolis?" Jake blinked as he skidded to a stop. "What are you—I mean—I didn't expect to see you today."

The hotel magnate rose and walked from behind the desk. "And why not?"

"Your personal assistant," said Jake, shaking his hand. "I spoke with her yesterday, and she said—"

"Personal assistant? I don't have a personal assistant. At least, not one who spoke to you." He glanced around the sparsely furnished space. "What possessed you to take an office here in the dungeon?"

Jake dragged a chair from a corner of the room and took a seat, still trying to mask his surprise. "It was Rupert Ardmore's decision, but I didn't mind. It kept me close to Herb and the surveillance cameras."

"Herb's the best. I'm going to throw him the biggest retirement party this hotel has ever seen in just about three months. But first things first. I was getting concerned. I had hoped to hear from you before this."

Jake stumbled for an answer. He'd left word on the man's private line a dozen times or more. If anyone had been unreachable, it was Mr. T. But how could he explain without sounding as if he were making excuses?

"I have called, and I've left messages. I have no idea why you didn't get them, but I spoke to a woman yesterday, and she told me you weren't attending the Voice of Vegas."

"Why wouldn't I attend? Besides the positive publicity, this is the most sensational event the Acropolis has sponsored in years." He raised a brow. "And what made you get involved, when you had an investigation to run."

"That's one of the things I wanted to talk to you about. I left a voicemail the night Ardmore gave me the job."

"Didn't get a single voicemail, and I certainly didn't get a message from any woman. What was her name?"

"She didn't say." Jake ran his fingers through his hair, ticked at sounding so lame. "I guess the wires got crossed. But you're here now. Have you had breakfast? Can I order something from room service?"

Mr. T rested an elbow on the desk. "Coffee would be fine, just don't tell the kitchen it's for me. No one but Herb knows I'm here. He's the one who let me in."

No one but Herb? "Uh, why is that?"

"Because I hate fanfare and all the kiss-up crap that goes with it. The staff in this place runs on a revolving door; the last thing I want is a gaggle of newbies fawning as if I were some sort of god. I sneak in after midnight, carry my own bags, and use the key I keep in my wallet to let myself into my suite. It gives me a bird's-eye view of how the hotel really operates, instead of the exaggerated reports I get from my managers."

Jake ordered coffee and pastries for two. The hotel magnate's arrival had put a crimp in his plans, which meant speaking with Kyra would have to go on the back burner while he discussed Ardmore with his boss. He decided to begin with the big lie. Things could only go up from there.

"So," said Themopolis, when Jake set down the phone. "What have you got for me?"

"A confession, for starters," Jake began. "I should have told you this years ago, but I didn't have the guts. As time passed it got easier and easier to keep up the charade, but you need to know the truth." He explained why and how he'd kept his mom in the dark about his lifestyle. Mr. T interrupted with a question or two, but allowed Jake to continue until the end.

"It's never a good idea to lie to a woman, son, even for a noble reason. I always wondered why I never saw the two of you together. Luckily, your mother is a forgiving soul."

Just then, room service arrived. After filling their cups with the strong black brew, Jake moved on to a more important topic. "You sent me here to do a job. With Herb's help, and the assistance of another employee, it's done. The only step left is calling the authorities."

"That bad, is it?" Mr. T asked, sipping his coffee.

"It's worse than bad." Jake pushed the file he'd tossed on the blotter across the desk. Themopolis studied the evidence while Jake spent the next fifteen minutes going over the details, including his theory on how Ardmore had accomplished the embezzlement.

"I think he hooked me up with the hotel's special events coordinator, just to keep me out of his hair."

"Deep down, I suspected Ardmore all along, but didn't want to believe it. Good thing I had you to depend on." Themopolis sorted through the photos and documents. "I have an army of lawyers, and a buddy in the Nevada attorney general's office. We'll have an arrest warrant within twenty-four hours."

"That's too long to wait," said Jake. "I suspect Ardmore's going to make his getaway during the contest. Just about everyone in the hotel will be at the pavilion, which will give him the opportunity to clean out his desk, destroy evidence, and leave without drawing attention to himself."

"Give me a minute to make a couple of phone calls. I'll tell him to put a rush on the paperwork. If things go well, we might be able to surprise Ardmore within the next couple of hours."

Kyra spent the morning finalizing the competition details with the director, producer, and musical

Judi McCoy

coordinator, then attended an uneventful meeting with the celebrity judges. Jake hadn't stopped by the pavilion for the last rehearsal, and she imagined he was spending time with his mother or going over competition security with Herb.

Ever since yesterday's gift of flowers, she'd been preparing for his absence. Though difficult, she'd managed to keep thoughts of him at bay while she steeled her heart for her return to Mount Olympus. If she could keep him out of her mind, she could hide her true feelings from Zeus long enough to be declared victorious in the father god's challenge. Then she'd be free to mourn Jake for the remainder of her immortal life.

Arriving in the lobby, she noted a commotion. Socrates Themopolis stood next to Jake at the bottom of the main staircase while two men wearing business suits and dour expressions escorted a snarling Rupert Ardmore from his office and down the steps. Four hotel guards and Herb met them at the base of the stairs, where Mr. T scowled at Ardmore and shook his head. He nodded to the men in suits, who then led the hotel manager away.

When Kyra's eyes met Jake's, his deep blue gaze cut straight to her heart. He waved her over and, unable to be rude, she walked toward him.

"Kyra, have you met Mr. T?" Jake asked, catching hold of her elbow and drawing her near.

Mr. Themopolis smiled as he shook her hand. "It's

a pleasure to see you again. You worked under Ms. Simmons last time I was here, correct?"

"Yes, sir."

"Kyra now has Ms. Simmons's position," Jake interjected. "And she's doing a terrific job."

"Good, good. Jake, if anyone wants me, I'll be in the surveillance room with Herb."

"What's going on?" Kyra asked as the men left for the elevators. "What happened to Mr. Ardmore?"

"It's a long story, but thanks to the spreadsheet you pulled up on your computer, I nabbed Ardmore embezzling money from the Acropolis. With Rob and Herb's help, the police have him in custody. He's no longer in charge here." His eyes glittered. "It's one of the things I've been trying to talk to you about. Do you have a few minutes?"

Not sure she was capable of holding her feelings in check if they were alone together, she put on her best business demeanor. "I have a lot to do before the afternoon run-through, then I have to speak to the VIP hostesses and—"

"Damn it, Kyra, this is important." Jake led her up the stairs, lecturing as he walked. "You've been giving me the brush-off and I want to know why."

She'd been giving *him* the brush-off?

He marched to her office, opened the door, and pulled her inside. Then he backed her into the wall, nestled his hips against hers, and kissed her as if his life depended on it.

Kyra fought his firm yet gentle hold, but found herself incapable of ignoring the pressure of his lips, the desperation in his demand. Like a desert flower welcoming the rain, she opened her mouth and met his thrusting tongue. The kiss seemed to last an eternity as it quenched her dry and hardened heart.

Jake drew back and gazed at her, his expression filled with longing. "I've been wanting to do that for three days. Thank God I finally got the chance."

Kyra wrenched away and paced to her desk, unwilling to let him see the pain in her eyes. "I've been right here, listening to the excuses and apologies, Jake. You're the one who's been absent."

He sauntered toward her, sporting his *come here, baby* grin. "For a good reason. I'm not Mr. T's nephew, Kyra. He sent me here to catch a thief. Since I've succeeded, he's going to offer me Ardmore's job."

"You're going to manage this hotel?"

"Damn right, and I have so many plans I don't know where to begin." Scooping her into his arms, he rounded her desk and plopped down in the chair.

"What are you doing?" she shrieked.

"What I should have done two mornings ago."

She opened her mouth to argue, and he kissed her again. Kyra pushed at his shoulders, but couldn't budge the mass of muscle and bone holding her captive. The kiss turned soft, teasing . . . tender. Unable to form a coherent thought, she melted into his arms.

He pulled back and nuzzled her lips with his nose. "I've missed you."

"I've missed you, too." She sighed her confusion. This was not the path she'd expected their next meeting to take. "Now, please, get out of here. I have a lot to do." She almost added "before I go," but caught herself.

"No more ignoring me. What I have to say can't wait."

If this was the big brush-off, it wasn't a thing like she'd expected. In fact, it was starting to sound more like a plea. A true apology. A confession.

"I love you."

Chapter 23

"Excuse me?" Kyra's heart skipped a beat, maybe two. She raised a brow. "That is *so* not funny. Let me go."

Jake held her in place without an inch of wiggle room. "I'm not a comic, sweetheart. I figured it out a few days ago, but the timing always seemed off whenever I tried to tell you. After two nights of tossing and turning, I couldn't wait another second."

Kyra opened and closed her mouth. "You love me?"

"I'm crazy about you."

"It's just the fantastic sex," she countered. "You can't be in love with me."

"Glad to hear you thought it was fantastic, because there's more bedroom aerobics where that came from. About sixty years more, if things work out right."

"But—but I thought you wanted a no-strings relationship. A fun time without commitments. You promised—"

"I didn't plan on falling in love with you, Kyra, but it happened. Now that I know how I feel, I want us to take the next step, and move in together, but first . . ." He pulled a wrapped package from his jacket and handed it to her. "This is for you."

Kyra stared, unable to move her fingers.

"Here, I'll open it."

He tore through the paper and flipped up the lid. Inside lay a stunning gold necklace showcasing two whimsical, laughing dolphins with sapphire-studded eyes linked mouth to mouth, locked in a kiss for eternity. She held the gift in both hands, considered its worth, and refused to cry or let herself feel.

"I can't accept this. It's too expensive, too big a commitment. Too . . . much."

"I thought about getting you an engagement ring," Jake continued, as if she hadn't spoken. Lifting the intricate rope, he held it to her neck and fastened the clasp, adjusting the dolphins so they lay in the center of her collarbone. "But I figured we'd have more fun doing something that important together."

Judi McCoy

An engagement ring?

Fingering the silky ribbon of gold, Kyra slipped from his hold and backed away. "I have work to do. You have to go."

"But there's a lot more to explain."

"Not now," she whispered, wishing Zeus would summon her home immediately. That way, she wouldn't have to hear Jake's pleas or have her heart torn in two by his words. If she confessed her love for him, the father god had the right to banish her to Hades, turn her into a piece of coal, anything he wanted. And if that happened she would never see Jake again.

"Okay, okay. I know you're busy, and so am I." His gaze turned serious. "I'll leave you to your chores, but there's one more thing. I want to introduce you to someone after the show."

"Introduce me?"

"My mother's in town, and she's dying to meet you. I meant to do it in the lobby, after the Mercedes drawing, but when I was ready you'd disappeared."

"You want me to meet your mother?"

"Her name is Laura, and she'll be in the audience tonight. I'll bring her backstage when the show's over."

Before Kyra could protest, he gave her another searing kiss. "I love you, sweetheart. And remember, our life officially begins from this moment."

* * *

"What do you think?" Lou stood in the hall leading to the stage steps. Twirling in place, she fingered her upswept hair. "Is it too much?"

Kyra bit her lip to keep from crying as she faced her two best friends, and concentrated on Lou, a vision in her hostess gown, and Rob, dressed in a designer tuxedo that fit as if tailored especially for him. He held Lou's hand, and Kyra realized this was the last time she'd be with either of them.

"You look fantastic. Like a princess."

The buzzing of the crowd seated in the pavilion seeped through the doors, almost obliterating the orchestra's rendition of songs the contestants would sing during the competition. With a hand on her earpiece, a production assistant guided the three female performers up the stairs. "Two minutes to showtime," she announced as she rushed past.

"Better than fantastic," Rob said, grinning at Lou. "We owe you a huge thanks, Kyra, for a lot of reasons."

"Rob's right," said Lou. "And we'll thank you properly when the show is finished. I've got to run." She waggled her fingers and took off for the VIP lounge.

Kyra smiled past the lump in her throat. "I guess you'd better get on stage." After Jake's amazing revelation, she'd hid backstage for the rest of the day as an excuse to stay out of sight. She couldn't bear to see him again, listen to his sweet words, or be warmed by the emotion burning in his eyes. She had promised herself she wouldn't cry until she was alone in her room on Mount Olympus, and she was determined to keep that vow. "You're going to knock them dead."

They hugged, and from over Rob's shoulder Kyra saw another production assistant hurry by, clipboard in hand. "One minute, Garrett," she muttered, striding toward the stairs.

Rob stepped back and held both her hands. "That was some surprise Jake pulled today, huh? The man can keep a secret, but I guess he told you all about it."

"Most of it. You'd better go."

"I warned him you'd be pissed when you found out he thought you were the thief." Rob shook his head. "But look on the bright side. It was an honest mistake. If he didn't suspect you, he wouldn't have asked you out, and you wouldn't be together now."

Jake had thought she was the thief? Kyra kept her smile in place. "The clock's ticking. Get going."

She followed Rob to the stairs, where he climbed them and turned. "We'll get together when this is over. Jake, too. We'll celebrate with Gram and his mother."

As if in a daze, Kyra watched Rob disappear, then heard thunderous applause fill the pavilion. Buddy Blue welcomed the audience, and began to read the rules of competition, and list the first place contestant's prizes. Then he introduced each judge with a toned down but still raunchy spin, and finished by calling out the performers.

The contestants were scheduled to sing in a specific order, interspersed with commercial breaks. First, a woman, then a man, then a number by Missy Malone; another woman, a second man, and a number by Dr. Slick; then the third woman, third man, and a monologue by Buddy while the votes were tabulated. Rob had drawn the final male position, a spot Kyra hoped would work to his advantage.

From start to finish, the show would take three hours, ending at midnight. Kyra had hoped to be in Las Vegas long enough to hear Rob perform, but his innocent comment about Jake rang in her head. The sooner Zeus snapped her back to Mount Olympus, the better. She needed time to sort everything out, including the fact that Jake had thought she was a thief.

She listened to the first competitor, then the second, without really hearing their performances. When Missy Malone began a song in her signature, taunting wail, Kyra made a beeline for the most comfortable backstage room, the celebrity judges' lounge. There she would change into a basic chiton, and plan for her confrontation with Zeus.

In the lounge, she stood before a full-length mirror and appraised herself. Undoing the top three buttons of her suit, her fingers brushed the golden rope and laughing dolphins. She closed her eyes, but still saw Jake's image as he walked the stands, spoke to the ushers and monitored the guards, or roved the VIP lounge as he checked the security staff, joked with Eddie, or chatted with Lou. She knew he'd be backstage eventually, where he was sure to search for her.

But she would be gone.

Kyra lifted her arms, and her suit and high heels were instantly replaced by a sheer and snow-white chiton and a pair of thin-strapped leather sandals. Raising her hands, she circled her hair, and her red tresses became a neatly arranged up-do with ringlets trailing down her cheeks and nape.

If she were on Olympus, she would have fussed with her hair or tried on several gowns and a dozen pairs of shoes until satisfied she looked her best. But tonight was different.

Tonight, she was going to face her destiny.

Dropping into the nearest cushy chair, Kyra heaved a sigh, and pressed two fingers to each temple. How could a year that had begun so well end in such a disaster? So what if Jake had thought her guilty of stealing? He'd told her he loved her, and she loved him. There had to be a way to save herself and be with him.

She just had to find it.

As if from nowhere, thunder rumbled. The lounge doors slammed open on a gust of frigid wind so strong it rattled the glasses on the service trays. Hermes, in all his winged and lavender glory, entered the room and reached out his hand.

Shedding her mind of all earthly things, Kyra stood and walked slowly toward him.

Jake made his final pass through the main level, noting the guards were doing a fine job with crowd control and seating. In the VIP lounge, he found the whales and their guests behaving, and the hostesses on top of things. Eddie had a way about him that made the customers laugh, and Lou was handling her job in a breezy and professional manner. Even Mr. T, who sat in a corner holding court, seemed to be enjoying himself.

He decided to head downstairs. The production was in commercial mode with only two contestants left, a girl from the Luxor and Rob. After they finished, the judges would hand in their voting cards and it was his responsibility to deliver them to the independent accountants ensconced backstage in a private room. After they tallied the scores, he was to bring the names of the first runner-up and the winner to Buddy, where the emcee would make the grand announcement.

In between supervising security and making certain everything ran like clockwork, he'd concentrated on Kyra. The curve he'd thrown her in her office had taken her completely by surprise. At first he'd thought she was going to send him packing, then he realized her reaction was due to a bad case of the jitters. It was obvious she had too much on her mind to think coherently.

Due to the time, he figured she would be somewhere behind the stage, pacing as she waited for

Rob to sing. Making his way down a side aisle, he inched open the door marked "principals only," determined to find her.

When he didn't immediately see Kyra on the stairs or in the hall, he checked the dressing rooms, the singers' waiting rooms, and the ladies' powder room. Then he went to the judges' lounge, the last place left to explore.

The doors were wide open, but the room was empty, though there was the usual array of leftover glasses, half full soda cans, and open liquor bottles. Hands on his hips, he gazed about the space with its flocked wallpaper and plush seating area. A female voice with a beautiful tone echoed down the corridor, her song filling the auditorium, and he guessed she was the next to last singer. Rob would perform in about five minutes. Kyra was probably in the wings, rooting for her friend.

He turned to leave, and his eyes caught a glittering object near his feet. Squatting, he poked through a pile of small white feathers and met the shining, sapphire blue eye of a smiling gold dolphin.

A variety of scenarios raced through Jake's brain as he retrieved the necklace. The dolphins were still clasped mouth to mouth, so it was unlikely the token had fallen from Kyra's neck, but it might have dropped from her pocket or tote bag. There weren't many more possibilities.

Standing, he stuffed the necklace in his trouser

pocket and took off for the stage, positive he'd find Kyra cheering Rob on.

Kyra stood in silence, her face set in a polite smile as she greeted the immortals lounging on the marble steps of the grand staircase. Under Hermes's watchful eyes, she'd been allowed to go to her room and prepare herself for her meeting with Zeus. The winged messenger had delivered her here a short while ago, and she had yet to calm her racing heart.

"Kyra, darling," mouthed Hebe, as she moved toward Zeus's office carrying a golden cup. "We've missed you. We trust you managed to reach your goal."

Sure you have, thought Kyra, noting the other gods sneering faces and sly expressions.

Zonás, a self-serving minor god, shot her a smarmy glance. "I heard you weren't successful, a truly unremarkable muse. It's a pity, but we shall try to think kindly of you when you are remanded to the stables."

Kyra sighed inwardly. She was doomed before the interview began if a creep like Zonas knew she'd failed. She gazed up and squinted at the bright cerulean sky and its flotilla of fluffy clouds. Between the pillars, far in the distance, mountaintops hosted identical cottony balls of white. She was home. The only place she'd longed to be for the past year. Home, where she could see her sisters, gossip with her cousins, and look forward to an eternity of pleasure.

Home, without the one man with whom she longed to share her future.

She took stock of the prying eyes that watched her every move, and realized this was also a place where the gods were jealous, spiteful, and *so* not deserving of her time.

Thunder shook the halls, lightning flashed, and Kyra cringed at the display. Thanks to Hera, Zeus wasn't in the best of moods, Hermes had warned. Apparently the mother god had spent too much time on Earth of late, instead of ministering to her husband's needs. If so, Kyra had to double-guard her heart, because it was the one thing the father god could cut to ribbons with a thought.

The doors to his office sprang open. Kyra threw her shoulders back, walked into Zeus's chamber, and strode directly to his massive desk.

"Father." She bowed, then straightened.

"Daughter." Zeus didn't so much as nod his craggy head. "It has been too long since I've seen your beautiful face."

"And I your . . ." *Grumpy, miserable grimace?* ". . . humbling magnificence."

"I will begin this performance review as I do all others. First, tell me how *you* think you did this past year."

Kyra cleared her throat on a cough, reminding

herself to be firm. The year had been filled with good deeds. "I believe I did well. I inspired good fortune in hundreds of mortals, many of whom were despondent and in need of aid. In doing so, they went on to overcome their misfortune, care for their spouses and children, and assist others."

Zeus raised a bushy brow. "And what of the impossible ones? Those who didn't believe in good fortune before you arrived, and those who still do not, since you have left?"

"I don't think there were any of those," Kyra said, keeping her tone respectful. "I believe I inspired each mortal I touched."

"What of the one called Louise?"

It figured Zeus would know about Lou. But now that the girl had Rob, Lou had to think her luck had changed. "Inspiring Louise without using my powers is something of which I am proud," Kyra said, crossing mental fingers.

"So say you, but I need to see for myself." He turned to his computer monitor and clicked the mouse. Rob and Lou appeared, standing to the side of the stage while the young woman from the Luxor accepted first prize as the Voice of Vegas.

Kyra's heart went out to Rob, but when Zeus zoomed in for a close-up, there were tears of joy in both Rob's and Lou's eyes. The chief god raised the sound and Lou said clearly, "It doesn't matter if you came in second. I'm still the luckiest woman on the planet."

Her father turned, his expression noncommittal. "It does seem you worked your magic on the girl."

Told you so, Kyra chanted in her brain. "Since I was the one who brought these mortals together, I take credit for Louise finding her belief both in true love and good fortune, and claim her as one of my successes."

"Are there any others?" asked Zeus, stroking his flowing white beard. "Because if I decide to add Louise to those I've chosen to count, you have two hundred-ninety-nine. A nice round number, say three hundred, would make my decision easier. Can you think of one I have yet to hear about?"

Before Kyra could speak or even think, Hera sauntered through the door. Dressed in red, with her black hair piled on her head, she appeared more regal than a queen. "If I show you a mortal to whom our Muse of Good Fortune has brought no luck, but has instead inspired despair, would you subtract one from her score?"

Zeus raised his leonine head. "What's this, wife? Have you been meddling again on Earth?"

Hera's smile turned feral, mirroring the evil in her heart. "I did it only to make certain the truth came to light, husband. And I found that not only did Kyra *uninspire* good fortune, she was the direct cause of a mortal's misery."

Zeus rose and thrust his hand in the direction of his computer. "Show me."

Taking a seat, Hera clicked the mouse. Jake

appeared on the screen, sitting on the sofa in his suite, his expression one of utter hopelessness as he stared at the gold necklace in his hands.

Kyra's eyes threatened tears, her heart burned to be with him again, to stop his pain and take it into herself. He'd fallen in love with her, even when he thought she might be a thief, which had to mean his love was real.

If only there was a way to return to him.

Zeus swung toward her the moment the emotions swirled through her system. "You have feelings for this . . . mortal?"

"He was but a diversion, oh mighty one," she lied, closing off her thoughts. "He meant nothing to me."

Hera gave a snort. When she guided the mouse to expand the picture, Jake's mother popped into view.

"Jake, are you going to bed?"

"Maybe." He stood and paced to the window, focused on the heavens, and breathed so deeply he shuddered.

His mother placed a hand on his shoulder. "You're a lucky man to have found her. Kyra will be back."

"Kyra wouldn't have left the necklace if she planned on returning. She never loved me. I should have realized it when I told her how I felt, and she didn't return the sentiment." He heaved a sigh. "Like I've said all along, there's no such thing as luck, at least where I'm concerned."

Hera gazed over her shoulder, her smile one of

triumph. "When he found himself in love with you, the mortal had hopes of good fortune, Kyra dear. Now, his despair cuts to the bone. And he has you to thank for it."

Zeus raised his head, his expression unreadable. "Do you value your life here, daughter, or do you find it tedious and dull?"

"I value life of any kind," Kyra answered, still focused on the screen. When Jake returned to the sofa and rested his head in his hands, she felt his pain reach out and clutch her very core. Suddenly, everything became as clear as water from a mountain spring. She did believe in good fortune. If she and Jake were meant to be together, it would see them through. "Especially the life of that man."

"Then you have fallen in love with a mortal," Zeus stated, his face a stony mask. "Even though it was a condition of the rules I warned against."

"Send her to the kitchens, husband. I've a hunger for honeyed fruit and cool, sweet wine. Then my gowns need a good washing, and my hair—"

"'Tis true, I love the human, father," Kyra interrupted. Her head high, she faced Zeus with pride. "And I'm prepared to accept my punishment."

"Perhaps the pigsty would be a better choice," Hera continued, tapping a finger to her chin. "So much slop, so little time for such a pathetic excuse of a muse."

Zeus stared at his wife, then closed his eyes and shook his head. "Will you ever learn to listen, wife?

Your plotting has been for naught, as I am a god of mercy as well as fear."

"Plotting?" Hera's tone was sweet innocence.

"I know about the mortal's intercepted telephone calls, wife. My question is, what purpose did they serve?"

"Did they have to serve a purpose? It was fun to keep the mortal guessing, for a hundred different reasons. I am the mother goddess. I owe no one an explanation for what I do."

"Except me, Hera." Zeus thumbed his chest. "Except me."

"But, my lord—"

He held up a hand. "I promised Kyra a lifetime of toil here on Mount Olympus if she failed in her quest. Though she succeeded, she disobeyed me, so there can be only one decision that will both reward and punish. I condemn her to live and die as a mortal. In this way, her life will be cut short and she will lose her godly powers, but she will be with the man she loves as a reward for her inspiration."

Kyra trembled at her father's pronouncement, from both joy and fear. If he sent her back and Jake decided he no longer wanted her . . .

"It should not—cannot—be possible," Hera sputtered. "She didn't meet her quota, she disobeyed your direct order. You must—she must— they all must—"

"All?" Zeus curled his lips. "My, but you have been a busy goddess."

"I trifled, as does every god—"

"Silence!" He thrust a finger toward Kyra. "Muse of Good Fortune, you may no longer be, so I send you to Earth for eternity . . ." Pausing, he glared openly at Hera. "And on my word, this I decree. No meddling from Olympus will there ever be."

Hera stomped a foot, her ear-splitting screech ringing throughout the hall.

Kyra smiled and Zeus gave her a naughty wink. Then he raised both arms. Darkness overtook her as she was lifted up and tossed skyward.

Then she found herself falling . . . falling . . . falling . . .

Jake ran a hand over his jaw and checked the time. No way in hell could he go to sleep now, not only because it was almost daybreak, but because every time he closed his eyes he saw Kyra's face, heard her joyous laughter, felt her presence.

He'd spent the night scouring the Acropolis, talking to the production crew, Rob and Lou, and his mother. No one had a clue as to where she'd gone, and a couple of people had acted as if they didn't know who he was talking about. Rob and Lou had narrowed their eyes, as if trying to picture Kyra in their minds before saying they had no idea what had happened to her.

He'd even taxied to her condo and found the door wide open, but without a sign of her, as if she'd never lived there . . . as if she'd never existed.

When he'd phoned the police, they'd told him the best he could do was wait twenty-four hours and file a missing persons report. But Jake knew that, by then, it would be too late. Kyra's trail would be cold.

He slumped into the couch and rested his head on the sofa. He'd blown it. Too many half-baked apologies and lame excuses, and too much concern for a job he no longer wanted, had caused him to lose the most important person in his life.

He'd already made the decision to turn down the manager's position when Themopolis offered it to him. Kyra had no next-of-kin listed in her papers, but she'd often spoken of Greece and her father. Since it was his only lead, Jake planned to go on the road. He'd continue to gamble, but he'd use the money to search for Kyra. And when he did, he was going to demand she hear him out.

His throat swelled and tears stung his eyelids. His mother's trust in him was so unshakeable, Laura had said she'd support him in whatever he chose to do about Kyra, even if she'd never met the woman.

Breathing deeply, Jake willed himself not to cry. He had no room for pity in his life, never had. He was a man of action. He had to find Kyra and plead his case. He owed it to both of them to convince her to give him one final chance.

He stared into space, plotting his next move. Rob might be able to hack into the airline computers and check the flight departures for Kyra's name, or he could hire an investigator . . .

At the sound of a knock, he took a look at his watch. Had his mother ordered room service? He raced to the door and swung it open while he said, "Just set it on the table."

"I really don't want to sit on the table, but I am willing to sit on one of the chairs. Or the couch."

Jake opened his mouth, but no sound came out. Kyra brushed past him, dropped onto the sofa, and grinned. Torn between anger and elation, he stuffed his hands in his pockets and clutched the smiling dolphins in his fist.

"Where have you been?"

Kyra continued to smile, as if nothing were wrong. "You said we'd talk about the future after the show." She glanced around the room. "As soon as the contest was over, I went for a walk to clear my head. I was bummed that Rob didn't win, and I didn't want my feelings to ruin our discussion."

"You stayed out all night *clearing your head?*"

"Hey, I had a lot of stuff in there. It took a while."

"You know Rob didn't win?" asked Jake, too shocked to speak sensibly.

"Second place isn't so bad. He might still get a recording deal. And he did have a great ride."

"Lou didn't seem to mind that he'd lost," muttered Jake. "She stood by him at the end."

Kyra scooted to the edge of the sofa. "Same as you stood by me, even when you thought I was stealing from the Acropolis."

"How did you find out . . . ?" Jake ran his fingers

through his hair. "Hell, Kyra. What else was I supposed to think? Whenever you did that crazy shoulder-tap thing, the casino lost money. It had to be a scheme of some kind."

"But it wasn't," she noted, folding her arms.

Jake shook himself awake. Had he been dreaming . . . or out of his mind for the past six hours? He walked to the couch and sat next to her, intent on making certain Kyra wasn't a figment of his imagination. "Where did you go?"

She shrugged. "Here and there. Did you miss me?"

"Miss you?" He tried to blink away his anger, but it didn't quite work. "I went nuts looking for you."

"Sorry. I guess I should have called, but I didn't have my cell phone and I—There's something else. Please don't be angry, but I lost the necklace you gave me."

He pulled the golden rope from his pocket. "You mean this necklace."

Kyra's smile brightened the room. "Then Hermes must have—oh, never mind." She swiped it from his fingers, slipped it over her curls, and settled the dolphins in the center of her neck. "I thought it was lost for good."

Jake's insides began to thaw. Kyra was here, sitting by his side, acting as if she'd never been away. He took in her tissue-paper thin, full-length white gown and wondered where in the heck he'd seen it before. Even her glorious hair looked a little different. If he didn't know better, he'd think she was at an X-rated costume party from another era, which was ridiculous.

"I realize you have a lot of questions, and I'm sorry if I worried you. I had to take care of something before we had our talk, and it consumed a bit more of my time than I anticipated."

"That's a pretty piss-poor apology," Jake said, coming to his senses. He swiveled on the cushion and inched closer. "You scared the living crap out of me. Take care of what?"

"Something I'll never have to deal with again, and that's the best explanation I can give at the moment." She glanced toward his bedroom door. "Is your mother still here?"

"Mom's staying the week."

"When are you going to introduce us?"

"When I've had time to cool down." He rose to his knees and loomed over her. "You deserve a spanking for pulling such a stupid stunt."

Kyra copied his pose, grinning at his threat. Their gazes locked and Jake's lips twitched. Then he brought his mouth to hers and Kyra gentled in his arms, forcing him to soften his hold and put his heart into the kiss. Minutes passed before they broke apart.

"I'm so sorry I—"

"God, but I missed—"

Smiling when they spoke at the same time, they

shared another kiss. Jake settled against her, and Kyra leaned back to recline on the cushions. Nestled between her open thighs, he drew away and rested his forehead on her chin.

"I love you."

"I love you too."

He raised his head and stared into her eyes, "Truth?"

"Always," she answered, nuzzling her nose to his lips. "I will love you for eternity. Even longer if you let me."

Jake's impressive erection prodded the V of her legs. "My mother is in the other room. Knowing her, she's probably heard every word we've just said."

Kyra sighed with happiness. She was mortal and it felt fabulous. Lying beneath Jake felt fabulous, too, exactly as she suspected it would sixty years from now. What was that earthly adage again? It's not the quantity but the quality?

Then and there she made herself and Jake a silent promise. The quality of their love and their life would be top-notch, A-one, more beautiful than a sunny day on Olympus, sweeter than the finest nectar of the gods.

She'd see to it personally.

"What are you thinking?" Jake asked her.

Unable to contain her happiness, she giggled. "We should probably get up so you can introduce me to your mother."

"Very funny."

Judi McCoy

Jake kissed her again, as if he had no intention of stopping, and Kyra thought the heated embrace had melted him into her skin, as if from this moment they were bonded as one being.

"How about we wait on that," he panted, slipping down the strap of her gown to reveal the upper curve of her breasts. "You'll have plenty of time to talk to Laura. I want to remember this moment forever."

"For a lifetime," Kyra whispered. "However long it might be."

"A lifetime? If that's the case, I guess I'll have to readjust my thinking." He grinned. "Because that makes me the luckiest man in the world."

Next month, don't miss these exciting new love stories only from Avon Books

The Duke in Disguise by Gayle Callen

An Avon Romantic Treasure

A dashing duke is hiding a dangerous secret, and loving him might be the most daring thing governess Meriel has ever done. But what will happen to their passionate union once she learns the truth?

Silence the Whispers by Cait London

An Avon Contemporary Romance

Cameron's life has been marred by tragedy, but when hunky Hayden Olson moves in next door things begin looking up...if only she'd accept his brazen overtures. But can she find the way to silence the whispers of her past . . . and end the nightmares of her present . . . in his strong arms?

Sins of Midnight by Kimberly Logan

An Avon Romance

Lady Jillian Daventry promises to behave—at least until her sister's coming out! But how can she resist solving a mystery, especially when it brings her into daily contact with handsome Bow Street Runner Connor Monroe.

Be Mine Tonight by Kathryn Smith

An Avon Romance

For nearly six centuries he has roamed the earth . . . a mortal man no longer. But when Prudence Ryland touches his heart, he knows that he must sacrifice everything to save her body . . . and her soul.

Visit www.AuthorTracker.com for exclusive information on your favorite HarperCollins authors.

REL 0606

Available wherever books are sold or please call 1-800-331-3761 to order.

Avon Romances

the best in
exceptional authors and unforgettable novels!